SINFUL SALVATION BOOK ONE

JUDAS

AMANDA EAST &
JANUARY KELLY

Wandering Reads
PRESS

Trigger Warning

Welcome, dear readers.

We are so excited to have you here in our sinful little universe. We have lots of spicy and thrilling fun planned for you within these pages and we think you'll love the ride we take you on.

But first, remember to take care of your mental health. Some of the characters in this book are truly horrific humans that don't deserve to take away your joy. We give them hell for it, but they're still in there. While we strive to bring you a story you will love, be aware that this book contains:

- Sexual Abuse (Discussed, not depicted.)

- Mentions of Abortion

- Mentions of Suicide and Self Harm

- Biblical Themes (Don't worry, we use them for our own gain.)

- Racism (It's disgusting, we know.)

- Sexism and Misogyny (Gag.)

- Attempted Murder (But in a good way.)

- Pregnancy

- Christian Nationalism (Double gag.)

- Death of a Parent

and, of course,
  - Explicit Sexual Content (No fade to black here, friends.)

If any of these things may cause you any mental harm, please proceed with caution. We love you from the very bottoms of our sacrilegious, smut loving hearts and we just want what's best for you.

Now, if you're ready, let the fun begin. We are pleased to officially introduce you to the first member of the Sinful Salvation Series.

Happy reading, friends.

Love Always,
Amanda and January

To the Girls, Gays, Theys
To the ones who questioned, deconstructed, and studied
May your books always be as spicy as your attitude,
May you never stop loving the most fabulous things the world has to
offer,
May you always seek the truth and speak the truth
and
May you always be the weird and wonderful you.

But you will exceed all of them. For you will sacrifice
the man that clothes me.

Already your horn has been raised, your wrath has
been kindled,

your star has shown brightly,

and your heart has become strong.

Jesus to Judas, The Gnostic Gospels

Prologue

"**C**an I get you a coffee to go?" Her sweet offer soothed his soul. Judas nodded, "That would be great, thank you."

The bouncy, middle-aged woman with bright red lips turned on her sneaker-covered heel to find a to-go cup. After filling it with the rich, dark bean water, she snapped the lid on tightly, handing it to the only person brave enough to sit at the old diner counter.

She thought he was handsome. His pale caramel, sultry eyes called to her from somewhere beyond time. She imagined for a moment what it would be like to dive deep and swim in them. To let herself be consumed by this vagabond passing through her small town only to be whisked away to someplace new and exotic.

"Here you go, sugar. Stay awake out there, you hear?" she blinked.

He put on a friendly smile before laying a fifty dollar bill next to his plate; an amount more than three times the cost of his meal. "It was nice meeting you, Darlene."

She winked, dropping her eyes to the Formica counter. But before she could protest and offer him change, the extraordinarily beautiful man and his coffee were gone.

The bluesy rock of KALEO blared from the speakers of the silver Audi and a darkening twilight settled over the open expanse of New Mexico landscape, the little town and the diner disappearing in his rearview mirror. The reflective green sign glowed in the car's headlights and Judas relaxed a bit knowing he was just within a few miles of the Texas state line. The grueling drive from Tacoma to Dallas took him the better part of three days to complete. But, to be honest, car travel across the country was leaps and bounds better than on horseback, and definitely better than by foot.

This wasn't his first time traveling across this slice of the desert or even on this highway, but it had been at least a century or more since he visited the second-largest state in the union. Judas couldn't say he recognized much of the area. The last time he was here, for starters, Raton was called Willow Springs. Admittedly over a few centuries, the specifically local scenery began to look the same anyway.

He was pleased that his new apartment was well-managed by a super attentive older gentleman who, after a haggle about a price for his time, graciously allowed the movers access to the space today. Judas wouldn't need to worry about lifting or assembling furniture, he paid extra for that as well, and all he would be responsible for was unpacking the boxes. Thankfully, relocations were becoming much easier with time.

He considered how many more of them he would have to undertake.

This *gift*, as his friend Yesh called it, was tiresome. While the locations changed, the repetition of life did not. In the beginning, he made friends and built communities only to watch them succumb to the inevitable ravages of time and death. After a while, he stopped making so many connections because his heart just couldn't bear the loss. But the real mind game came as Judas lived on the fringes of his old life for more than two thousand years not only to hear it retold in stories and rumors, but even worse, lies.

For the first three or four hundred of those years, the gossip infuriated him to the point of near madness. Judas made it his mission to tell people the truth in places like Assos and Apollonia, but it only got him labeled as an apostate and heretic by certain groups of a new, fledgling religion at the time. He held onto some hope with a sect of this radical group, the Gnostics, but even they were vilified by this new theology and lost to the sands of time. No one wanted to hear the truth it seemed, so over time, he gave up trying to tell it.

Judas assimilated into the world again and again. He made his way to the territories of the Franks and Visigoths, eventually settling for several hundred years in the Western Rhaetia Alps. Keeping his head down and out of sight, he watched humanity evolve around him. He witnessed wars, famines, and plagues. By the middle of the French Revolution, society and its technology encroached upon him, and moving every thirty years to a different town, country, or continent became his new gamble. After barely escaping the fighting during the Reign of Terror, Judas made the arduous journey to the newly formed United States of America, a land he eventually grew to love for its expansive landscape and restless wandering spirit. He found he could blend in and out of circles more easily here in this land of plenty, but this young nation of promised opportunity wasn't without its own challenges or dangers.

While he preferred to disarm an opponent with words, Jude, as he called himself in public, had known from his first day in his new country that he was looked upon as different because of the color of his skin. It had been that way in Europe, and it was for sure a struggle here. For this reason, among others, he'd established himself in northern states and territories to ease his transition. Until as recently as fifty years ago, Judas lived a delicate balance of being the helpful outsider while also staying in the shadows. He was perfectly content in being the apprentice or assistant and mostly took odd jobs that required the use of his brain instead of his brawn.

That wasn't to say that Judas wouldn't or couldn't fight as he had done plenty of it before even arriving on American shores. But shortly after realizing that he couldn't die, he devoted himself to learning everything his mind could hold including strategies of war, fighting, and self-defense. He defended a fair amount of interlopers on his remote Alpine farm and he had even taken ranks in more than one war in Europe.

But all of that was in the past now, and his immediate future lay almost six hundred miles within the next state's border. Allowing his mind to wander, Judas reminisced on how much of this country he had seen. In a little more than two hundred and thirty years, he moved no less than nine times. He knew he had not begun to scratch the surface of his adopted homeland but he did have his favorite places.

It was in the mid-1960s that he first moved to Oakland, California and began studying under a young martial artist named Lee Jun-fan who was known to his friends and students as Bruce. A striking person, both literally and figuratively, Judas was stunned that he could be in awe of such a *young* man. Bruce was incredibly intelligent, loved philosophy, and had an infinite sense of humor. The pair had an immediate, friendly rapport and often spoke at length after class hours about their love of the taste of a freshly caught fish and the mutual dislike of the racial tensions of that time.

The memory of his friend made Judas smile. He was always fond of Bruce's teaching style and life ideology, mostly because it reminded him a bit of Yesh. And, not unlike Yesh, he was gone from the world before anyone was really able to know and appreciate him.

The blanket of stars was bright overhead as the car hummed along the desolate highway and song lyrics floated out the window. He pulled his mind back to living in the present and felt the cool air on his face. He had never lived in Dallas before and the thought of what potentially awaited him excited him a tiny bit. It amused him that, after all this time, he could still get excited about a new city. Although, if this were his last move, that would excite him more. The soothing voice of the car's electronic voice from the GPS pulled him from his daydreaming.

"Welcome to Texas."

Chapter One

The oppressive Texas sun bounced off the mirrored glass of the eighteen-story downtown building as Judas raised his hand to block his eyes from the glare. It was his third interview today, but he felt more confident as the day continued that he would find the right fit soon. He had accumulated enough wealth in his lifetime that he could easily choose not to work, but he found that having a job or a duty to report to for made life pass more easily. Boredom was soul-sucking in unbearable ways.

Pulling on the oversized chrome handle of the door, a rush of icy, air-conditioned air met him like a sentinel, slamming into his face. He strode to the building directory at the center of the spacious, mostly empty lobby. Names of various companies and law offices were etched in the black marble monolith, the letters carefully gilded with gold paint.

Arthur and Branson, floors seventeen and eighteen.

Most of the names on the stone slab listed at least two destinations on each floor, but evidently, the top two were reserved for only the law firm of Arthur and Branson. Judas would like to pretend he was impressed a tiny bit but after several hundred years on earth, there was little that did. The chime on the elevator pinged softly as its doors opened and he slipped inside the empty car.

As the door chimed again, Judas was greeted by an enormous reception area decorated in rich wood tones and gold. Stepping out of the lift, his spotless Lafitte oxfords sunk into plush snow-white carpeting. Taking in his surroundings momentarily, he waited patiently for the older woman with curly graying locks to finish her phone call and tap her headset before he approached.

"Welcome to Arthur and Branson. Do you have an appointment?" she smiled pleasantly, her accent dripping with southern hospitality.

"I have an interview... Jude Christian," Judas nodded.

Looking at him curiously, the woman motioned for the man to sit, "Oh, yes, Mr. Arthur will be with you shortly."

Before he could get comfortable on the soft nubuck sofa, a beautiful woman with piercing blue eyes approached, "You are Mr. Christian?"

Judas turned quickly, only to draw a sharp breath as he stared at one of the most beautiful women he'd ever seen. A quick question crossed his mind; was it luck that Mr. Arthur and his partner were surrounded by such beauty or was it by design? He saw beyond even the soft wrinkles of the receptionist's face that she was once gorgeous in her youth and now another exquisite woman stood before him. Either way, Judas was having a difficult time finding his words. It wasn't something that ever happened to him and it made his mind race with more questions.

"Uhhh...yes. I'm Judas...Jude Christian." Reaching out, he shook her hand. It felt soft and delicate in his, and for a split second, he considered not letting it go.

The woman took him in with her eyes as he stood before her. He looked like he worked out and his firm body occupied his pricey suit quite well. She noticed his hair was long and silky but he kept it tied back neatly at the nape of his neck. His beard and mustache were equally tidy and she noticed he smelled expensive. But it was the glow of his pale brown eyes that drew her in and his entire presence made her wonder why he would want a job as a bodyguard for a political candidate. He did not appear to be a man in need of cash flow.

"This way," turning on her heel, she led him down a long hallway.

Judas took note of the artwork lining the walls. Most of it depicted moments in Texas history, except for the large piece at the end where the corridor made a T. The colossal piece seemed almost out of place from the rest. A field of red, yellow, and pink flowers was set on a backdrop of midnight blue. It reminded him of Monet's work. The beautiful woman with sapphire eyes and blonde hair pulled into a taut bun turned right at the picture and knocked once on the door before letting herself and Judas inside.

"Your interview is here," she stated before turning back to Judas and lowering her voice, "Don't let him intimidate you and you'll be fine."

He heard the door click as she left.

Paul Arthur, Attorney at Law, and Republican candidate for the Texas State senate, sat behind a gargantuan dark mahogany desk. Judas saw that his silver hair nearly matched the grey pinstripe in his dark suit as he rocked back in his large leather chair. Behind him, a wall of glass overlooked the Dallas city skyline. Leaning forward slowly, Paul never offered Judas a seat but placed his elbows over an open file in front of him.

"Where you from, boy?" Paul's eyebrow arched as slowly as his Texas drawl.

Judas cleared his throat, "Seattle, sir."

"Well, you sure sound like a northerner. I wasn't sure if you were one of these people from the border towns," Paul searched the file with his eyes as Judas realized it must be his resume. "You look like you could be."

The desire to laugh in the man's face and tell him where he could put this job was overwhelming. It wasn't as if Judas *needed* the money, but having moved to the area just a few months prior, he knew he had to set down roots for as long as he could. In twenty years or so, he would have to relocate. It was best practice to get settled as quickly as possible so he could enjoy what time he could in a new city.

"Yes, sir. My family is actually from around Israel...many generations ago," Judas' hazel eyes smiled.

"Judas Christian. That's a rather unfortunate name...why would your parents name you that?" Paul continued studying the paper in front of him. "I wouldn't name my hound after a traitor."

Judas seethed but he almost expected this reaction, "Jude, sir. I go by Jude.

Paul quietly eyed the tall man for a silent moment. It may have only been a moment but, to Jude, it felt heavy. Almost menacing and ill fitting. It was as if he was being inspected for quality assurance. Judas held his head a little higher. He wasn't lying to the man, at least not entirely. His family was from Israel, but his definition of the word *few* was as wide as the Texas plain since it had been more like eighty generations since he was home.

"I would as well," Paul muttered and flipped a page in the folder. "So, your family...are they?"

Judas shook his head, confused, "Are they what, sir?"

The older man's eyes finally met him again, "Christian."

Judas bit the inside of his cheek, hard. What a racist piece of shit. Who did this man think he was? Angry thoughts and comments roiled in his mind.

"Yes sir," he held back what he really wanted to say. "Long-standing."

"Humph," the man grumbled before continuing, "Says here you're trained in a couple of different kinds of martial arts and weapons. You military?"

"Not anymore, sir," Judas was ready to walk out. He wasn't sure he could work for another tyrant; especially one that hid his autocracy under a cheaply tailored suit.

Paul's smile spread across his face slowly, "Well...I do appreciate any boy willing to serve his country. And it looks like you've got all the necessary training and papers. I think you'll do. You'll be heading up and building my security team for the duration of my election." He paused to inspect Judas again, "You own a tuxedo, boy? If not, you'll need to rent a nice one. We have fundraisers to attend. I'll have Betsy take you down to Human Resources for the paperwork."

Before Judas could answer or object, Paul pressed the intercom button on his phone and spoke into the air, "Betsy...can you please come in here?"

Both men were silent for several awkward moments until the beautiful woman with ocean-colored eyes reappeared in the doorway, leather portfolio in hand.

"There she is!" Paul rose from his perch to meet the stunning woman halfway. "Betsy, I'd like you to meet Mr. Christian. He will be our new head of security. Mr. Christian, I'd like you to meet my campaign coordinator, Betsy. You'll work together on all the event planning over the next few months." He turned to the much younger woman, "Darlin', can you take Mr. Christian down to Alice? Let's get him started tomorrow morning with the meeting for the gala."

Her smile was angelic radiance lighting a halo around her entire face. Judas' heart beat hard in his chest and he felt oddly off balance being next to her. But there was something behind her luminous grin. It took him back for a split second but then he thought he saw a twinge of tired sadness. There was heartache there, he could feel it.

"Certainly. Shall we?" she motioned quickly for him to follow her. Once in the hallway, her pace slowed as she paused to check her phone.

Judas, certain there was no way he was taking this job just a short minute ago, followed along beside her without question, "So, Betsy–"

Her sapphire eyes looked up sharply, "Please, no. The *only* person that calls me by that awful name is my dad."

"Oh." Judas thumbed over his shoulder as they continued walking, "Mr. Arthur is your *father*. Good to know."

She turned back to him, smiling, "I'm Eliza. You're Judas?"

The sound of his name off her lips was the most enticing sound he had ever heard. He hated to correct her because he wanted her to say it again... or maybe he didn't. He couldn't get involved because it always ended in abandonment and pain. He made mistakes in his past and he promised himself a very long time ago that they wouldn't be repeated.

"Actually, I go by Jude...for obvious reasons," he shrugged as if he needed no further explanation. If Paul Arthur was right about anything, it was that his name seemed to be poison to a lot of lips. To his surprise though, she insisted on one.

"Why is that? Judas is a perfectly fine name," Eliza held her notebook close to her chest.

"Why do you hate Betsy?" the corner of his mouth pulled into a grin. His attraction to this woman overrode the little voice that insisted on emotional distance.

Eliza pursed her lips as she studied him, "Betsy is a horrible nickname...one that is juvenile, completely outdated, and is like fingernails on a chalkboard."

Judas nodded, "Yes ma'am. Eliza, it is."

He wanted another one of her glorious smiles and she did not disappoint. This time though, he received the full version; bright, natural, and alluring. His entire body felt warm and he hoped she wouldn't notice.

"We're here," she rapped twice on the door. "Alice will get you sorted. It was nice to meet you, *Judas*."

Eliza turned on her heel, walking away. Judas stared at her glorious form as she disappeared down the hallway. The emphasis she placed on saying his full name had warmed him in the coldest corners of his soul. He knew he would hate every second of being near Paul, but he was also certain it would be worth it to be near Eliza. At least for a while. There was just something... a feeling deep in his gut... that he felt he needed from her before he walked away. And, so, into the office he went, head spinning the whole time.

Eliza was feeling that same kind of questioning. When she made it around the corner and was certain she was out of sight, she paused for a moment, swallowing hard and taking a few steadying breaths. No man had made her feel quite as hot and bothered as Judas in a very long time. That was going to be a problem for sure, she just knew it.

Chapter Two

Walking back into the monstrous building the next morning felt different to Judas. He'd never really been excited to start a new job. Not that anyone could blame him, he'd worked so many over the millennia that it'd become hard to get first-day butterflies. He'd woke this morning thinking it was just another day, but when he remembered that he could possibly be spending his day with the beautiful daughter of the would-be congressman changed how he felt. Judas walked into the boardroom with a bounce in his step instead of his usual boredom.

When he looked around the room, he was disappointed to see just Paul and a few other faces he didn't know yet. No smile full of sunshine to greet him. As he took a moment to stare dejectedly around the room, a small hand slid along his shoulder startling him. Looking to his side, Eliza beamed up at him.

"Good morning, Judas," she said pleasantly.

He smiled back the weight of his disappointment fading instantly, "Good morning, Eliza."

"Are you ready for this?" she asked under her breath.

"I'm sure I can handle it," he murmured back knowing that he'd already had the opportunity to deal with just about any situation that could arise at one point or another in his life.

Eliza stared ahead at her father, sighing, "I'm glad one of us can."

Judas watched as she walked away from him. She seemed less than enthusiastic about her job here. He was sure there must be a story behind that sigh and Judas made a mental note to ask her someday. He walked further into the room and greeted his new boss, "Good morning, sir."

Paul ignored Jude's outstretched hand and barked out his first, of many, orders for the day, "Christian, stand over there and take in the meeting. We can talk about security needs and the rally later. The gala is priority number one."

Eliza glared in her father's direction, "Dad, we need to plan security for the gala and the event. He needs to be a part of the meeting, not just a fixture in the room."

Paul waved his daughter off, "You can talk about those details later, I want to get to the good stuff first. Where's Georgia?"

Eliza was clearly displeased, but carried on, "She's bringing up the handouts for the event. She should be here anytime."

Right on cue, a young girl entered the room lugging a large box nearly as big as she was, dropping it on the table in front of Paul. She looked as though she wanted to talk but her words were hindered by the gasping breaths of exertion she was taking.

"These... are the... uhh... the campaign b-buttons, sir," she managed to force out between exhausted breaths.

Paul smiled brightly and rubbed his hands together in excitement as he stood, tearing open the box. Greedily he reached inside, grabbing a handful of buttons. Quickly, his smile faded into a dark scowl. He dropped the buttons back in the box and slowly looked up at the young intern. Her smile faded as well when she saw his face redden.

Without warning, Paul swept the box off the table sending thousands of buttons flying across the room. Georgia squealed in surprise and Eliza jumped to her feet.

"Dad!" Eliza exclaimed, "Have you lost your mind?!"

Paul turned dangerously to look at his daughter, "No, Betsy. I have not lost my mind. I have just been completely let down by this sorry staff of mine."

"What are you talking about?" Eliza asked.

Paul threw a handful of stray buttons toward his daughter and Judas immediately saw red. He watched this scene unfold and thought the guy was an asshole, but seeing him treat his own daughter in such a way enraged Judas beyond anything he had experienced in a very long time. He wanted to tear this mediocre man to pieces, but the small voice inside his head steadied him.

To his utter surprise, Eliza took it all in stride. It was clear she had seen this kind of behavior before and wasn't fazed even in the slightest. Staring coldly at her father, she stooped to pick up a button. She studied it closely and then a small giggle escaped her. Judas was certain it was the sweetest sound he had ever heard. He smiled in spite of the chaos before him. She was entertained by whatever the issue was while her father was turning a deeper red with each passing second.

"Betsy, it is NOT funny," Paul shrieked, veins popping in his neck.

She rolled her eyes then stared straight into his, "Dad! No one is going to care that your middle name is on these buttons. Lots of men are named Lindsey. It's not that big of a deal."

Judas held in his chuckle and watched as Paul swept all the paperwork off the conference table as well. Judas was in disbelief as the man lost his ever-loving shit over people knowing his middle name. The irony that Paul Arthur had the audacity to question his name was not lost on Judas and made him laugh a bit more to himself.

"Senator Lindsey Graham would be very disappointed in this behavior," Eliza admonished.

Judas couldn't be certain, because she had a wonderful poker face, but he imagined for a quick moment that Eliza might just be enjoying her father's madness.

Paul, still full of rage, turned to the poor intern who was shaking at his side and screamed in her face, "Are you stupid, girl? Who told you to put that name on there?" He leaned in close, yelling, "Are you trying to sabotage me?"

Eliza, furious that he had turned his attention to the young girl, moved around the table in an instant, pushing her father away. Standing between them, Eliza squared her shoulders, "Enough, Dad! Get out. Go work somewhere else until you can calm down. Now!"

He never argued but stalked out of the room, slamming the door before the other men in the room, except Judas, gathered their belongings and quickly followed behind. The crying intern scrambled to pick up the buttons but Eliza stopped her instantly.

"I'm so sorry, he acted that way, Georgia. This has nothing to do with you and I fully understand if you want to walk away from this whole mess and never come back," Eliza whispered earnestly.

Georgia wiped at the frantic tears threatening to roll down her cheeks, but waved Eliza off, "No, really. I'm fine. It's fine. I had no idea he would be so mad. I had no idea they would say his middle name." She added with a shrug, "I didn't even know his middle name."

Eliza hugged her, "Please don't blame yourself for any of this. You had no way of knowing what was going to happen and he had no right to treat you that way. Genuinely, I am so sorry for my father's behavior."

Georgia smiled at Eliza, "Thank you. I'm just in a bit of shock, I think. He just scared me, but I'm okay."

Eliza held her at arm's length, "No one should ever scare you in the workplace. Or anywhere else for that matter. Please, take the day and do whatever you need for yourself. Tell Lydia at the front desk that I want you to have the company card for the day. Take yourself to brunch. Go to the spa. Buy yourself something nice. All of the above. Whatever you want. It's on my insufferable father today."

Georgia shook her head aggressively, "Oh, no. I could never. Really. I'm okay."

Eliza stilled the young woman, "No, Georgia. I insist. Take the day. Take the card."

Georgia was still unsure but softly nodded her head and seemed to relax as relief flooded her. She turned, heading out of the room with a small wave.

Judas watched this entire scene unfold from his perch in the corner and was speechless, but he stayed to watch Eliza. She folded her arms across her chest and walked to the wall of windows overlooking the city. She stared out into the expanse, shaking her head, trying to come to terms with what this job would mean for her in the long run. She felt trapped, but couldn't leave because who would rein in her father when he needed it if she was gone?

Judas crossed silently to stand behind her. She saw his reflection in the windows before she saw him. She dropped her head in defeat realizing he was still here watching the whole sad scene unfold.

She turned to face him, "Still think you're ready for this?"

Judas, fully composed and calm, drew a breath without hesitation, "Are you okay?"

Eliza was so overcome with emotion she nearly fell into his arms. No one ever asked her how she felt after one of her father's outbursts and she had no idea how desperately she needed to hear it. She's kept it all inside and nothing about this man would change that. She couldn't let him see the weakness for even a second. Instead, she painted on her smile, straightened her suit, and touched his shoulder as she walked past.

"I don't even know what okay is most days," she replied, walking out the door, and leaving Judas alone in the room.

He watched the closed door willing her to walk back through it. She may have been raised by that man, but he knew she was nothing like him. Judas could already tell that Eliza was good, kind, and full of integrity. He wished he could take her away from all this and see who she really was inside. He wanted to know her more than he'd ever wanted to know another person. That truth was more painful than he would like to admit because he understood the accompanying truth as well.

Her father would never allow her to spend her days or her nights with the hired help.

Chapter Three

The rest of the morning passed as any other first day would. Judas was shown around the office, introduced to all the key figures in the firm, and left to fill out piles of HR paperwork in a small, but nicely decorated office just off what would be the security office. Once finished with the monotony of tax forms and emergency contact number, something he had to make up since he had no one, Judas set to work pulling resumes to build a full security detail for Paul. Just before noon, the kind receptionist stuck her head just inside the door to alert Judas to a lunch meeting with Paul, Eliza, and Chet Branson, Paul's business partner. He was eager to arrive first and waited for the arrival of the woman behind those complicated blue eyes that had completely captivated him so quickly.

Judas stood in the lobby of the Dallas Ritz-Carlton waiting for the rest of his party to arrive. Being on time was something Judas was exceptionally good at, but it always felt like the rest of the world struggled. He'd always considered ten minutes early to be almost late while most seemed to think ten minutes late was right on time. He added this to the list of things he would just never understand about the human race.

All his years of waiting for everyone else made him an expert at occupying his own time though. Judas found a quiet spot just outside of the hustle and bustle of the busy hotel lobby to play one of his favorite games: Fact or Bullshit. Hotels were truly the best venue for this sport because there was always a bible lying around somewhere. He'd appreciated Gideons International for their exhaustive efforts in making sure every room where the weary laid their heads there was a copy of King James' version.

Leaning against the hard stone wall, Judas slid the bible off the small lobby table and flipped to a random page. The book of Matthew, chapter eight, verse thirty.

Some distance from them a large herd of pigs was feeding. The demons begged Jesus, "If you drive us out, send us into the herd of pigs." He said to them, "Go!" So they came out and went into the pigs, and the whole herd rushed down the steep bank into the lake and died in the water.

This one was technically bullshit, but with a tiny grain of truth and Judas smiled recalling that night. There had been no demons. It had simply been a juvenile prank gone wrong. Just he and Yesh walking the rural paths and drinking a little too much wine. Stupidly, they decided it would be a good idea to let the shepherd's pigs loose. What they envisioned was a glorious scene of chaos as the farmer attempted to corral his herd, but the pigs had gone straight to the water and were washed away by the rapid current. Judas and his friend exchanged a look of wide-eyed horror and quietly slipped away into the night. They would recall the story some nights and laugh with each other as the others were apparently building their own version of the story in their heads.

Shaking off the soured memory, Judas flipped back to another random page. Leviticus 15: 16 to 18

If a man has an emission of semen, he shall bathe his whole body in water and be unclean until the evening. And every garment and every skin on which the semen comes shall be washed with water and be unclean until the evening. If a man lies with a woman and has an emission of semen, both of them shall bathe themselves in water and be unclean until the evening.

Judas laughed out loud at this one and a woman nearby cut her eyes at him. Even though this was a law of his own people, he had to call absolute bullshit. Sexual piety was a modern concept. Especially for men. They spread their seed wherever they pleased with little regard for hygiene or cleanliness. Not that much had changed in that regard over the centuries.

Book of Romans.

Judas rolled his eyes refusing to even read on. If it was written by Paul, he knew it was garbage because Paul was so completely full of shit and himself. Seemed to be a theme with the name.

As if right on cue, the small hairs on the back of his neck rose as Judas felt the eyes of an onlooker. Glancing up from the book full of lies and half-truths all written by men, Judas met Eliza's gaze watching him.

"Are you reading the bible right now?" she chuckled, a little stupefied.

He smiled at her and closed the book, returning it to the table, "Just fact-checking." He grinned wider.

Eliza's eyebrows furrowed and she stared at him in a way that made him think she was trying to figure him out.

'Good luck with that, dear Eliza', his internal monologue chimed in, still amused by her confusion.

Eliza shook her head, walking toward the entrance of the restaurant.

Following her into the hotel's premier restaurant, Fearing's, Judas watched her body move confidently through the crowd. He would've given anything to know what was going through her head at any given moment. The way she so quickly had taken over his frequent thoughts intrigued him in ways he couldn't explain. But it also frightened him a little.

If he could've seen inside her head, he would've known that she was just as consumed with thoughts of him. He seemed so wonderfully strange and different from what Eliza was used to finding around her. It was refreshing like white wine on a hot night.

After a quick few moments of conversation with the maître D', Eliza motioned to Judas to follow the restaurant staff to their waiting table. Judas watched the older, well-dressed seated man rise with a smile as they approached.

Meeting Paul's business partner, Chet Branson, was everything Judas had expected it to be. Here was a good ole boy clearly born and raised in the heart of Texas. His charm was much more genuine than Paul's, however, it was clear they shared the same kind of upbringing. Chet had logged a few more hours of manual labor than Paul, though. Judas could feel the calluses on his hands as they greeted one another for the first time.

"Welcome to the team, Mr. Christian," Chet smiled as he shook hands with Judas.

Judas felt Chet's genuine enthusiasm, "Happy to be of service, sir."

Eliza stepped close, greeting Chet with a huge smile. Chet beamed, immediately wrapping her in a tight hug. First instinct would ordinarily lead Judas to believe these two were involved somehow beyond business, but the embrace looked almost fatherly. Eliza squeezed him back and Judas studied them closely. This man was a person of importance to Eliza and that gave him instant esteem in Judas' eyes. Already, without understanding why, Judas trusted Eliza's judgment.

"How are you, Eliza?" Chet released her from their hug.

"Good as ever, Uncle Chet. How's the family?" she smiled.

"Same ole, same ole," he replied warmly before turning to Judas to offer a seat at the table.

Commotion from the entrance drew all of their attention. They turned to see the last member of their party arrive with massive fanfare, from other patrons, however self-induced it may have been.

Paul, forgetting all about the morning's woes, morphed into public servant mode as he greeted everyone willing to acknowledge his presence as he walked across the room toward them. Waving and shaking hands like he was on the actual campaign trail, Judas was surprised Paul didn't track down a baby or two to kiss. Finally, reaching the table, he took the seat next to Chet.

"Good to see you, old man," Chet drawled as he shook Paul's hand.

Paul mocked a scowl at his partner as unfolded the white napkin, placing it in his lap.

"What did I miss, folks?" he asked loudly to their small group.

Eliza did her best to hold in her eye roll at her father's entrance as Chet gave her a look of amused approval. Judas saw the camaraderie between them and Paul had absolutely no clue. It made him smile.

"We've only just exchanged pleasantries, Paul," Chet explained, clapping Paul on the back, "You haven't missed anything yet, you old coot."

Paul scowled for real this time, "Now, I just don't know why you always have to call me that. I'm only two years your senior, I'll have you recall."

Chet laughed as Paul relented, play-punching Chet in the shoulder.

"You met my new security man, I see," Paul boomed.

"I did. Seems like a strong capable man to keep you safe out there on the campaign," Chet replied.

Judas smiled in response, nodding in Chet's direction as a way of thanks for the endorsement and acceptance. He still wasn't sure at any given moment how Paul actually felt about him, but Eliza's warm smile in his direction was enough.

"I was just about to tell Eliza Neveah's exciting news," Chet said, turning his attention back to her.

"Neveah is Chet's daughter," Eliza explained to Judas, "She's kind of like my little sister."

The pride in Eliza's voice when talking about this new name was evident. Judas realized there was a lot of love around the table even if Paul hadn't.

Chet paused for dramatic effect, "She got her acceptance letter to the University of Texas at Austin!"

Eliza squealed with joy and clapped her hands. Judas was delighted to watch her in a moment of true pure happiness and smiled brightly alongside her.

"Hmph," Paul grumbled, "We'll throw the real party when she gets her letter for Texas Christian University."

Chet shook his head, "No, no. This was her first choice. This was the one we were waiting for."

"You see, Dad," Eliza purred. "Some of us want an education, not indoctrination."

Paul waved off his daughter's words and seemed entirely uninterested in the current conversation as it didn't revolve around himself. He pulled a vibrating cell phone from his pocket. Waving everyone off, Paul rose from the table mid-conversation, "Sorry folks, I've gotta take this."

Eliza glared at him as he walked away from the table.

Chet leaned toward Judas meeting his gaze, "I have known that man for most of my life. I know he is rough around the edges and a lot of times an absolute fool, but he does have some good in there. I promise. After all, he raised her." Chet gestured toward Eliza.

"Yes," Judas agreed, "I can't imagine a more poised, intelligent, beautiful testament to that than Miss Eliza."

Before the words had even fully left his mouth, Judas regretted them. Not their sentiment, just that he'd spoken them out loud. Eliza turned toward him, their gazes locking. The immense tension that passed between them in the moment was so thick you could slice it with the steak knife gripped in her hand.

She was momentarily frozen. She thought she'd been imagining the feeling his eyes gave her every time he looked at her, but right now she thought she'd been right all along. Maybe there really was a spark between them. The idea caused red heat to spread across her features and she wanted to hide under the tablecloth so no one could see it, but it was too late. Both Eliza and Judas felt Chet's gaze move between them as he laced his fingers on the table and leaned back in his chair.

"Well, isn't that interesting," he stated quietly, bringing Eliza and Judas back to reality.

Eliza cleared her throat, "About Austin, yes! So exciting and wonderful!"

Chet gave them both a look that said *'I saw that'* but allowed them the courtesy of moving on.

"Uh-huh... Anyway, yeah. She's over the moon excited to follow in your footsteps, Eliza."

She beamed, before asking about the rest of the kids. The table quickly filled with conversation as they reminisced while Judas took it all in. He was surprised to hear that Chet and his wife, Reba, share five children. All of them boys, except the youngest, Neveah, who was seventeen. Their oldest was the same age as Eliza and had grown up side by side with her. Through listening to their stories it seemed they'd always had a close relationship, Eliza and this oldest son. His name was Davy and Judas had already decided he didn't like him. He had no reason, he just didn't.

Upon further reflection, Judas realized that this unwarranted distaste was the bitter roots of jealousy weaving their way through him. How could he feel jealousy over a man he'd never met and for a woman he barely knew? This was so foreign to him and he wasn't sure what to do with it, but he couldn't stop its path through him as he watched his blonde-haired, sapphire-eyed lunch companion through the rest of the meal.

She watched him too and she knew she was right.

There was definitely a spark there.

***

Paul wasted no time putting Judas straight to work after their lunch.

"Listen, Jude," Paul whispered conspiratorially as they walked toward the exit, "When we walk outside, I'm likely to have some fans waiting around to see me. I may need you to help us make it through the crowd, understand?"

Judas nodded in agreement with a blank expression, but inside his head was full of laughter. This man was clearly delusional if he thought that many people truly enjoyed him enough to gather just for a glimpse of him. He was, by no means, a prize to spend any time with, that was for certain. Sure enough, though, walking out into the sunshine revealed a small crowd of about fifteen to twenty people who seemed to be waiting for the hopeful senator.

Like a practiced actor, the old man's shoulders lifted and he plastered on the politician's smile as he called out to the supporters, "Good to see you, folks!"

His leathery fingers, likely more used to wagging in people's faces, were spread wide in a frantic, childlike wave as he oozed the smarmy political charm, "Support from regular, working class people like you all's what's going to help me win that senate seat and start changing this country back to the good old days."

Judas took position in a protective stance behind Paul as they made their way through the crowd that was now gaining additional attention from strangers on the street, craning their necks to see who might be in the middle of this scene. Paul shook their hands, posed for selfies, and actually found a baby cradled in its mother's arms to kiss on the forehead for the perfect photo opportunity. He actually did it. He was out here kissing babies. Judas could hardly believe this scene was real life. It all felt so cliche and so scripted.

Scanning their surroundings, Judas caught a glimpse of the blustering old man's daughter and had to work hard to not react to the look on her face. She rolled her eyes so hard in her father's direction that Judas had to wonder if the movement was painful.

Her eyes recovered and were now locked with Judas'. She shook her head shrugging her shoulders at his look of bewilderment. Yes, her father was insufferable. No, she didn't know how to explain how anyone might believe a single slimy word from his mouth.

As Paul completed his walk through his fans, he turned to face them all, "Remember folks. Come November, a vote for Paul Arthur is a vote for the Bible. Good to see you all and God bless." He then ducked into the car waiting for Eliza to join him.

Judas gestured for Eliza to climb into the town car and as she passed him she laid a hand on his arm.

She spoke quietly, "Don't let the fanfare fool you. That call he took at the beginning of lunch? Yeah, it was to set all this up. These faces are all paid actors so that intern over there could take some promotional videos." She sighed with another shrug, "All of this is of his own making."

Judas watched her climb into the car and shut the door behind her. He tapped the top of the car to let the driver know they were safe to depart. Walking slowly back to his own car now, Judas could think of only one thing.

Eliza Arthur.

She was clearly intelligent and composed. She didn't seem to like anything about her father or working for him, yet she does. The way she interacts with others tells Judas she has a good and kind heart. Everything about her work with Paul felt like a complete contradiction to who she is. Why does she do it?

Judas wanted nothing more than to climb inside her mind and read her every thought. He needed to know who she was under all the layers of herself that she portrayed to the world. He wanted to hold her hand and tell her she didn't have to work so hard to be someone she wasn't. That being just her is enough.

He dragged a hand down his face as he climbed into the driver's seat. He doesn't even know her. Why does he think he can tell her anything about herself? Why does he want to know her so badly?

He sits behind the wheel for a long moment and stares up at the sky. He speaks aloud to someone he isn't sure is even listening anymore, "Yesh, why? Why now? Why her? Why am I here? Is this part of the plan? Is there even a plan at all? I have been wandering this planet since you left and never once have I felt this kind of pull to a person. Why?"

There was no answer, but that's what he expected. No answer had ever come before, why would it now? It's just that all these centuries of living have always felt like a punishment. His entire existence, just a way of saying he deserved pain and suffering.

Eliza didn't feel like that to him. She seemed to lift that burden instead. She felt like the gift of light at the end of a too long darkness. He had known her for two days and he already craved her presence. Every second he had spent learning who she was felt like breathing fresh air into dying lungs. She was a reminder of why life was worth living, but her glow could not outshine one glaring truth.

Even if he stuck around and got to have her as his, which had quickly become obvious to him as his only desire, he would lose her. One way or another, she would be gone and he would go on living. Living on eternally in a world without her light just watching as forever became his very own hell.

Chapter Four

Judas was only employed by Paul Arthur for a week and yet he had managed to pull together an entire security team, vet a location for the first fundraiser gala, and fully orchestrate a safe event for the would-be senator. Tonight marked the official beginning of Judas proving his worth to his new employer and he knew he had done the job well. If Paul was disappointed in any facet of the evening, it would simply be because he was an impossible-to-please, racist old man. Of that, Judas was entirely sure. Still, he completed his every duty with professionalism. This was not the first in his very long lifetime that he had encountered someone like Paul.

Judas opened the car door and watched Paul stumble from the car in the most uncoordinated way possible. Judas rolled his eyes while Paul straightened his tie and brushed off his suit. This man was nothing more than bluster and Judas had figured him out entirely in just his first couple of days. How on earth was anyone else fooled by his make believe bravado? Still, Judas followed behind him dutifully as he walked into the law office lobby.

As they walked through the familiar doors, Judas was blown away. Eliza mentioned plans for transforming the business setting into a real life gala, but the result was beyond anything he'd expected. The walls draped with delicate satin curtains, the ceiling as well; the fabric had softened the lighting to intimate glow. Decadently dressed tables were arranged around the room creating private spaces for potential donors to sit while the middle of the room stood empty except for the lone, raised stage. No one would know that just hours ago this place had seemed outdated and truly nothing remarkable. The catalyst for this transformation started walking to the podium, welcoming the guests as they began to filter into the room.

Judas felt his heart thudding in his chest, his skin growing warm just looking at her. She was radiant. Her hair, always in a tightly wound bun, was looser with a few golden curls escaping as they trailed down her neck and framed her face. Her usual suit had been exchanged for loose, flowing wide leg pants and a snug, white lace top. She was absolutely stunning. She took his breath away. She's was as close to heaven as Judas would ever get. All his doubts and fears aside, he fought an overwhelming urge to steal her away from the room and never let her go. He had no idea what to do with the feelings, but they were becoming harder and harder to ignore the longer he knew this woman.

As crowds gathered, Judas floated discretely between Paul and Eliza as his eyes continued to scan the room. He watched every face as they sipped drinks and ate appetizers being served by the wait staff. At eight o'clock sharp, Eliza took the stage as the room erupted in applause. She smiled as she announced the evening's schedule and her father's desire to raise funds to run for office as a long standing pillar in the community. No one else noticed her slight grimace as she gave this last bit of information, but Judas did and it made him smile. She clearly loved her father, but he also mortified her in so many ways. Judas fully understood the feeling.

At the conclusion of her speech, Eliza handed the microphone off to Paul and made her way to the sidelines alongside Judas.

"That was torture," she whispered.

Judas smiled down at her, "You did wonderful."

She rolled her eyes and shook off the last of her nerves, "Thank you, but unless I'm in a courtroom, public speaking is not my thing."

"You seem like a natural. You were eloquent and perfectly professional up there," he told her earnestly.

Eliza wrinkled her nose at his words playfully, "Are you flirting with me, sir?"

Judas felt the blush in his cheeks and hoped the lighting was dim enough to hide it, but Eliza's matching red cheeks suggested otherwise. They both stared awkwardly toward the floor in hopes that the heat was leaving their faces.

After several quiet moments passed, Judas offered "You were beautiful up there too, for what it's worth."

Eliza's lashes fluttered as she gazed up at him, "I think that might actually be flirting."

Judas, feeling brave by her side, shrugged his shoulders, "And if it is, what would you do?"

Eliza pondered over her answer before responding. The butterfly feeling in her stomach was back. Looking up at him was the sweetest reward but absolute torture all at once. She wanted to touch him. She wanted him to touch her. She wondered what his lips would taste like.

Sucking in a sharp breath from the weight of her own thoughts, Eliza played coy, "A lady never reveals her secrets."

Chuckling, he nodded his head head. She was absolutely captivating and without a single second of hesitation he decided to dive in headfirst. "You are absolutely right, but I have to tell you," he said leaning down closer to her and whispering in her ear, "This man will walk to the ends of the earth to learn every secret you have to offer, Eliza."

His cheek brushed against hers as he pulled away and Eliza desperately wanted to grab hold of him and keep him near. His words made her head spin, her pulse quicken. She wasn't used to feeling this out of control. She didn't know what to think about how she felt or about him. Thankfully, the crowd began to clap as her father ended his speech and she was catapulted back into the here and now.

She turned her attention back to the podium in time to see her father walking toward them. He was beaming with joy at all the attention and immediately wrapped Eliza in a bear hug.

"How'd I do, Betsy?" he asked in his signature drawl.

Eliza cringed, but recovered quickly, smiling as she escaped the hug, "It was great, dad! Completely perfect and the crowd loved it!"

She, in fact, had absolutely no idea what her father had said up there. Every moment he was speaking, she was staring into the eyes of a man she barely knew and, undressing him in her mind. Recalling this in her father's presence caused Eliza to stiffen and stare around the room to avoid her father's eye contact at all costs. She was hopeful feigning boredom would cause him to move on to a more willing conversationalist, but luck was not on her side.

Instead, Paul frowned at his daughter's seeming disinterest in this party just for him, "Listen, sugar, you need to lighten up. This is a party. Get out there on the dance floor and celebrate your daddy!"

Eliza looked horrified, "Oh, absolutely not."

Paul was not the kind of man that liked being told no, especially by his daughter, and insisted she take his advice, "I'm not offering ideas, Betsy. I'm telling you to get out there and have fun. Looks tacky if we don't enjoy our own party."

She firmly shook her head, "Dad, people are out there slow dancing. What do you want me to do? Go out there and sway by myself?"

Paul's brows furrowed as he considered this dilemma before he glanced at his bodyguard, "I'm plenty safe in here surrounded by friends. Take the boy. Christian, take my daughter on the dance floor for a while. She needs to get with the program. This is a party."

Judas had to use every ounce of self-control in his being to not react in the way he would've liked to. Instead of grinning from ear to ear, Judas simply nodded solemnly and extended a hand to Eliza.

She stared from Judas to her father, biting her lip in uncertainty, but couldn't resist this delicious opportunity that just fell into her lap.

Eliza took his hand and let him lead her into the middle of the crowded dance floor.

Judas moved her across the floor like he had done this a thousand times before. He was graceful and sure on his feet. Eliza easily let her body lean into his as he twirled her through the notes of a slow, country ballad. She felt like Ginger Rogers to his Fred Astaire. Being in his arms was the most grounded she had felt in more years than she could count.

As the music faded into the faster melody of a new song, Judas changed up their movements, shifting seamlessly into a two-step.

Eliza smiled up at him, "You're a very good dancer."

He twirled her away from him then pulled her back in even closer than before, "I've not had a chance to dance in a long time, but it's something I very much loved to do once upon a time."

"You are a constant surprise, sir," she said, "Did you have lessons when you were growing up?"

He laughed, "Oh, no. We never did much dancing when I was a child, not like this. I was once friends with a tremendous jazz singer and she taught me everything I know. She was a wonderful teacher."

Judas revels in the flooding memories of all the nights he spent in Harlem listening to Billie singing and all the mornings they shared, still sitting by the bar or tearing up the dance floor. She was such a beautiful woman, inside and out. He felt extremely lucky to have known her.

"You look so wistful, thinking about her," Eliza said. She would never admit it, but the look on his face when talking about this woman who taught him to dance, sent shockwaves of jealousy through her. "Is she the one that got away?"

Reading the look on Eliza's face, Judas realized what his trip down memory lane must have looked like. He laughed, "Nothing like that. She was my friend. I enjoyed her company and she enjoyed mine. No, hanky panky or innuendo. I promise."

She was embarrassed that he so clearly read her intentions. She bowed her head and looked at the floor. He squeezed Eliza tighter against him and checked their surroundings to make sure they weren't being watched too closely. He then leaned closer to her and lifted her chin to meet his gaze. He bit his lip, overcome with the weight of their close proximity. Their faces so close he felt the warmth of her breath.

He seemed to stare straight to her soul, "With each passing day, I get the feeling that the one that got away may end up being you."

Chapter Five

Eliza stared at him, breathless, only the fading out of the music into a new song about red, white, and blue patriotism registered in her mind. Nothing else in the room even slightly penetrated her consciousness. At that moment, she stared only at Judas and his sparkling hazel eyes.

He seemed just as swept away as he took her by the hand whisking her away from the busy room. Leading her out a doorway and into the hallway, he released her the second they were away from prying eyes. She wanted to plead with him to wrap her up in his arms. She wanted to feel him as close to her as she could get him. He wanted the same but was too desperate to clear his mind from the fog she'd placed him in to take any action other than to create space between them. He paced the hallway for a few moments, running his hands through his black, shoulder length hair. This woman was quickly turning his world upside down. He was usually cool, calm, and collected, but Eliza seemed to steal away all of his careful thoughtfulness. She made him feel impulsive, needy. She made him want to give up everything for every stolen moment he could have with her.

After a few steadying breaths, Judas returned to her side, "I have to make rounds to check in with the rest of my security staff. I'm sorry I was so forward and distracted you from your night. You can go back in and enjoy yourself. I'll see you later, okay?"

Eliza stared at him for a long moment. Did he seriously think he was bothering her? Has he lost his mind? How can he not see that she was feeling equally drawn to him if not more?

"Can I come with you?" she asked.

He was taken aback by the request, "Would you want to?"

A giggle spilled from her, "I would rather be anywhere but back at the party. Especially if it's somewhere with you."

Judas felt warmth spread through him as a smile took over his face. Eliza delighted in his obvious joy at spending more time with her.

She threaded her arm through his as they began to make their way down the darkened hallways. The only lighting was the red glow of the exit signs and the moon shining through the few windows. It set a candlelight-like glow on their skin. Almost simultaneously, they thought to themselves how perfectly the ambiance compliments the other. How his eyes sparkled in the dim light. How her hair shone against the darkness. So completely in sync, both feeling the same, but neither really brave enough to admit it.

They walked a distance in companionable silence, but Eliza had so many questions about this beautiful stranger and was finding it impossible not to ask. Inquisitive by nature she contained herself as much as possible already. "So... security? How did you get into that? Are you like an ex-CIA operative or something?"

Judas raised an eyebrow at her, "What kind of back story have you created for me in that head of yours?"

Eliza humored him with all her wildest ideas, "Well, I think first you were probably in the military and they decided that you were so smart and wonderful that some super secret government agency scooped you up and placed you in the heart of danger and let you fight your way out. You probably know jiu-jitsu and taekwondo and how to kill a man with nothing but a ballpoint pen." She sighs now, as if picturing him in all his glory, "But then you grew tired of the assassin's life and decided to put down roots in good ole small town Texas." She looked up at him expectantly, "How'd I do?"

Laughter filled the space, "So very, very bad. Excuse me for a moment."

Judas stepped away to check in with the man in a black suit standing at the rear exit of the building. After just a few seconds, he returned and offered Eliza his arm once more before continuing, "I've spent some time in military service, but I was never more than a foot soldier. I do know several variations of martial arts, but I'm really more partial to yoga. Never been in the CIA or any other secret government agency and definitely never been an assassin. I just like to protect people and I think I'm pretty good at it."

"Someone in the CIA would *so* say all that," she responded with a grin.

Judas shook his head laughing out loud as he left her side to speak with another shadowy figure, this one larger than the first. He was out of sight for a much longer period, but when he returned, he some-how magically materialized two champagne flutes full of the bubbling spirit. She took hers from his hand and they cheered one another in the darkness. The bubbles tickled Eliza's nose and Judas felt his heart squeeze looking at her silly, scrunched up face. She was absolutely perfect in every way.

They continued their journey down the halls, "What about you, Miss Eliza? How did you end up as a political coordinator?"

She made a gagging noise and stuck out her tongue before answer-ing. "I'm most definitely not in or into politics of any kind. I'm simply the resourceful daughter of a wealthy man who decided to run for office for some god-forsaken reason," she finished with a roll of her eyes.

"I can't imagine you not doing this professionally. You are very good at it," Judas offered.

"I am just good at handling my father," she said with a snort, "The rest is all just leftovers from finishing school and cotillion classes."

"So what do you really do? I can't imagine you don't have a profession of some kind."

"I started out as a prosecuting attorney for the county. I put bad guys away all day, every day. Pretty easy to do in a state that prioritizes law and order over everything. One day I just came to the realization that we weren't just putting bad guys away. They were fathers, mothers, sons, daughters. And a lot of them, more than I'm comfortable admitting, could very likely have been innocent. I couldn't live with knowing that my job was tearing families apart like that, ruining lives. So, I quit and I started a non-profit to help innocent people who were wrongly convicted get the justice they deserve." She shrugged nonchalantly.

Her words slammed into him in the deepest parts of his soul. Judas had always felt like an outsider because of his past. He always felt as though he was unredeemable because of the assumptions made and lies told about him. This woman before him made an entire career out of giving others in the same kind of torment respite. She forgave and redeemed the wrongly accused as her day job. He had never felt more safe with another human on this planet and it filled his throat with emotion.

He stopped her cold and turned her gently to face him, "You just said that like it's nothing special. Eliza, that's truly something to be proud of. You are doing something that makes the world a better place. You're saving lives. You should own that. Say it with pride."

She blushed, not at all used to having her work praised, "I guess I'm used to downplaying it. It is pretty cool. My dad hates it. Thinks it's a waste of time so I guess that's why I don't lead with that. Texas isn't known for loving criminal defense issues." She shrugged her shoulders again as if this foregone conclusion was just the way it was.

He shook his head, "No, that's bullshit. What you do is amazing. I'm really proud to know you."

Eliza's heart soared with pride. She knew that her job was important but it was not often she heard it, especially lately. Just looking at him, she knew he was being honest and that truly did things to her that she could not fully comprehend in the moment. All she knew was that right now she wanted to kiss him. She had to, needed to.

She reached for him, placing her hands on either side of his face. He moaned and leaned into her touch, setting her on fire. She lifted herself onto tiptoes, pulling him to her. Their lips nearly colliding...

A loud thud startled them back to reality. They quickly moved as far away from one another as possible while waiting to see who'd invaded their moment.

Chet rounded the corner swiftly, looking concerned. Was Paul suspicious of where the two have disappeared to? Was Chet here to warn them?

Relief washed over his face as he spotted them, "Eliza, I know you're probably busy, but I wanted to let you know that your dad has had a few drinks and I- uh... You know how it is... I just wanted to let you know before things get too out of hand..."

Eliza didn't even need to ask. She knew exactly what Chet's concern was. Her father was about to make an absolute fool of himself and ruin everything he was trying to build before he even got it started. Eliza knew this scene well as she'd lived it and cleaned it up too many times to count. She threw back the last gulp of her champagne and walked back into the gala resigned to her duties as Paul Arthur's only child.

Judas watched as she lost all the shine she'd had with him all night. Her shoulders dropped. The blood faded from her cheeks. It was devastating to see her shoved dutifully into the role of fixer for a man that had little if any decency to offer the world. Still, Judas followed behind her knowing he would be there for her the entire way, no questions asked.

As they re-entered the room they escaped from earlier, Eliza saw him immediately. Thankfully, the crowd was busy listening to a speaker from their team so it still appeared to be an isolated incident, but Paul was belligerently drunk and appeared to be hitting on the same poor intern he screamed at just yesterday.

Honestly, hitting on was too kind of a term. He was pawing at her. Placing his hands on her in ways that made it clear what his intentions were. He was bordering on sexual assault and committing human resources violations that could easily get him sued if the girl was willing to fight him on it.

Eliza hated him at this very moment. She wanted to yell and scream and cause a scene so everyone could see him for what he really was. She wanted to end his whole facade right now, but she knew she wouldn't as the tears threatened to spill from her eyes as she came to terms with this truth. No matter how terrible he was, he was her father. He was the only parent she had left and he gave her everything he could after her mother died. She owed him this, no matter how crushing it was.

Eyes now red and brimming with unshed tears, Eliza turned to Judas. She couldn't say anything because if she did she was afraid her emotions would betray her. She hated to cry in front of anyone and she was certain crying in front of him, strong and kind Judas, would be something she would never forgive herself for allowing to happen So, instead, she just looked at him, while trying her best to regain composure, but he didn't need her to do anything.

Judas took her hand saying, "I'm here and I'll do whatever you need."

Chapter Six

I t took some heavy persuasion to get Paul to leave his own party, but the fraudulent promise of an after party dinner consisting of the donors with the biggest wallets did the trick.

Juda, behind the wheel, watched Paul in the backseat smiling like he'd already won the damn election. He showed no signs of understanding that he'd almost cost himself the whole race in an instant. If his pious and conservative donors had seen him lewdly groping at a young staff member, they would've dropped him without hesitation. Not because they hadn't done the same kinds of things all through their own lives, but because his actions did not fit the kind of image they wanted their party to portray in public. He'd become a liability.

Judas turned his gaze to Eliza sitting next to her father. Her eyes were vacant and dull. She looked like a victim trapped in her own head and he just wanted to stop the vehicle to go to her. He wanted to take her in his arms and hold her until everything was okay again. He wanted all the things that he knew should be off limits. Seeing her powerful and secure made Judas lust for her, but seeing her broken makes him want to make her his. It made him want to be the one that she could depend on when she felt like she had no one. He wanted to be her someone.

'Damn it, Yesh,' he thought to himself. '*All these years of being utterly alone and now you make me want a woman that I will have to leave or watch age and die without me. Why the fuck would you do this to me? Was this a gift after all?'*

Heaving a heavy sigh full of contempt, Judas turned his attention back to the road but could hear Eliza placating her father from the backseat.

"Dad, stop," she said.

"Oh, calm down, Betsy. It's all in good fun," Paul slurs back at her.

Looking back in the mirror Judas saw the look of discomfort on Eliza's face and Paul's red-faced stare boring into her. Paul's hand was stroking Eliza's cheek and she was wincing away from his touch. Judas felt rage boiling up inside him to see that sleazy man lay a single finger on Eliza.

"My pretty, pretty Eliza," Paul drawled, "So pretty and perfect like your momma."

The remark made Eliza cringe and sent sparks of fury through Judas. He quickly slammed his foot onto the brake and jerked the steering wheel, sending Paul flying forward out of his seat until he was crumpled onto the floor of the large SUV.

"My apologies," Judas said, "There was something in the road that I had to avoid."

He expected Paul to be infuriated, but instead, Paul laughed as he climbed back into the seat and leaned forward, resting a hand on Judas' shoulder.

"Thanks, my boy. You're always looking out for me," Paul chuckled jovially. "I really never expected you to work out so well, seeing as you're an exotic type and all, but so far you've been a mighty fine help."

Judas nodded but rolled his eyes before looking into the rearview mirror again. Eliza smiled back at him and mouthed, "Thank you."

Judas smiled back and she could read his expression through his piercing honey brown eyes. She was certain she could see a whole world in them and she very much wanted to explore that world. She could not be more grateful to the man in the driver's seat. He was a complete stranger just days ago and now she knew she wanted him to be a part of her life. Being drawn to him was an understatement. She was completely trapped in his gravitational pull in ways she loved tremendously.

Settling back into their seats the three rode in silence for several minutes until Paul began to recognize his own gated neighborhood.

"Oh, no," he said bitterly, "No, no, no. This is all wrong. This isn't where we were going. I'm ready for the dinner party you promised me. I won't be going home right now. Turn the car around." With every word, Paul became more angry.

Judas and Eliza both ignored his rising outburst like they would a tantrum throwing toddler. The car pulled up the long driveway and Judas parked in front of the columned entryway. Paul continued to protest loudly and Eliza wasn't sure how they would ever get him out of the car.

Without missing a single beat, Judas exited the vehicle and walked to Paul's car door. Opening the door to a grumbling Paul, he leaned in, and grabbed hold of the ranting old man. Judas picked Paul up and easily tossed him over his shoulder. Paul's eyes grew large with shock and his protests stopped instantly. Eliza watched in astonishment as Judas carried her father up the sidewalk and to the front door effortlessly.

Judas turned to her, "Where to?"

Eliza scrambled out of the car and led Judas inside and to Paul's bedroom. Judas deposited a stunned Paul onto the edge of his bed before turning to Eliza.

"What else can I do?" he asked.

Eliza, blown away by the ease and grace with which he handled this whole debacle, smiled up at him and touched her palm to his cheek. Judas leaned into her touch and closed his eyes. Eliza would normally be worried about her father seeing this moment of intimacy between his daughter and a stranger, but she was certain Paul would remember very little of this evening in the morning.

"I can handle it from here," she assured Judas letting her hand fall to her side. "Would you mind giving me a ride home, though?"

Judas broke into a wide grin, "It would be my pleasure, Eliza."

He loved the feel of her name on his mouth. For a brief moment, he allowed himself the privilege of imagining how sweet her skin would taste on his lips as well but quickly dashed away the thought with another mental round of curses to the heavens. He quickly turned to leave the room.

"Judas," Eliza called out.

He turned back to face her and felt nearly weak in the knees seeing her in the soft light before him.

She smiled at him, "You were my hero tonight."

Her words filled him with a warmth that he couldn't fully explain or comprehend. Without another word, Judas left the room heading back toward the car. He spent the entire walk recalling how her hand on his cheek had been the most electrifying touch of his entire life.

Chapter Seven

With her father safely tucked into his bed and a raging hangover waiting for him in the morning, Eliza returned to the car and slid into the passenger seat. Judas watched her intently as she sat still and silent, staring out at the cloudy skies through the windshield. He wondered what she was thinking, but didn't have long to contemplate what was going through her mind.

Without warning, Eliza howled out her frustration in a bellowing cry. Clenching her fists, she pushed her tight palms into her eyes and laid her head against the headrest of the passenger seat. Judas didn't react and didn't ask questions. Five minutes spent with Paul was more than enough to make him want to scream as well. Eliza had been doing this her entire life. He was amazed by her patience but did wonder why she wasn't always screaming at the top of her lungs in absolute disgust at the man-child who raised her.

Forever thinking of the part she played in her father's world was exhausting for her. Taking a moment to fully express her feverish disgust was therapeutic. When she was finished, she took a steadying breath. She pursed her lips, closed her eyes, and seemed to completely recompose herself. It was like magic how she was able to just let it all slide off her and return to the prim and proper lady her father expected from her, so instantaneously. Judas was certain he'd never been so fascinated by another living creature in all the years he'd lived. Eliza was a puzzle and, though he knew he shouldn't, he desperately wanted to put all her pieces together to see her as the full masterpiece he already knew she was. He wanted her in ways he had never dared to want another person. He was more and more certain with every passing moment that he had to have her, consequences be damned.

She looked over at him sitting behind the wheel watching her. She noticed while he waited for her to return, he had removed his jacket and rolled the sleeves of his shirt up to his elbows. The muscles of his forearm flexed as his fingers traced the stitching of the steering wheel. Their eyes locked and a spark of attraction flickered again.

The interior of the car suddenly grew very warm and he wanted to reach out and touch her. He didn't. But he wanted to.

Eliza wanted his touch, as well. She felt exposed and vulnerable after letting a stranger see into her imperfect world. She worked so hard to keep their family dysfunction quiet. She was constantly on the defense, fighting off compromising situations her very public father always wound up in. She was tired and the way his eyes looked into her made her want to give up the whole charade and let him hold her until it all went away. She didn't even know him, yet she wanted to lay herself bare for him. Tell him all her secrets.

"I'm sorry," she offered. She could only imagine what he was thinking after her outburst. She was certain he thought her out of her mind.

"You're allowed to express any feelings you have," Judas told her with as much sincerity as he could fill his words with hoping she knew and believed him.

It worked and his tenor filled her with warmth. Suddenly, the confines of her alter ego were suffocating. She clawed at her now too tight updo until every tendril of blonde hair was free around her shoulders. She began to tear at her lacy top, desperately needing to be free of its confines. She sat quietly in just in her tank top and pants, feeling a little more like herself.

Judas even more enraptured to see her morph into a truer version of herself, couldn't help but run his eyes over every inch of her exposed skin. His eyes came to an abrupt stop on a sliver of color not quite hidden beneath her skimpy top. He was surprised to find the brilliant green of what looked like a snake.

"Do you have a tattoo?" he smirked.

Eliza blushed, instinctively pulling her shirt down to cover the evidence, "My secret rebellion against dear old dad."

Judas laughed, "You are a constant surprise, Eliza."

She laughed as well, fully relaxing for the first time in as long as she could remember. She lifted her top to reveal the delicate lines along her ribcage and trailing down toward her hip. It was truly beautiful. Shades of vibrant green and deep black were placed so perfectly that the entire snake seemed to shimmer and shine like it was alive. Its rounded off head pointed its nose just under her right breast as the body curved into an intricate S-pattern down her side.

Without even realizing what he was doing, Judas reached out and ran his fingers along the coiled snake. Eliza trembled at his touch and he felt goosebumps rise on her skin. He quickly pulled his hand away as they stared at one another for a long moment. Pulling himself together, he turned his attention to the windshield and put the car in drive. Eliza typed her address into the GPS as he pulled out of her father's long driveway. The silence between them felt tense but only because it was so loaded with the chemistry building between them. Without even realizing it, they both were thinking the same thing at the same moment: that resisting the temptation of one another might be more than they could withstand.

"So why a snake?" he asked, desperate to fill the space with conversation that might drown out his thoughts.

A giggle bubbled up from Eliza, "Because I couldn't think of a single thing that would make my father more mad than a literal serpent."

He smiled, "So what did he have to say about it when you showed him?"

"Ha!" she cried out with the most beautiful smile Judas could imagine, "I didn't have the guts to show him. I must have known I wouldn't since I put it somewhere he would absolutely never see."

Judas glanced at her as he drove, "You really think he would be that mad? So mad that you can't show him?"

"Oh, most definitely," Eliza said with a sigh, "He would never forgive me. Your body is a temple and all that."

Judas felt an unexpected pang of intense protectiveness for her. He itched to fight this man who couldn't love this amazing woman, his own daughter, sacrilegious tattoo and all, "I'm sorry,"

Eliza waved off this apology, "It's fine. That's just who he is. Set in his ways and stubborn." She shrugged her shoulders and changed the subject, "What about you, Mr. Christian? Any tattoos of your own hidden under there somewhere?" She bit her lip at the thought of his flesh beneath what remained of his suit.

He caught her flirtation from the corner of his eye, "Please, call me Judas. And no. My body is a temple and all that." He smiled at her as she giggled. "I have a feeling my family wouldn't approve either."

"If your body is a temple, you should decorate it as you please," Eliza replied.

He slowly depressed the brake at a stoplight before turning to look at her, "I suppose you're right. What should I get?"

Unable to withstand the intensity of his gaze, Eliza moved her eyes back to the road, "Hmm... Well, that depends. What's important to you?"

This question sent Judas' mind racing. What *was* important to him? He didn't know. He rarely took the time to know anyone well enough that they might ask anything like that of him. How would one answer a question they hadn't considered in literal eons?

"I'm sorry if that was too personal," Eliza said softly, seeing the wrinkle forming between his eyebrows.

"No, not at all," he responded before pressing on the gas. "It's just that no one has asked me anything like that in a very long time and I'm not sure how to answer."

"Well, we're a good four minutes away from my apartment. I have time," she said and they shared another laugh.

"I guess," he said with hesitation, "Honor. Home. Doing what's right."

Taking his answer in, she found herself appreciating the man more and more with each passing second.

He shook his head, "That's a stupid answer, sorry."

"I mean, it would be hard to pick a tattoo for those things," Eliza said with a laugh before reaching out to place a hand on his arm, "but I can't imagine anything better to hold near and dear."

Hearing her words of affirmation to his inner thoughts and feeling her hand gently on him knowing the only thing between them was his shirt sleeve sent waves through his body that sent him reeling, just like every time before. He wasn't sure he had ever felt that kind of... what?

Contentment?

Joy?

Understanding?

Whatever the emotion was, he never wanted to stop feeling it. It put warmth through his entire being. It made him glad he had lived as many years as he did just to have felt what this moment gave him.

"Thank you," he said, looking directly into her sapphire eyes, "Thank you."

Giving him another smile, Eliza motioned towards the buildings that surrounded them, "This next one is me. Thank you for your help tonight. I appreciate all of it more than you know. Especially, the chance to talk and just be myself. I don't get to do that very often."

Pulling into a parking spot just outside her building, Judas was disappointed that the night was coming to and end. He reminded himself that he had a job to do and he would have to ignore any spark he may have felt and any desire to sweep her into his arms. He settled for taking her hand, still resting on his arm, and kissing her soft skin. It sent electricity through them both and Eliza hesitated leaving the car. She could stay with him forever. She wanted to, but she couldn't. She knew they were something that just could never be for so many reasons, no matter how many times tonight she had tried to convince herself otherwise.

Instead, she climbed from the car and gave a wave as she walked away from him. He watched her jog up the stairs toward her apartment door, and felt a giant hole in her absence. Watching her go was like watching the last golden rays of sunshine fade into dusk. He would be crazy to chase after her. He barely knew this woman. He couldn't reasonably follow after her for just another moment of her presence. He just couldn't. She would think he was insane.

'Are you happy now, Yesh? Is this what you wanted? You fucking sadist.'

Throwing the car door open, Judas jumped from the seat and raced toward her as she opened her apartment door. Reaching her, she stared at him in stunned silence.

He stood as near to her as he could and leaned his body towards her, completely lost in temptation. Resting one hand on the door behind her, their faces were so close they nearly touched noses. She was breathless. He was overcome with need.

His voice heavy and sultry with want for her, "Are you still into doing things that would make your dad mad? Because I thought of a way to really piss him off."

Without a second of hesitation, Eliza smiled up at his beautiful face and pulled him to her. Tangling her fingers through his long hair, she kissed him with a passion neither of them had ever felt before. When their lips collided, it seemed as though the earth shifted beneath them. Hunger overcame them.

They were all hands, grasping for whatever hold they could get on one another. Tearing each other's clothes off before they were even through the door.

The sound of her needy breaths against his ear set his soul on fire.

The feel of his lips on her skin sent waves of pleasure through to her core.

Neither of them had ever felt more alive than they did in those delicate seconds.

Judas pushed her away from him, "Are you sure this is okay?"

Eliza stared at him, eyes crazed and body aching for him. She crashed her mouth back into his and pushed him against the wall. Pressing her entire body into his, she felt his hardened need against her. Yes, this was okay. This was the most beyond okay thing she had done in years. She more than wanted this. She needed it.

Judas tangled his fingers in her hair and ran his other hand along the length of her body. His arm wrapped around her waist and pulled her tighter against him. She moaned against his lips and he growled his response. Not another second wasted, he grabbed her by the thighs and lifted her body off the floor. Wrapping her legs around his waist, he carried her to the counter behind them.

The cold granite against her skin was jarring, but not enough to bring her out of the fever dream. Judas locked eyes with her as he used one skilled hand to unhook her bra and slid it down her arms. He placed a hand against her bare chest pushing her back onto the counter. With her lying before him, back arched against the frigid stone, Judas tucked his fingers beneath the waist of her slacks and the elastic of her panties. Slowly, he slid them down her legs and let them fall to the floor. Completely exposed before him, she was the most beautiful thing he had ever laid eyes on. His eyes met hers again and she bit her lip.

"In all my years, I never dreamed of seeing something this glorious before me," he whispered, apparent awe overtaking his voice.

His words made her tremble and she begged for him, "Touch me, Judas. Please, put your hands on me."

Never glancing away from the deep pools of her eyes, Judas ran one finger slowly from her chin, down her throat, between her breasts, down her stomach, and finally between her thighs. He opened her and felt her wet need for him. With painful slowness, he circled the sacred bundle of nerves with his finger then plunged it inside of her. She cried out at his touch and he felt all judgment and reason leave his body.

His free hand unbuttoned his slacks and they fell to his feet, freeing him. Without hesitation, he pressed his length against her.

Eliza reached for him, clawing for him, desperate to feel him fully possessing her, "Please, oh, God. Please. I want to feel you."

Judas obeyed and penetrated her completely. Pressing against her inner walls, he filled her. Both moaned in absolute ecstasy. Eliza rose from the counter and wrapped her arms around his neck. Their bodies pressed together, Judas thrust into her again and again with a thirst that was completely foreign to him. He'd had a hundred women before, but not like this.

He needed to find release in her like he'd never needed anything. More than he needed water in the desert of his homeland. He had to feel this glorious woman wrapped around him in every conceivable way.

Eliza continued to cry out with every pounding thrust. She had never experienced anything quite this primal. She never had anything that wasn't polite sex. Missionary, lights off, and gentle movement. It had gotten the job done, or so she thought, but this was otherworldly. Her entire world was on fire feeling him inside of her.

As his pace quickened, she clung even tighter to him and felt her own body's rhythm match his urgency. She felt flames climbing within her, threatening to consume her. She threw her head back as she cried out his name, "Judas!"

His lips claimed her throat and he was sure it would leave a mark, but he wanted it to. He wanted to claim her body as his. He had to know that she was his. He wanted the entire world to know. Eliza was his.

He could tell she was close to falling over the edge of orgasm as her muscles tightened around him and she trembled with each movement.

He wanted to be sure that she left this encounter devoted to him and ordered her, "Look at me. I want you to look at me when I make you cum."

Eliza gasped but obeyed. As she stared into his eyes, he placed one hand between their bodies and rubbed her sensitive bundle of nerves with skill. He continued pushing into her as his fingers glided through her wetness. All the while, he watched her.

As her skin flushed red.

As her mouth cried out for him.

As her eyes rolled back in complete loss of control.

He watched her.

She had become his complete undoing and he crashed his lips onto hers while spilling his orgasm into her. They rode the wave of pleasure together until they were both left panting, dripping with their own pleasure.

Eliza, completely spent, laid her body back against the counter again and stared up at this beautiful man standing between her thighs, still sheathed inside of her.

"Holy shit," she breathed, "This cannot be real. You have got to be a god or something."

Judas couldn't help but laugh at her statement. If she only knew.

Chapter Eight

Eliza was called a workaholic on more than one occasion and it had been an issue with every partner Eliza had even attempted to have a relationship with. They would always want her to drop everything for them on a whim and all she wanted to do was work on research for her next big case. She loved her job and that had always been priority one for her. Plain and simple.

While working for her father had not been the same kind of obsession as her own personal work, Eliza could never be considered a lackluster employee. Doing her job and doing it well was something Eliza held near and dear. Being presented as an above and beyond employee was something she had never been willing to compromise.

Until this morning.

Nearly 48 hours passed since Judas rocked her body fully, but she hadn't stopped thinking about it for even one second. Sitting at her desk with Monday's to-do list staring up at her did nothing to correct that either. Every time she closed her eyes, she saw him standing over her, heard him claiming her as his, and felt him touching parts of her soul she didn't know existed. Recalling it in that moment, sent shivers down her spine in delicious ways. She cradled her head in her hands and wondered how she would ever make it through the day. Especially once he arrived.

Shaking her head to try and hold off the flashing images of his divine body, Eliza trudged through the office to make a cup of coffee. Coffee tended to at least slightly calm her nerves and bring peace to her mind. This morning, though, it seemed it would be served with a side of Judas Christian and that would do nothing to take him off of her mind.

He was in the kitchen pouring himself a cup as Eliza stood frozen in the doorway staring at him. She saw him naked not two days ago and that was all she could see when she looked at him. Wanting to enjoy the view, she took in the sight of him as long as she could without getting caught. Unfortunately, she'd underestimated how long that was and she was sure he saw her out of the corner of his eye as he turned toward her. Without waiting to find out, Eliza whipped on her heel, marching away from the kitchen as if she never intended to go there in the first place.

As she spun, Lydia smiled at her in that conspiratorial way that said she knew exactly what Eliza was just doing.

Walking past her at lightning speed, Eliza muttered, "Shut up, Lydia."

The woman's laugh followed her as she hid behind her office door.

Meanwhile, Judas, having immensely enjoyed catching her staring at him as he poured his morning brew, slowly sauntered behind her as she ran away. He nodded cooly as he passed Lydia's desk.

"Good morning, Mr. Christian," Lydia said with a smile.

He paused to be polite and offered his own greeting, "Good morning, Lydia."

The woman continued smiling up at him with a twinkle in her eye, "Seems our Eliza is quite distracted this morning."

Judas hated that he felt a warm heat flood his cheeks and feigned ignorance, "I'm sure she is. She's a busy woman."

Lydia winked at him now, "I'm sure she is. Have a great day, Mr. Christian. Tell Eliza she forgot to get her coffee, would you?"

Judas laughed, unable to contain himself, "How about I just bring her one myself?" He walked back into the kitchen and poured a cup for Eliza before heading to her office. Lydia smirked as he walked by.

Shaking his head, Judas knocked on Eliza's door. There was no response but he knew she was hidden away inside. He cracked open the door and held the cup of coffee through the opening. From directly behind the door, Eliza's hand shot out and snatched the cup away.

"Thank you," she mumbled.

He chuckled, pushing the door open further, and with it, her body away from the doorway. He peeked around and saw Eliza sipping her coffee in hiding. "Can I come in?" he asked.

Eliza's face burned bright red but she nodded her head.

Walking inside, Judas took a seat at her desk. He looked over his shoulder and gestured toward another chair, "Join me."

Swallowing a large gulp of coffee, she crossed the room to sit across from the most sexually gifted man she ever met. They stared at one another for a full three minutes of complete silence.

Judas cracked first, "Are we good? I'm sorry if I crossed boundaries I shouldn't have."

"Sir, you have not crossed any boundaries. I gave willing consent and active participation. It's just..." she let out a hysterical cackle before falling quiet.

Her silence seemed weighted and it frightened Judas. He was terrified she was about to say they could never do that again, he was certain it might actually break his heart. He leaned forward with a solemn expression on his face, "It's just... what?"

Eliza set down her coffee, moving closer to him, whispering, "It's just that I can't focus on a goddamn thing and all I can do is picture you naked every single time I look at you!"

Letting it sink in, Judas burst out with bellowing laughter. That's it? He could definitely work with that.

Eliza shushed him, "It's not funny, Judas! I am about to meet with my father, probably with you standing right behind him and I can't concentrate on anything but having sex with you!"

"If it makes you feel any better, seeing you naked is quite a distraction as well," he replied, calming his laughter. His eyes scanned her body and he could feel his own respond to her instantly.

Eliza dropped her head in a sigh, "Thank you, but I don't think that is going to help me make it through the day."

"I was worried," he admitted.

She looked back at him, seeing the serious expression that had overtaken his features, "Worried about what?"

"When you very abruptly kicked me out of your apartment the other night, I was afraid you would want nothing to do with me," he said.

Eliza felt a wave of warmth wash over her. She hadn't meant to kick him out, she just needed to process what just happened, not that the time helped at all. Not feeling the need to hide anything from him, she tried to explain, "What we did felt like some kind of religious experience. That's how good it was. I needed time to process all that and there was no way I was going to be able to process jackshit with your body in the same space as mine. I didn't mean to make you worry."

Judas smiled, "A religious experience?"

She glared at him playfully, "It's the only thing I could think of to describe it."

"I think that's a perfect description," he said, moving to the other side of the desk. Sitting on the edge, he was so close to her that their legs brushed, "I look forward to continued worship of you, if you'll have me."

She felt flames burst to life within her and she wanted to answer, but the words just wouldn't come to her. She fiddled with her watch instead and noticed the time. Panic set in as she jumped to her feet,

"I would love to continue this conversation later, but my dad will be walking through that door at any moment and I think it will look a whole lot better if he walks in to you sitting on that side of the desk." She gestured to the chair he just vacated, praising the universe when he obeyed.

And just in time.

Not more than two seconds after Judas seated himself a respectable proximity away from her, Paul burst through the door without even a warning knock.

"Good morning, Betsy! Jude, fancy seeing you here," Paul nearly shouted in his exuberance.

Judas nodded, "Yes, we were just discussing how well security handled the event, sir."

Paul smiled widely, "Good, good! It was a hell of a night, wasn't it? We raised a boatload!"

Judas turned to Eliza with a grin from ear to ear, "It was, indeed, a truly incredible night."

Eliza bit her cheek to avoid returning his smile, trying her best to ignore her newly acquired paramour. Turning her attention to her father instead, she found it easier than she had thought it would be to focus on the conversation she needed to have with him, "Dad, we need to talk. Judas, would you excuse us?"

Paul cringed at the mention of his real name, but from her lips, Judas never loved a word more dearly. He nodded and stepped outside. Taking up a post outside the door, he could hear their conversation.

Eliza's voice started calm and cool and her words were muffled through the door, but her volume rose which triggered Paul's to rise as well. Before long there was a full on screaming match behind Eliza's closed door. After the many interactions he had been privy to, Judas had his money on Eliza winning this one for sure.

He took pleasure in listening to her completely eviscerate her father. She told him he was a petulant child. She told him he was going to get himself sued. She set the clear boundary that he needed to get his act together right then and there or he was going to ruin any chance he may have had at the election. She told him, plain and simple, he must treat this staff with respect and civility or she planned to walk out the door to let him fend for himself.

Once she got going, Paul was mostly silent and let her rant. When she was finished, Paul walked out of the office looking like a scolded child leaving the principal's office. He was feeling the wrath of her words fully and looked to be taking them seriously. Judas dutifully followed behind Paul as he made his way to his office, but all he could think about was Eliza.

She was a force to be reckoned with; full of power and bravery even in the face of the man that raised her. Judas swelled with pride in knowing this incredible woman. He made a mental note to show her just how much the next chance he got.

***

Finally, Eliza reached the end of her day. She let out a heavy sigh as she walked down the hallway toward the exit. Others were still working into the night to make plans for an upcoming rally, but she was leaving and was beyond ready. Walking past each empty office, she let her thoughts drift back to where they were this morning. She smiled to herself as she recalled Judas asking to worship her. She thought he was crazy. It should be her worshipping him. His intense, honey eyes that saw into her soul. His broad chest. His olive skin. But she was happy to let him be the worshipper, either way.

As she approached the elevators and passed the very last doorway on her way out, a strong arm reached out into the hall and wrapped itself around her waist. She squealed out in alarm but calmed the second she saw it was the very subject of her current daydreams.

Snatching her away from the open hallway and into darkness, Judas caged her against the wall. His entire body pressed into her and they both felt their pulses quicken with the contact.

Judas leaned in almost close enough to taste, "You are the grandest surprise of my life. You're strong. You're intelligent beyond words. You're capable and kind. You're good, through and through. I'm thankful to know you."

He pressed his lips to hers in a kiss that stole away her breath. She moaned into him and pressed herself against him. But then he ended the kiss too quickly for them both. Gazing longingly down at her as she panted beneath the weight of his body and of his words, he traced a finger across her lips and smiled.

"Until next time, my Eliza," he whispered before walking away into the darkness.

Chapter Nine

While unusual for Judas' position in Paul Arthur's campaign, he was randomly given the day off when leaving the office the night prior. All of his growing security team and a few interns worked late into the night preparing for a rally Paul was scheduled to attend in one week. Paul had been so excited about the outing that, to conclude the meeting, Paul promised each of them the next day off. He reasoned they all needed to rest before he blew up on the political scene and they had to work twenty-four-seven. His poll numbers were on the rise and his justification seemed solid. Judas rolled his eyes but was still riding the high from his last kiss with Eliza so he didn't raise his concerns.

On his random Tuesday off, he attempted to spend his morning in meditation and practicing some yoga poses in his living room but struggled to concentrate on anything but Eliza. He wanted to call her and spend the day together doing whatever she pleased. Getting to be by her side and getting to know everything about her was the only leisure he desired. If he wasn't afraid of scaring her away, he would just show up on her doorstep. He felt fairly confident that she would welcome him with open arms, but he didn't want to intrude on her life so much that she got tired of him. He wanted to be sure he was giving her the time and space she needed to crave him in her life. He needed her to want him and fear of jeopardizing that was terrifying to him.

It was a brand new feeling for him. He hadn't feared the loss of another's affection in literal eons. Of course, there had been friends he had grown close with over the years and those had all been losses he mourned, but he knew they were inevitable. All just a part of the price one pays to have eternal life. This... this felt different somehow. He knew, logically, that this story would end in the same way all his others had, but it didn't feel the same somehow this time. This time felt like if he didn't have her in his life, he could actually perish. While that was something he wanted for many hundreds of years, now it felt unfair and cheap. At least as long as she was among living.

While he contemplated this irony, legs crossed in lotus position in the middle of his living room with both eyes shut tightly, Judas heard the buzz of his cell phone on the counter. Opening one eye to gaze at the offensive noise, Judas sighed and pulled himself up off the floor. Very few people had his number. If anyone called, it was usually work related. Walking over to the device, he glanced down and ground his teeth in frustration seeing Paul Arthur's name illuminated on the screen. He considered not answering, but unfortunately, that just wasn't who he was.

Groaning, Judas picked up the phone and nearly growled, "This is Jude."

"Hey, boy. Good morning," comes Paul's drawl through the speaker.

Judas rolled his eyes as exaggeratedly as Eliza would, but put on a facade, "Good morning, sir. What can I do for you?"

The excitement in Paul's voice caused his words to rise in pitch as he spoke, "I need you to get down to the county courthouse in two hours and meet me. I've got an invite to Senator Reed's rally this afternoon and I'm going to need you there."

"I'm not sure if I can be available for that, sir," Judas replied even though he knew for a fact that he was available. He just didn't want to. Senator Reed was possibly even more insufferable than Paul and Judas had no desire to spend the day with the sort of individuals that would be attending that rally.

Paul completely dismissed Judas and insisted, "Oh, you'll be fine. I'll see you there in two hours. Pick Eliza up on the way. She needs to be there, too. Tell her I insist and don't let her give you any argument about it."

A smile spread across his face and Judas knew he would be going, "We'll see you there, sir."

They ended the call and Judas threw more suitable clothing into a bag and raced out the door.

***

Eliza had chosen to spend this unexpected day off in the comfort of her bed while wearing comfortable clothes and watching her favorite movies. She was so dedicated to this cause, that she wasn't even leaving for food. She had brunch on the way and Steel Magnolias playing on the TV in her bedroom. She was certain this vibe was absolute perfection.

Upon hearing the doorbell ring, Eliza leaped from the bed, in a near run to the door, already salivating over the crepes she knew were waiting on the other side. When she swung the door open, however, she gasped to see the god-like face of Judas staring back at her. He smirked as he looked her up and down while she wanted to crawl into a hole and disappear.

Judas took in every inch of her, feeling as though he was falling quickly in love with this perfect lady before him. She was completely free of makeup, her hair was woven into two perfect French braids, and she was wearing baggy sweatpants with her college sweatshirt. Seeing her so unguarded and free made his heart race.

"Coffee?" he offered, extending a cup to her.

Eyes wide and disbelieving, she took the cup but didn't move from her spot.

Judas laughed softly, "I take it your father didn't call?"

Eliza scowled, "Should have known he would find a way to ruin a day off that he literally gave me himself."

"Well," Judas said with a sly smirk, "just because he's the reason it was interrupted doesn't mean we can't make the most of it. We don't have to meet him for another hour and a half and the venue is only twenty minutes from here."

She caught his meaning immediately and smiled back as she reached for his t-shirt and yanked him into the apartment. As soon as she had him through the doorway, she slammed it shut, shoving him against it. His head hit the door with force and he laughed as he held her slightly away from him.

"Slow down, killer," he teased, "We have time."

Eliza bit her lip and checked his head, "Oh my goodness, I'm so sorry! Are you okay?"

He calmed her fretting hands, "Trust me. I'll be fine. Just slow down. I want to enjoy you."

He stroked a loose strand of hair away from her face and suddenly she remembered what she must look like.

She gasped, pulling away immediately, "Sweet Jesus, Judas. I'm a mess. I'm so sorry!"

Judas raised an eyebrow, "A mess. Eliza, this is the most beautiful I have ever seen you." He advanced toward her, "This is you. The real you, under all the pretense and manners. This is who you really are."

Eliza looked toward the floor and shook her head, "Oh no. I am the put together version, I assure you. This is just me when I'm alone and don't have anywhere to be."

He closed the distance between them and slipped his arm around her waist, "Exactly. The real you. The rest is all smoke and mirrors.

This is Eliza," he wrapped his other arm around her as well and pulled her tight against him. "And I like it tremendously."

Eliza sucked in a harsh breath as his lips met hers and his kiss made her weak in the knees. Her body melted into his as his hand tangled in her hair and pulled her head back to expose her throat. His lips claimed the soft skin along her jaw and Eliza moaned out in bliss. His touch drove her to the point of madness and for the first time in her life, it didn't scare her in the slightest. She craved it, instead. Begged it to take her over.

Clawing at his hard body, she tried to close any gap left between them. No amount of him was ever enough. He responded to her need and began to shed her clothing, one item at a time. He needed her against him with nothing to separate them. They needed the contact of nothing but skin to feel human again. They needed one another in a way neither of them expected, but it grew every day. It went beyond hunger.

With shaking hands, Eliza slid his shirt over his head and ran her hands greedily over his bronzed body. She untied the drawstring of his sweatpants letting them fall to the floor, freeing him to take her completely. Guiding him to the couch, she pushed his shoulder so he fell to the soft cushions below. He gazed up at her beauty and could almost see a glow around her. She was an absolute goddess standing over him and any thought of taking his time flew off somewhere into the ether. His hands reached for her as she glided her open thighs around him and sat herself in his lap, fully sheathing his length within her wet warmth. She cried out as she felt him fill her. He grabbed her thighs and pulled her even further onto him throwing his head back at the ecstasy of feeling her tight walls demanding his pleasure.

She began to grind her body against him, feeling the sweet friction of her pleasure center rubbing deliciously against him. He pulled her mouth to his exploring, probing with his tongue as she continued to ride him into oblivion. Sweat glistened on their skin and he tasted it as his lips ran down her throat and to her shoulder. Every so lightly, his teeth nipped her flesh as he tried to take her in as fully as possible. Eliza moaned his name quickening her pace, delighting in the pleasure and light sting of pain. She threw her head back as her body bounced along his shaft again and again until they both neared complete explosion. Their bodies were as one as they ascended to the peaks of pleasure and climax together. Panting and vibrating with orgasm, they clung to one another as if their lives depended on it.

An hour later, Eliza emerged from the bathroom, fully polished and dressed for the day, to see Judas standing at the full-length mirror in her bedroom tying his tie. Watching him like this felt intimate in a way she wasn't familiar with. It felt like he belonged here, among her things, in her space. She fantasized about waking up with him here every morning but shook the nonsense from her head. How could she possibly be thinking of such things after knowing this man for such a short amount of time? How had he so quickly wound himself in her thoughts so fully?

He caught a glimpse of her in the mirror and turned. He had never, in all his many years, found himself so completely absorbed in thoughts of a woman. She had entirely bewitched him in ways he would never trade for anything in the world.

He extended a hand to her in invitation to stand by his side. She joined him and he pulled her in front of his body, wrapping his arms around her and resting his chin on her soft blonde hair. They gazed at their reflection in the mirror and seeing themselves together sent tingles of contentment through them both.

"Your hair is down today," he pointed out.

Eliza leaned fulling into his body, "I'm feeling brave today."

Judas smiled down at her, "I can't imagine why."

Turning to face him, she gazed up at him, "You make me feel... different. In a good way. You make me want to be... free."

"You deserve to be free," he replied with a kiss on her nose.

She closed her eyes and breathed him in, luxuriating in his magnificent scent. She murmured simply, "Thank you."

His face is puzzled, looking down at her, "For what?"

"For reminding me that there are truly magical things to feel in this world," she replied. Her words caught him off guard as he felt that she was the one with magic to offer. She giggled at his look of surprise before standing on tiptoes to kiss his nose just as he did hers.

Judas had heard others talk about the feeling of butterflies in the presence of others, but only Eliza had ever been able to give him that feeling.

Chapter Ten

As Judas and Eliza pulled into the parking lot next to the courthouse, a dark cloud descending over their earlier lust induced joy. A large crowd had already begun to assemble on the surrounding sidewalk and around the raised platform on the lawn. Eliza let out a long sigh taking in the signs in the rally-goer's hands. Things like *Deport All Illegals, Build the Wall,* and *Stop Immigration, Stop the Invasion* printed in red, white, and blue on homemade poster boards and custom printed banners. She didn't want to be seen here, at all. She wanted to crawl into the floorboard of this car and not come out until Judas had returned her home safely.

Judas surveyed the crowd, as well, and was instantly on high alert. Crowds gathered for tenuous issues such as this could be volatile and it seemed wrong to bring Eliza right into the middle of such an event, but he also felt that his presence was exactly what these people needed to be exposed to here. He wanted them to have to look into the face of a man they claim to hate, while they screamed their taunts and threats.

Judas glanced toward Eliza in the passenger seat, "There's a lot of anger in that group."

Eliza cringed in acknowledgment of the truth, "Yeah, this is not the sort of event I want my dad to be associated with. I definitely don't want to be associated with it myself."

"Well," Judas said with a sigh, "He's here already and waiting for us."

Judas pointed out the window to her father, standing by his own vehicle waving wildly at them, two of his bodyguards flanked mere inches from his side. Eliza held the bridge of her nose with two fingers and closed her eyes. Seeing her father more excited than a toddler with a stolen bag of candy, was fundamentally in opposition to everything Eliza believed in and was, honestly, mind bending. The moral implications of standing behind this man that represented everything she wasn't made Eliza feel as though her karma was going to take a serious hit after this.

She turned to Judas, placing a hand over his, "We shouldn't be here. Dad and the others can manage this one on their own if he really feels like this is where he needs to be. I can't take part in this and you shouldn't be expected to."

Judas nodded and placed a hand over hers, "Trust me when I say that this is not where I would ever want to spend my day but running is exactly what these kinds of people want. They see my skin and they want to intimidate me. I won't give them that. I've faced far more danger, I assure you. I will stand up there on that stage and let them see me doing my job in spite of their hate. They want to call themselves children of God while they hate me for being different, yet the man they call their savior looked like me. I won't give them the satisfaction. Let them look at my face while they spew their hate."

His words touched Eliza in a part of her soul that made her admiration for him bloom into a shining beacon. She smiled solemnly toward him, "Okay. Let's do this."

She waited for Judas to place the small earpiece in his left ear before they exited the car.

If Judas could use the moment as a silent reprimand and protest, she could too. She felt an obligation to be here for her father in a way that would guide him to better things. She could stand here today but tomorrow explain to him why she would never attend something of this sort again and neither should he. Today, she would gather evidence and tomorrow she would present her case whether he wanted to hear it or not.

Judas refused to have Eliza on the stage with her father but took up a post behind him with another of his staff, Bobby. They would run point allowing Travis, an extremely large former linebacker for the Texans football team to stand at Eliza's side. He knew she didn't want to be a part of this nonsense, but he also didn't want to place her in any further risk. He just couldn't bear the thought. She protested but a promise to worship her body later finally got her to obey.

Judas felt the ever familiar pull of resistance as he listened to the empty platitudes of these modern day false prophets. One after another they stood at the microphone and listed off all the reasons God himself had called them to stand before this crowd and save them from a *'woke'* and sinful future as Americans. Their words were full of hate and thinly veiled racism. They didn't come right out and say the quiet part out loud, but they tiptoed so close to the line that Judas had to use every ounce of self-control in his highly trained body just to avoid wincing at their words.

In his many lifetimes, Judas had heard similar speeches and watched entire generations of people fall under persecution. First, it was the brand new and evolving Christian sects that were vilified by a very pagan Roman Empire. Then, during the fourth crusade, and while Judas was living as a small farmer outside of Rome, Pope Innocent III declared Jews were a threat to society and would be moved to seg-regated areas away from Christians. It seemed whoever was in charge at the time gained their power by oppressing someone else and Judas watched it all. The poor, the infirm, the disabled, homosexuals, the Roma, the Jews. He saw the hatefulness of history. The rhetoric from the powerful was the same, it was just wrapped in another country's flag.

The crowd itself wasn't any better.

They chanted hateful words and rhymes meant to denigrate anyone who was different from them. They were gullible people raised to believe that their prejudices and backward thinking had value and rich and powerful people, like Paul actually cared about them. With every promise of a '*Godly America*' they screamed amen not even remotely realizing the irony of claiming to follow a religion based on the opposite of what they believed.

Yesh would hate every second of this, of that, Judas had no doubt. He would bow his head and likely shed angry tears for the things being spoken here in his name. He might even kick over the microphone. He would stand up against them and they would tear him apart just as the Romans had. This wasn't new. It was nothing more than a repetition of history. This was hate for nothing, all of it based on a bastardization of who Yesh was. He was an immigrant himself and every single one of these degenerates would probably demand he be deported if he showed up on their doorstep today, all of them guilty of the sin of being inhospitable. Judas looked toward the ground to hide his rueful laugh. Their savior was exactly who they proudly proclaimed unbridled hate and disgust for.

In the short seconds it took him to glanced up, things were beginning to worsen. While the crowd in and of itself was a rowdy bunch, a group of protesters had assembled along the edges of the gathering. This group in no way carried the same energy. Their signs asked for tolerance and love. They yelled out demands for respect for their fellow man regardless of skin color or country of origin. They truly wanted nothing but peace, but their presence only further ignited the chaos already in attendance. Mere moments passed before Judas heard the back and forth arguments of the crowd growing out of control. Normally, this would be just another day. He was no stranger to rebellion or revolt. Somehow, though, today felt different, and it made the hairs on the back of his neck stand straight.

His eyes slid over to Eliza standing behind the scenes and fear clenched his gut. He wanted to scoop her up, throw her over his shoulder and get her the hell out of here. He wanted to carry her far away from all this nonsense. He just wanted to disappear with her and to live their lives together in peace.

Judas sucked in a sharp breath. The immense weight and magnitude of that last thought startled him. He'd known he was getting in over his head with the beautiful blonde who smiled back at him, but he had no idea how out of control those feelings were truly becoming. His mind worked to wrap itself around the immense need he suddenly had for her. How could he so deeply desire Eliza when he has lived all these centuries without that heartfelt pull?

He had become so wrapped up in his thoughts that he didn't notice the change in the air around him. It was only when the churning crowd pushed through the barrier in front of Eliza, shoving her backward, as Travis caught her, that he realized a fight had broken out between the crowd and the protesters. His heart clenched at the sight. He mentally reprimanded his lapse in vigilance as he jumped into action.

He grabbed Paul first, not wasting any time to be polite, latching his fingers around his suit's collar. He yanked the wide-eyed man from his stunned stupor and towards the edge of the stage. The stage itself was becoming unstable as the crowd pushed and pulled against its infrastructure. Paul didn't even hesitate with the floor beginning to wobble and sway beneath his feet, just following along while gasping at the crowd churning into a frenzy before his eyes.

When they reached the bottom of the stairs off the stage, Eliza's terrified face met Judas's protective gaze. He handed Paul to the linebacker before wrapping his arm around Eliza's waist, pulling her along with him as he led them all to safety. All the while, one sentence echoed in his mind.

You should have been paying attention.

You should have been paying attention.

You should have been paying attention.

Bodies jostled around them, bumping them along their journey. Expletives and slurs hurled through the air. Judas didn't know for certain if the words were meant as attacks against him personally, but he knew that he would feel responsible if anything happened to Eliza. Of course, his job demanded his protection of Paul above all, but Judas knew that Paul put himself here in this mess. Paul helped add to the rhetoric that stirred the violence unfolding before them. Paul was responsible for his own well being in this situation, but Eliza...

She was better than all of this. She deserved nothing but a safe departure from a scene she wanted nothing to do with. She deserved complete protection and Judas delivered. While he continued to lead their small contingent through the crowd to the parking lot, Judas tucked Eliza into the curve of his body. Nothing was going to happen to her today, of that he was completely sure.

But someone decided to test that resolve.

A man wearing a homemade t-shirt sporting a sharpie design proclaiming *'Make America White Again'* rushed the group from the sidelines and latched his greedy fingers around Eliza's arm. She cried out in pain as the man pulled her away from her guardian. Judas turned toward her bellow and locked eyes with the would-be assailant.

"Just where do you think you're going with her, goat fucker? She's definitely one of ours," the man drawled while leering down at Eliza.

Rage and disbelief bloomed to life in Judas and he moved to tear the tiny minded man to shreds. Without a word, Judas faced the man, everything left his mind, except his desire to remove this man's hate-fueled existence. Towering over him, Judas wrapped one hand tightly around the man's throat and lifted him from the ground. The man's shock caused him to let go and Eliza stumbled away from the fight.

Looking deeply into the man's eyes, Judas growled, "You will never put your hands on a woman without her permission ever again or I will personally find you and break every bone in your body. Do you understand me?"

"Sir!" Travis yelled, his hand clutched gently around Eliza.

The man managed a nod and Judas dropped him to the ground. The man crumbled at Judas's feet and crawled away. Turning back toward Eliza, Judas saw his team had swept both her and Paul into the outskirts of what had become an all out brawl. The shoving from both groups quickly turned into fists being thrown and people covered in blood. It was full on war and Judas was getting swept away in the chaos.

Just a few feet from the barricade, Judas felt a sharp pain in his lower back. He turned just in time to catch a large fist to his left eye. His stoked anger turned to fury as Judas grabbed the man by the front of his shirt and drove his fist into his nose. The man screamed in pain and blood spewed in all directions as he pinballed off others in the crowd before collapsing in a heap on the asphalt.

His earpiece crackled and Bobby's voice boomed, "Sir, we've got the packages out of the hot zone."

Still fuming, Judas pushed his way out of the crowd and hopped over the barrier. He wiped at the last of a small trickle of blood from his quickly healing cheek as he jogged toward Eliza and Paul. Pulling Eliza to his side and wrapping his other arm around Paul's shoulders, they scuttled back to the vehicles. When he determined they were a safe distance, Judas let his grip on the pair loosen. Travis tucked Paul inside while Bobby slid behind the wheel as Judas and Eliza watched his cowardly retreat in awe.

Now locked safely inside his vehicle, Paul cracked the window yelling out to the pair watching him in silence, "Thanks for the quick escape there, Jude. And for keeping my Betsy safe! I'll see you both in the morning. Gotta get out of here before those ANTIFA bastards get any crazier!"

Without a moment of hesitation, the man with no conscience pulled out of the lot with a wave. Judas continued to shield Eliza all the way to her car door, shaking his head in disgust.

Leaning against the car, he looked out over the crowd, still violently stirring before him. He watched them hate each other with fists and furious screams. The sight made his gut feel queasy and he instinctively brushed his eye once more, but the area was clean and undamaged. Today could have gone so differently. Judas reminded himself that he couldn't allow lapses like that one again. He must remain on high alert in these situations or something far worse could happen to Eliza.

And, for the first time in his very long life, he knew that he would not survive that heartbreak.

Most of the car ride back to Eliza's apartment they sat in silence. Judas was still in his own thoughts about how he nearly failed the angel sitting next to him, while Eliza wrestled deeply with her recriminations.

The idea of attending today's rally had disgusted her from the start, but now she fully understood the gravity of what she had done. The shame she felt inside her was daunting and heavy on her soul. She never should have been there. She should have told her father no. That's it.

Holding the distaste for being there inside her while standing on the sidelines felt excusable in the moment, but while walking under Judas's hold as the crowd screamed every filthy word of hate they could dream of at him Eliza's faith in her own decisions had crumbled. She hated herself in those long torturous moments. Nothing about this rally was acceptable. Nothing about her presence there was okay in any way.

She finally had to admit to herself that using her blind support of her father was a cop out for the responsibility she needed to own. She knew it was wrong, yet still, she'd said nothing in the moment. That was what cowards did and Eliza refused to be a coward ever again. She would start from this moment forward by being a loud voice against hate of any kind, but first, she owed something to Judas.

As he parked in front of Eliza's building, she turned to him. She knew she'd hurt him with her inaction today and she would do anything to erase it all. To somehow take it back, but she couldn't. All she could do was take accountability. He gazed back at her with profound sadness pouring from his deep eyes.

Holding his gaze with her own, Eliza spoke, "Judas, I owe you an apology for today."

Confusion crossed his face and his forehead crinkled, "For what? I don't understand."

For a moment, Eliza dropped her eyes to her feet fidgeting nervously on the floorboard, but then shaking her head she looked him in the eye. He deserved that, "We never should have been at that rally today. I never should have allowed my father to have any of us there. I knew it was wrong, but I still went and I will forever regret that decision. You shouldn't have had to stand there and hear all those terrible things those atrocious people were saying. I understand you're hurt and I just wanted you to know that I'm eternally sorry."

Silence fell between them for a moment and Eliza let it sink its teeth into her. She deserved his silence.

But then his deep laugh filled the car and she stared at him with confusion.

"Oh, dear, wonderful Eliza. No apologies needed. I promise. I know your heart. I know you aren't one of those people and I told you why I stayed. That was my choice." His smile now is warm and he placed a gentle hand on her cheek.

She leaned into his warm palm but then shook off his easy acceptance, "No, Judas. You don't have to do that. I can take the reproach. I promise. I should have put my foot down with Dad and none of us would have been there. I know I deserve any bad feelings you have about it and I can tell you're upset. It's okay, really."

Judas leaned toward her and spoke directly to her pleading eyes, "I'm upset because I was too distracted thinking about you to realize we were in danger until it had already begun. It's my job to do better. I am not upset with you. I am upset with myself."

Hearing how completely selfless this man truly was did things to Eliza that she couldn't quite understand. The only thing she did know for certain was that she wanted him more than she had ever wanted anything in her life. Without hesitation, she climbed over the console and into his lap. She straddled him, placing one hand on either side of his beautiful face. He licked his lips as a warm blush rose into his face. As she lowered her mouth to his, and Judas wrapped his arms around her tightly, fusing them together. Their tongues tangled and desire flickered to life inside them.

Short of breath, Eliza leaned back, staring down at him, "Would you like to come inside and wash this awful day off with me?"

Immediate thoughts of water running down her bare skin and seeing her body pressed against the slick shower walls took over his every thought. Without a word, he climbed out of the car with Eliza still on his lap. A squeak of surprise escaped her as he effortlessly threw her over his shoulder and began walking up the stairs with her. She giggled uncontrollably and handed him the keys.

Chapter Eleven

Eliza was doing her best to focus on the task at hand, but laying out all her father's tasks for the day was not nearly as entrancing as her memories of the scandalous things Judas did to her last night. She simply couldn't process a single coherent thought without quickly flashing to the memory of his body against her, his skin on her skin. His lips on her in places she should not be thinking about at work. She could feel the blush overtaking her fair skin just with the memory. This was all so unlike her and the weight of it was overwhelming.

Right as she took a steadying breath to calm her inappropriate urges, an arm snaked around her waist and she gasped in shock. In one fluid movement, the arm spun her around and she saw his perfect face smiling down at her. She melted into him instantly. With his arms tightly wound around her, Judas felt complete. Seeing her smile back up at him made everything in the world right.

"What has you blushing so much this morning, Harzr Shli?" he asked, knowing the answer already.

His words sent a shiver through her, even though they were completely foreign to her. "What does that mean?" she asked.

"It's Hebrew. It means, my treasure," he responded with no hesitation because that was what she was to him. She was the only treasure he had ever felt the need to possess.

She smiled at him, "You speak Hebrew?"

He tilted his head as he contemplated how much he should reveal, "I speak many languages. Someday I will tell you how valuable you are in every one of them."

Warmth filled her soul from top to bottom. As he brought his mouth down to meet hers, that heat morphed into scorching flames. Their tongues danced. Their hands roamed. He slid a leg between her knees, opening her to him.

He broke their kiss and slid his cheek against hers to whisper in her ear with a laugh, "Maybe you should start wearing skirts to work after all."

Eliza laughed out loud and squeezed him tight against her, nuzzling into his neck. She breathed in his scent, committing it to memory for possible candle buying later. She wanted to smell his sultry skin at all times.

Judas slowly began to move his thigh against the warmth between her legs, knowing without doubt that she wanted him as much as he wanted her. He knew they were at work, but she was a temptation that was almost too much to resist.

"I want to be right here," he said as he slid a hand down to touch her.

She moaned as the friction of his touch against the thin fabric of her suit aroused her to the point of losing rational thought.

His free hand grabbed her hair and tilted her head back to look at him, "I want to worship your body for as long as you'll let me."

Eliza licked her lips moaning, "I would let you for a thousand years."

Judas smiled down at her, "Don't tempt me."

They were both lost in a haze of newfound desire with one another. When they touched, the rest of the world fell away. Reality disappeared and they forgot that the bubble they were sheltered in could be easily broken. Popped in an instant.

That realization came quickly back into focus as the latch to the office door clicked just before the door swung open wide. They both scrambled to move as far away from one another as possible, but the evidence of their heated exchange was still written over every inch of their faces. Thankfully, Georgia was the first to walk into the room and she immediately read the chemistry.

"Oh, my!" she exclaimed with a giant grin on her face. She quickly shuffled backward bumping Paul back into the corridor before he could enter the room. "Oh, sir. That office is a mess! I wouldn't dare let you work like that. Let's head to the conference room while I let the cleaning staff know that your office needs a clean up ASAP!"

Eliza dropped her head into her hands in relief. She needed to remember to cut Georgia a check later. That woman was a godsend.

Once the voices of Georgia and Paul faded down the hallway, Judas and Eliza stared at each other from across the room for a long moment. They burst into laughter coming to meet each other in the center of the room. Judas slid an arm around her waist as she stood on tiptoe to kiss his face.

He looked down at her as they embraced, stars in their eyes, "Where were we?"

Eliza shoved at his chest and pulled out of the hug, "We were getting to work. Save it for later. You're going to be the death of me."

He smiled and leaned against the desk she was attempting to straighten once again, "I can't help it. You have me under a spell, Eliza."

She gave him a playful glare but loved his words.

"You make me feel young again," he confided as sentiment had been plaguing his mind. She made him feel like life was brand new, like all the years of aimless wandering were worth this time in his life.

She felt a warm tingle his words always inspired and smiled at him but continued re-composing herself. She shot him a coy smile, "You aren't even that old."

Judas laughed internally. If she only knew.

She shoved his shoulder, "Go do something useful, you sex fiend."

Judas chuckled but held his hands up in surrender, "Yes, ma'am." He bowed to her and he exited the room.

Once he was gone, Eliza walked around the desk and collapsed into her father's chair. She held her head in her hands and thought about how close they just came to being caught. Her father would want to have Judas killed if he knew. She was certain her father was actually that hateful and crazy. She didn't care one way or another how her father felt about who she chose to have in her bed, but she knew how much his knowledge of their relationship would complicate Judas's life. God, what was she doing? How did this happen?

Then she remembered what he does to her body and her mind and laughed hysterically. She couldn't resist that man if she tried.

They were going to need to be more careful, but she knew there was absolutely no going back.

Thirty minutes later, Eliza walked into the conference room to greet her father. Seated at the long table usually reserved for meetings and mergers, he grumbled a greeting as she came through the door.

"You're in a wonderful mood this morning," she tossed back.

He waved her off and went back to reading the local paper.

Eliza glanced over his shoulder and met Georgia's gaze. She mouthed a *thank you*. Georgia smiled in response then pointed at Judas and mouthed *oh my God* while giving two thumbs up. Judas caught this interaction and couldn't help but laugh, quickly disguising the sound as a cough.

Paul glanced around the room, sensing he was missing something. Everyone plastered on a perfect poker face. He scowled but returned to his paper as he grumbled, "Everyone has lost their damn minds today."

"So, what exactly has you so chipper this morning, Dad?" Eliza asked, voice dripping with tension, "Did you finally realize what a mistake yesterday was?"

Paul glared at his daughter now seated across from him, "Yesterday would have been an absolutely perfect day if those damn yahoos hadn't decided to protest and make a big scene out of it. It was supposed to be a peaceful gathering of conservative minds."

Eliza, quickly losing all patience for her job and father, barked out a sardonic laugh, "The conservative minds were the violent ones! Dad, you can be conservative without pandering to fools who live life with nothing but hate inside them. Those are not the real people of your party. Just the loudest."

"Puh-tay-toe, puh-tah-toe. You see it your way and I see it mine," Paul snapped as he returned to his newspaper, violently flipping the pages. Once he had made it through all the pages, he slammed it down on the table in disgust.

Eliza had entered the room in a delightful, Judas-fueled mood, but recalling the events of yesterday afternoon soured it quickly. Her father's inability to hold people accountable only made Eliza want to fight, "What in God's name is wrong with you today?!"

Paul yelled at her across the table, "Damn it, Betsy! Don't you take the Lord's name in vain with me! You know very well how I feel about that nonsense!" His skin flushed bright red with anger and a vein throbbed out of his forehead in ways that made Judas fear the old man may have a stroke.

Eliza rolled her eyes, relenting, "Sorry. Let me rephrase. What is wrong with you today?"

An obviously fake smile painted across her face.

Paul stood from the table and stalked over to the large windows overlooking the city. Staring out, he seemingly contemplated every last inch of the horizon before speaking quietly, "I wasn't even mentioned once in the article."

Eliza's brows drew together and a line formed between them. Judas took note and reminded himself to take extra care in gently rubbing away that little line later. He never wanted to see anything but relaxed bliss written across her features and would do anything to achieve that.

She stared at her father's back and reached for the newspaper as she spoke, "What are you talking about?" Her eyes scanned the pages as he just had with understanding dawning, "Oh."

Eliza walked the paper over to the other staff members in the room and pointed out an article taking up a large portion of the front page. The headline called out the drama from the rally yesterday. Not even one time was the hopeful senator, Paul Arthur, mentioned, even though the article continued on for several pages. Eliza stood next to her father, giving him the silence he needed to process his next words.

"I was there, Betsy. I stood right there on that stage when all hell broke loose. I was a part of all of it from start to finish, for goodness sake. Yet, not even one time does that article say my name. It's a disgrace. How am I ever going to get the votes I need if the local paper doesn't even feel the need to say my name?" His voice cracked with emotion at these last words.

Eliza looked at him and told him the truth but in a way that would make sense in his worldview, "That article is not the kind of place you want your name spoken. That article is the ugly side of politics and prejudice." He began to quarrel with this, but Eliza silenced him with a raised hand and calm demeanor. "We will get your name mentioned, Dad. That's what we're all here for, but let's try to do it in a way that makes you look like the old-fashioned, upstanding Texan that you are. Not for being a bigot. That's not the press you want and that's not the reputation you want to establish for yourself. Can we agree on that?"

The older man stared out the window for a long moment before nodding his head and looking toward his daughter, "I suppose you're right, Betsy."

She smiled at this small victory and placed an arm gently around her father's shoulders, "Good, now let's all sit down and brainstorm some ideas."

Judas watched as she guided her father back to the table and took control of the situation. As beautiful as it was to watch her work on any given day, this scene felt a little like a preschool teacher talking to a tantrum throwing toddler. He didn't know or understand where that woman got her copious amounts of patience, but he knew he admired it tremendously.

Chapter Twelve

Taking one final look in the mirror, Eliza appraised her appearance. Her hair was down and flowing around her shoulders, it perfectly framed the ample cleavage she worked so hard to produce under her silk nightie. It had two lace panels sewn into the sides that gave just the slightest glimpse of her tattoo beneath. The mid-thigh length gown was not something she would ever wear on a regular occasion, but tonight was different.

Inviting him over felt like the most foreign concept to her and she felt awkward the entire time she was doing it. Eliza was not the kind of woman that invited coworkers over for after work shenanigans. But then again, she had been doing a lot of things that weren't normal for her since Judas came into her life. She had never slept with someone she had known for such a short amount of time. She always waited until she knew them better. Being a woman meant never knowing if a man was trustworthy enough to be invited into your home and your bed until he had been fully vetted with dinners, drinks, and heavy online sleuthing. She just never felt the need to do that with Judas. She just felt that he had a good soul. She didn't know how she just knew that, but her intuition told her she was right. Tonight was different for her in so many ways, but it felt right.

Tonight she wanted Judas to see her not as someone he worked with and occasionally fucked, but as a woman that needed a man in her life to fill her nights. She wanted him to see her as a woman that he wanted to fill his nights.

Looking at herself in the mirror, she saw a pink heat crawl up her skin as this thought crossed over from her subconscious into her reality. She exhaled a shaky laugh and couldn't even believe this was in her mind. He would think she was completely insane if he could read her thoughts around him, but that didn't stop her from knowing he was absolutely what she wanted.

Suddenly her doorbell sounded and she felt an intense panic take hold of her. She desperately wanted him to want her in the same way. Taking one last look in the mirror, she grabbed the silk robe that matched her nightie and made her way to the door.

She took one last steadying breath and opened the door to see the most beautiful man she had ever laid eyes on standing before her.

He sucked in a sharp breath at the sight of her, "My Eliza, you are the most heavenly creature I have ever been blessed to see."

She knew her face was crimson from the weight of his compliment, but she managed a smile. She was certain she must look like a lovesick teenager staring back at him and it made her even more self-conscious.

Judas couldn't imagine anything more gorgeous than the glow that emanated from her. Every inch of her was perfection on a Godly level. Without hesitation, he reached for her and had his lips on hers before they had made it all the way inside. She moaned against his lips and it sent the most thrilling heat through his body.

Their tongues grazed one another while their hands explored every inch of reachable territory.

Suddenly, Eliza pulled away from him and backed up to the counter, bracing herself against its cold edge. She needed a moment of space because she feared she just might self combust. Panting with lust, she stared back at him and thrilled to see the same kind of need reflected back at her.

Looking at her, he saw her fully. Her robe came just to her mid-thigh and plunged low enough to reveal her silky gown beneath. Her hair, in tumbling waves around her shoulders, framed in the perfect curves of her breasts, heaving with her heavy breathing.

"I want you more than I've ever wanted anything," she admitted.

"I'm yours," he confirmed without question.

"This thing between us..." she said, "It's intense in ways I don't really know how to handle. I'm not used to feeling this... unhinged."

Judas laughed in agreement, "I completely understand."

Biting her lip, Eliza collected her thoughts, "I want this with you, but we work together so I have to make sure that there isn't going to be any kind of drama that might filter into the workplace. My dad is our boss and I'm afraid of how he might treat you if he finds out about us. I need to know that this isn't just a fleeting thing if we're going to risk that. I don't want that to happen to you."

Slowly approaching her, Judas locked his gaze with hers, "I'm not a fleeting thing kind of man." He stood against her, pressing their bodies into one another, and continued, "I have learned to be very patient in this life and if the current intensity is too much..." He paused to caress her soft cheek, "I'm more than happy to take things as slowly as you need. Until I can prove myself to you."

Leaning her face into his hand, Eliza knew that slow was not what she was aiming for. Not slow, just certain. She exhaled a shaky breath, "I'm comfortable with our *intensity* as long as I have your word that I'm not just one of many. I'm not a casual fling kind of woman."

He smiled down at her, "I adore that about you. Your body is sinfully enticing to me, but your mind is what has me on my knees before you begging for a chance to be the kind of man you want in your life."

Eliza smiled back, appreciation sparkling in her eyes, "Let the intensity continue."

Judas leaned toward her and laid his lips gently against hers. The kiss was unlike anything they had shared. It was tender. It was full of promise and potential. It was more erotic than a full night between the sheets.

When he pulled away, Eliza took his hand and led him to the couch. She gestured for him to sit before straddling his lap. His hands slid up her bare thighs and he felt goosebumps spread across her skin. She stared down at him as she untied her silk robe. Letting it slide down her shoulders, she could feel his eyes on her skin. He trailed his fingers across her collarbone then let one finger glide down to her cleavage. She bit her lip, sliding the thin straps down her shoulders.

Judas pulled her toward him and planted kisses against her neck. Eliza moaned out her acceptance and let her head fall back to give him access to her throat and chest. He took the invitation and let his mouth explore every inch of her sweet skin. She could feel his erection rubbing against her as she ground into him. He freed one breast with his gentle touch and took her nipple into his mouth, rolling it across his tongue, sending shivers down her spine.

Eliza gripped his long hair in her hand and pulled his head back to look at her.

He stared into her face for a long moment, "I'm yours as long as you'll have me."

His words made her come unglued and she pushed her mouth to his. Never breaking the kiss, Judas gripped her thighs and rolled her body beneath his on the couch. His mouth made a trail down her form until he reached her silk thong, he gripped it with his teeth and pulled at the delicate fabric until it strained against her skin. She moaned and raised her hips toward him, arching her back and begging for more. Judas smiled up at her and began to work the silk down her body as his nails scraped delightfully against her skin.

Every sensation sent her mind further into the fog of arousal. She was so deep in this place that she didn't even notice the sound of the frantic knocks on her front door until Judas stopped what he was doing and leaned away from her.

"Eliza, the door? Do you need to answer it?"

Eliza sat up on her elbows finally registering the sound and returning to reality. She'd never wanted to do something less than she wanted to climb out from beneath this man, but she thought of her elderly neighbor whom she'd promised to help if she ever needed it and groaned.

"Yes," she said against her own will, "I probably should. Stay here and I'll be right back."

"Oh, I will be right here waiting to pick up where we left off."

His grin was devilish and she wanted to leave his side even less. Against better judgment, Eliza stood, straightened her robe, quickly combed her fingers through her hair, and tried to appear as if she wasn't just about to have an orgasm eaten out of her body.

Pulling the door open, Eliza's pleasant smile slid completely off her face, "Uh, oh my God. Dad! What are you doing here?"

Paul didn't wait for an invitation and pushed past Eliza into the apartment, but stopped in his tracks seeing Judas sitting on the couch. He stared at his bodyguard then turned to stare at his daughter before turning back to Judas.

With a scowl overtaking his face, Paul spit out, "Boy, what are you doing here?"

Judas was tempted to tell the selfish old bigot the truth, that he was about to do things to his daughter that would make the finest sex worker blush. But instead stared past Paul to the look of horror on Eliza's face and couldn't bear what that might do to her.

He stood, bowed in greeting to this awful human, and lied, "Miss Eliza was having car trouble, sir. A flat tire. I helped her by replacing it and she invited me in to clean up." His eyes met Eliza's and her gratitude shone back at him, "She is a very kind woman, sir."

Paul turned his gaze to his daughter now, glancing up and down at her scantily clad body, "Dressed a little like the whore of Babylon to be going for a drive, aren't you?"

Eliza blinked at the absurdity of everything that came out of her father's mouth, "I got dirty helping with the tire. I cleaned up and threw on what I intended to sleep in. Didn't want to dirty up more clothes for no reason, but thanks for the flattering description, Dad."

Paul still seemed dubious at first, looking back and forth between the two, but could not wrap his mind around his daughter doing anything scandalous with the help and relented, "Well, thank you, Jude. I appreciate you being there for my Betsy."

Judas walked to meet the man's extended hand. The men shook and Paul handed Judas a twenty dollar bill from his pocket with a wink.

Eliza rolled her eyes and moved to stand before Paul, "Why are you here, Dad?"

Paul walked to the kitchen and began pouring himself a drink, "I had some ideas about more positive exposure as you called it and needed to get my ideas out there while they're still fresh in my head."

"Now is really not a good time," Eliza said, her voice betraying her desperate need for her father to leave as soon as absolutely possible.

Judas could read Paul's expression and knew that wouldn't be happening. He turned to Eliza and smiled apologetically, "Thank you for letting me clean up, Miss Eliza. I will see myself out so that you and Mr. Arthur can speak privately."

The look on her face was devastating. Judas wanted nothing more than to fix it, but he knew, now more than ever before, that he would not be able to do that. Maybe ever. He kissed Eliza's hand goodbye and walked toward the door. She followed and mouthed 'I'm sorry' as Judas left.

Walking down the stairs to his car, Judas felt a cold dread slide over his entire being. What had he been thinking? He wanted Eliza on a pure and true level, but having her was nothing but selfishness. His presence in her life beyond anything more than her father's security did nothing but complicate her life. He should have known better and he reprimanded himself all the way to his car.

As he slid into the driver's seat, he looked up to her window and vowed to distance himself from the crushing need he felt for her. He owed her more than giving in to his own self-serving wants and desires. She would be upset, he was sure, but he didn't want to make her life harder than it was. With all the stress her father put on her, she deserved to have all other stress removed.

He knew she feared the same things. She tried to tell him that tonight and he just hadn't fully heard what she had been trying to tell him. He should've given more weight to her words. She deserved peace.

If that meant removing himself, Judas was willing to make that sacrifice for her. No matter how badly it would hurt him to do so.

Chapter Thirteen

It has been one week since Paul interrupted Judas and Eliza. One week since they had touched. One week since Eliza received a voicemail from Judas telling her that she had been right and it wasn't a good idea for them to see each other. One whole entire week since Eliza had felt her heart break for a relationship she hadn't really even had yet.

And it was torturing them both without the other even knowing.

Eliza understood why he felt the need to end things. The way her father had spoken to him. The way he had treated Judas like an unwanted intruder in her space. It caused her heart to ache when she thought about how she's allowed it to happen. She cringed every time the entire scene replayed in her head. He deserved so much better than she knew how to offer him. She knew Judas was right, but she hated having that knowledge.

The sudden end to their encounters felt like being drenched in ice cold water. It was so abrupt and jarring to have the crazed, greedy moments they had shared ripped away without warning. She felt like an addict going through withdrawals and every encounter was a temptation she didn't know how to endure. Walking into the conference room now, Eliza passed by Judas and wouldn't even acknowledge his presence.

But, she knew he was there.

His scent filled her senses and caused her stomach to flutter to life with butterflies that seemed to remember exactly what his touch felt like. She wanted to turn to him and shove him against the wall, their lips tangled in a passionate embrace, but she didn't. She carefully held her poker face in place and strode past him, seemingly without a care in the world.

Judas could barely stand to see her go by him. He wanted to reach out for her. He wanted to hold her in his arms and never let her go. Seeing her so out of reach was torture of the soul and he had to fight every internal urge within him to not take her right there on the conference table in front of every single person in this crowded room. She felt like a compulsion he didn't know how to fight. He took a deep breath releasing it harshly in a bid to relax his inner turmoil. He knew maintaining this distance was what was right and he would never betray her trust by violating the boundary put in place to protect her.

She hadn't protested this separation and she knew she shouldn't. It would be selfish to put him through what her father would hurl at him if they were together, but hearing his sigh from behind her is almost enough to make her call the whole thing off. She was truly walking so close to falling already and hearing him exhale in frustration nearly sent her careening over the edge of temptation. She took a seat and gripped its edges in an attempt to ground herself to something tangible before she floated away willingly into his gravitational pull.

Her Uncle Chet had been meeting with her father about law firm business before their campaign meeting and he eyed her suspiciously as he stood to leave. She wondered if she was being that obvious. Apparently, she was.

Chet walked to her side and leaned down to whisper in her ear, "Are you okay, Eliza?"

She pulled away and smiled up at him, "Oh, yeah. I'm good, Uncle Chet. Just distracted. Thinking about campaign stuff." Her attempt to sound chipper about a job he knew she hated didn't fool him.

Chet looked from Eliza to the other stressed face in the room and very quickly put the pieces together.

"Huh," he said as matter of fact, "Well, I really thought that was going to work out. Dad complicate things?"

Eliza's painted-on smile faltered and she exhaled the sigh she had been holding inside her. She nodded.

Chet gave her a pat on the back, "That old man has no right to tell you how to live your life, okay? You outgrew him a long time ago. Do what makes you happy."

He winked at her and she wanted to disappear. How was it possible that they weren't even currently speaking and yet their chemistry was thick enough for the entire room to read? It made the ache in her chest grow in intensity.

Intensity.

Eliza lifted her eyes and stared across the room to Judas. Like he could feel her stare, his gaze met hers and a world of emotion passed between them. She was tempted, in the moment to rush directly into his arms. Witnesses be damned.

Before she could, Georgia plopped down in the seat next to her, "Intense stare there, lady friend."

Eliza broke eye contact with Judas and glared toward the floor, "Please don't use that word or I may scream. Nothing intense is happening here."

Georgia rolled her eyes, "Uh huh. You keep telling yourself that."

Eliza looked at Georgia seeing the empathy in her eyes, "Is it really that obvious?"

The younger woman laughed under her breath, "What? The original sexual tension so thick you could cut through it or the current angst that seems to have swallowed you both whole? Because they're both pretty clear."

"Well," Eliza began, "Well, I... We... It's done. So, I hope everyone will just move on and not worry about it."

Georgia looked even more sad, "Girl, that's a pity because whatever was happening between you two seemed like that super rare, special, thing of fairy tales, real deal kind of stuff. Not to mention, that man is a major snack."

Eliza couldn't help but smile at this, "It really seemed like that?"

She playfully shoved Eliza's shoulder, "Oh yeah. You two had that whole starry eyed, I just found my soulmate kind of buzz around you. I don't know... It was just kind of special, you know?"

Eliza did know. She'd been feeling that since the first moment she laid eyes on Judas. She didn't know what it was, but there was just... something. Romance and love, dare she call it that, had never really been on her radar. She was career minded. She wanted an education and a job she could love for the rest of her life. Aside from this little tangent into politics, she'd had that and she was happy. Wanting more wasn't something she craved or needed. She figured you could have one or the other and she chose work that filled her life with purpose. Then he walked in and, and for the first time in her life, she wondered if she might've been able to have both. Could she be that lucky? She now knew the answer was no.

It seemed silly to her to even be thinking something so crazy so fast, but somehow it just fit.

Eliza gazed toward Judas again and found him already looking back at her. She felt that spark in herself again and wanted what she'd had with him back again. She wanted it so badly that it felt like a necessity.

Georgia nudged her, "Listen, I'm usually only into the ladies but I would absolutely make an exception for that hunky dreamboat." Georgia shrugged her shoulders unapologetically, "I mean, if you're really done and it's really over. You just let me know."

Alarm spiked through Eliza's heart at the thought of seeing him look at another woman the way he was looking at her and she panicked, "It's not! It isn't done. Maybe I thought it was, but it's not. I'm still invested, okay?"

Georgia answered with a wide smile, "That's kind of what I figured, but now you know too, right?"

Eliza smiled back. Now she knew.

Chapter Fourteen

S oft, bluesy music wafted through the candlelit apartment as Judas poured himself two fingers of a sixty-year-old single malt scotch. He'd settled into his spot on the overstuffed sofa and just opened his book when the light rapping happened on his door. Judas took a sip of his drink before setting the glass on the table in front of him and getting up to turn the knob. Eliza's piercing eyes stared back at him.

"I'm...sorry for barging in unannounced," she apologized.

He noticed she looked a little disheveled as though she was in quite a hurry to leave wherever she came from and her demeanor radiated anger. Judas immediately hated the idea that someone had upset her and he could guess who that person was. He knew he shouldn't, because that same person would never allow it, but Judas would do anything to be everything for this woman.

Opening the door wider, he gestured for her to come inside, "No problem."

He watched her from behind as she sloughed off her blazer. He swore after their last tryst several weeks ago that he would keep his desires for her in check, but it was hard not to imagine his fingers tracing the tattoo on her ribcage again.

"Can I get you a drink?" he shut the door.

Eliza saw the tumbler of amber liquid sitting on the glass table, "Sure...whatever that is."

A small grin pulled at the edge of Judas's mouth as he plucked a glass from the bar and handed it to her.

"Do you know what it's like to work for the most infuriating and frustrating human on the face of the planet?" She railed suddenly. "I mean...he is such an asshole. I can't believe I chose to do this job. I mean, I could go anywhere else and not deal with half the bullshit I do with him." She took a quick look around the dim apartment, "Well, apparently my father pays you what *you're* worth. Too bad I can't say that about everyone else."

Judas poured the liquid slowly into her glass, listening intently.

Eliza took a quick sip, "It's almost like he does this crap to intentionally piss me off."

Taking his glass from the table, Judas sat on the corner of the sofa's arm, "I suspect we're talking about your father."

"Who else?" Eliza sat carefully on the sofa's edge next to him, savoring the burning sensation in her chest.

"Tell me what happened."

Sipping her drink again, she shook her head, "It doesn't matter. Nothing changes with him...his way or no way."

She sat her drink on the glass coffee table, hanging her head in silence for a long moment. She was making a choice by coming to his apartment tonight. She knew how to hit her father below the belt and having a relationship with his bodyguard openly; his brown-skinned bodyguard, would be the ultimate act of rebellion. She might even be lucky enough to be disowned.

From the minute he walked into her father's office, she knew this man would change her whole world and nobody had ever made her feel the way he did. Her thighs quaked thinking about every time he had touched her. Her mind flashed to her conversation with Georgia and the immediate jealousy that roared through her at the mention of him being with anyone else. She chewed her lip, contemplating her next move. She wasn't content with letting this go. There is no way she could let this go.

Judas leaned toward her, "Eliza, are you ok—"

Eliza pounced on him like a hungry lioness. Wrapping her arms around his neck, she kissed his lips in frenzied passion. Running her tongue around the curve of his ear and down his neck, she struggled to untuck his shirt.

Shock pervaded Judas's brain as his lips immediately returned her affections. He wanted to feel those pillows of desire all over him again, but in the same instant, a thought crossed his mind and he pulled away. His woody eyes gazed over her. As much as he wanted this woman, and as fun as he thought the idea was in the beginning, he would be damned if she would use him as a pawn in a power struggle with her father. He found himself caring for her more than he rightfully should and she deserved more than just fun for retribution's sake. She tried to kiss him again.

"Eliza, stop. What are you doing?" he frowned, placing the drink back on the table.

Blush flooded her face, "I...uhh-"

"Look, I understand you're mad at your dad, but I don't think this is the way to get back at him. Not this time," he whispered.

Eliza stared blankly as she slowly backed away, regret filling her soul, "I should go."

"No. Don't," Judas latched onto her hand. "Look...I know you miss what we had as badly as I do. Every single day I have a hard time keeping my eyes off you or my thoughts...*work-related*." He paused. "But, I want this to be right...not something we'll throw away. And not as a way to get back at him anymore. No games. Please...stay...let's just...talk. Let me know *you*."

Eliza's heart lightened. A small fear had been gnawing at her that this beautiful man was going to disappear in the middle of the night only to be a memory. She knew she hated breaking their connection and she hoped he felt the same, but until now, she wasn't sure.

Her arm relaxed in his hold as she stared at her hand in his.

"What do you want to know?" her heart beat faster. She never really knew a man who took a genuine interest in her and her life.

Judas smoothed his fingers over her soft skin, and laughed nervously, "Everything. Suddenly, I'm not sure what to ask."

With no awkward transition, no uncertainty, she found herself slipping back into the ease of their relationship. Just like that, being with him felt effortless again. Eliza pursed her lips in a delicate smirk, "Have you ever played Truth or Dare?"

"No," he looked at her suspiciously.

"Seriously? Not even as a kid?"

Judas shook his head, "I had a...sheltered childhood."

Eliza shrugged, "Well, the rules are pretty simple. You ask the person if they want to answer a question truthfully or take a dare."

"What kind of dare?" he narrowed his eyes on her.

"Well...anything. Like...I could dare you to run naked in your hallway outside," she took another sip from her glass. "Here, I'll go first; truth or dare?"

"Truth."

"Okay," she looked around the dim room, "What's with all the candles? Did you forget to pay your electric bill?"

Judas erupted in laughter, "No...I just...like it, I guess. It sets a mood."

It was the best he could offer. Telling her that he has spent more time without electricity than with it wasn't the conversation he was ready to have. At least, not yet, and probably never. Besides the fact he was serious; he genuinely enjoyed the feeling of candlelight.

"Sure does," she giggled. "Okay, your turn."

"Truth or dare?"

"Uhhhmmm..." she teased coyly. "Truth."

"Tell me about the tattoo," Judas's dark eyebrow arched. "The whole story."

Eliza grinned, "Now, how did I know you would ask that?" She didn't admit she knew because he traced it gently with his fingers every time they had been together.

He shrugged.

Relaxing against the soft back of the sofa, she took a deep breath, "I'd like to tell you one of those cool stories about how a bunch of girlfriends and I got drunk one weekend and woke up to new body art. But, like most everything else I do...it was well planned."

"Go on," he urged.

"I don't know if you've noticed, but my dad is kinda a control freak. About everything."

Judas sipped his scotch, nodding.

"Since I turned eighteen, I've done everything I could to find my own way, you know? He calls it rebellion...I call it making my own decisions." She rolled her eyes. "Something else you may have noticed about my dear dad is his radical adherence to this evangelicalism-right wing bunk. Since the day my mother died, he had me in only the most expensive private Christian schools. He was pissed when I moved to Austin for college...liberal heathens he called it."

Eliza laughed darkly, "For me, this tattoo represents something he can't take away from me...my free will. I just wish I would have remembered I had it when he wanted me to help him with this God-forsaken campaign. But, I guess I'll always be at daddy's beck and call."

Judas stared at her through flickering light. He saw so much pain in her eyes and his heart ached for her. He met a thousand men like her father; powerful, controlling, selfish. Not one of those men was as pious as they claimed. They caused misery with every word they spoke and their own actions were almost always their downfall.

He tucked a strand of golden hair behind her ear gently, "I don't think that will be your fate."

His fingers brushed against her cheek and she leaned into his touch. Eliza loved the way his hands were always warm against her skin and that his dark honey eyes seemed to see into her soul; as if he had the knowledge of all the ages locked inside them.

Judas continued caressing her face. "I think it's your turn," he whispered.

"Oh...yeah, truth or dare," she was finding it more difficult to concentrate on their game. The longer he touched her, the more she felt her life force vibrating with his. Closing her eyes, she leaned her head on the back of the sofa focusing on each stroke of his fingers.

"Dare," Judas breathed.

Eliza's eyes fluttered open to find his face lying mere centimeters from hers. Licking her lips she whispered, "Kiss me."

Studying her for a moment, Judas slowly moved closer until he felt the plump flesh of her lips on his. He tenderly urged her mouth open, allowing his tongue to dance with hers. Wrapping his large hands around her face, he pulled her closer until he felt the tautness of her nipples on his chest.

Eliza's hands ran tentatively through his long hair and it felt like silk in her fingers. Judas let out a small moan of pleasure that made her smile.

"My *Ahavah*," his voice muffled against her neck.

With a swift movement, Judas lifted her off the sofa and held her cradled in his thick arms. His stare spoke to her without words and told her that what he would do next would be because he wanted her, body and soul. It said that he would forever worship her very existence. It screamed that he loved her.

Judas carried her into his bedroom where the only light was filtered through long vertical blinds from the nearby streetlamps. As he placed her on the thick-down comforter, their eyes remained locked on one another. Eliza watched as Judas towered over her, unbuttoning his shirt and tossing it to the floor. It was then she noticed areas of stark white skin in sharp contrast to his naturally dark olive tone. They were of varying lengths and widths and were scattered like confetti. Every time they had slept together before this, it had been frantic and feverish. She had never taken the time to really see him like this.

Judas removed his belt and unzipped his dark slacks as her body throbbed with excitement. Eliza could see his hardened erection behind the cotton boxer briefs in the dappled light of the room. She felt her insides quaking with anticipation as he took her hand and slid it into his waistband to free him from the constraining fabric.

Eliza was anxious to rid herself of her own clothing, but as Judas knelt beside her, he took her hands above her head.

"Don't move," his breath was hot on her ear but sent a chill down her spine. His radiant eyes and dark lashes were seductive in their gaze.

She felt her thighs become wet as her arousal climbed to new peaks.

Slowly, Judas released each button on her linen blouse until the black lace of her bra was fully exposed. Her chest heaved steadily as he continued to work his way to her tight-fit jeans. Easily popping the button, he peeled them away to find the matching panties underneath. His fingers barely gracing her most sensitive spot, he felt what was waiting for him there and he smiled down at her.

He slid next to her as Eliza wrapped her arms around his broad shoulders. Continuing to concentrate on her face, he removed her panties and held her nude body next to his. He wanted to know what every inch of her felt like on him. Their first few times together had been quick and uninhibited. He needed to take his time; to give her everything she deserved.

Judas' lips found hers before making his way to her already firm nipples. His suckling only drew them tighter and her moaning grew louder. Eliza groaned in ecstasy as Judas's fingers found her swollen center and began rubbing it gently.

"I need to know what you taste like," he begged.

Eliza purred a soft, "Yes.." as he slid down her body, gently urging her legs apart. He found he could swim in her as he buried his face in her essence. Her honey was sweet and his mouth devoured every delightful drop. He opened her folds exposing her beauty and plunged his tongue inside her. Her hips bucked and the lascivious moans emanating from her rose louder. With each thrust of his mouth, her ocean flowed and her cries of pleasure grew.

Judas was familiar with the sounds of sex, but hearing her satisfaction brought him to an almost immediate climax. Needing to give her more, he focused his attention on her swollen clitoris while he stroked her plump breasts.

"Oh, Judas...oh my God...please...don't...stop," Eliza's words were sporadic and breathless. She felt her walls vibrating as his foreplay brought her closer to ecstasy. She grabbed for his long hair and tangled her fingers in the strands, pulling and holding his mouth against her.

The feeling of her unbridled need for him sent shockwaves through him. He knew he had to have all of her right now or he might burst into flames from desire alone. Self control wrapped around him and he continued running his tongue around her most sensitive bundle of nerves until he felt the shudder of orgasm spread through her. As her body pulsated from completion, he rose to stand over her. Looking down at the heavenly woman coming undone before him was the single most gratifying sight of his long life.

Bending her knees, he buried his entire length into her before she had even finished riding the waves of her pleasure. Filling her, he stroked her pleasure center into another orgasm. Her core pulsated around his wet erection and she screamed his name with each satisfying thrust. He drove himself into her as he looked down upon her arching body.

Eliza spread her legs wider now, wrapping them and her hands around Judas' ass and hips to drive him deeper, greedy for the intensity of the pleasure he gave her.

He looked down into her eyes before clasping their lips together, "Eliza... Oh, my Eliza..." Judas' growl of climax was only drowned out by the crashing of the headboard against the wall.

Completely spent, his thrusting slowed and Judas rested his shaking body next to Eliza, both panting in unison. With a quivering hand, he stroked strands of sweat-soaked hair from her forehead, "You are a wonder to behold."

He pulled her trembling body against his as the pair drifted to sleep.

Chapter Fifteen

The twinkling of dawn was just starting to lighten the central Texas sky when Eliza's eyes opened sleepily. For a moment, she forgot where she was until her drowsy orbs caught a glimpse of Judas' thick arms still wrapped around her. Her mouth was like a desert and she really needed to pee. Careful not to disturb him, she slipped out of his embrace to find the bathroom and a glass of water.

The thick carpeting felt luxurious under her feet as she quietly pattered to the kitchen. The barely burgeoning daylight brightened the apartment better than the candles that its owner preferred and it was the first time Eliza was able to get a good look at her surroundings.

The unit itself was located in uptown Dallas, just a simple two-minute walk to the Katy Trail. The apartment, perfect for a single person, was a one-bedroom, one-bath open floor plan space with an entire wall of glass that overlooked the city skyline. Eliza knew the general cost for a place like this was nearing a million dollars.

Standing at the farm-style sink of the spacious kitchen, she began to notice unique pieces of artwork decorating the walls. She moved closer to a long piece of stone mounted just above a small bar along the edge of the breakfast nook. Looking closer, she noticed it was actually two pieces, one smaller, oblong in shape hanging over the elongated one. The larger of the two looked as though it was worn smooth from years of use. Eliza remembered a college history class where they studied first-century methods of preparing food. The stones reminded her of pictures of a tool used to hand grind grain. She wanted to touch it to see if it was as smooth as it looked but was afraid it might fall.

The stones piqued her interest and she spent the next ten minutes or so admiring every piece that drew her attention. There were coins in a glass case that could have come from a pirate ship or long ago buried treasure chest. There were statues and face masks from various cultures and old pictures hung along the inner wall of the living room. Eliza suspected they were family photos because a few of the men resembled Judas dramatically.

The entire apartment was like a museum.

Getting a chill over her still nude body, Eliza walked quietly back to the bedroom only to find Judas propped on an elbow, waiting.

"I was beginning to think you got lost," he smirked.

A pleased smile spread across her lips, "Oh...naked and lost. I might need someone to save me." She collapsed onto the soft bedding and allowed him to wrap her body into his. "I was actually admiring your taste in decor. It looks like you've traveled a lot."

Judas narrowed his eyes on her, "Why would you say that?"

"I'm pretty sure those masks are authentic and they aren't something you can just pick up at any home store," she snorted a laugh. "And the pictures? Your family is clearly well-connected...I mean, one of those looks like your great-great-grandfather with President Lincoln."

She rolled over, pressing her back into his chest and he wrapped his arms around her exposed breasts. Her eyes gazed around the bedroom until they landed on a large rope whip hanging above the door; its nine fingers splayed out exposing the pieces of metal and rocks tied into each one.

"Like that!" Eliza jumped from the bed, pointing to the whip. "That looks...*old*...Judas." Turning to him, she raised her brow, "What kind of kink are you into?"

Her joke fell on a suddenly sullen face. For a moment she was confused but remembered the white scars from the night before. She turned back to the whip and flipped on the bedroom light. Judas squinted in the sudden illumination.

Eliza got as close as she could to the tool of torture and saw small areas where the old rope was darker than the rest. Tiny dots of deep brown scattered across the objects tied inside it and trailed far into the handle. Turning back to Judas, her face was horrified.

"Is that...blood?" she demanded. Judas sat on the edge of the bed, holding his head in his hands. "Judas? Is it? Your scars... Did someone... beat you with that?"

His head snapped to face her but he remained quiet.

"I see the scars...tell me. What happened?" she pleaded quietly.

To her surprise, Judas began to laugh maniacally, "You wouldn't believe me."

"Try me."

He looked to the ceiling considering his next few statements. For over two thousand years, Judas never revealed his true identity to anyone because he knew no one would believe him anyway. He would do anything this woman wanted. He never wanted to expose his soul to anyone like he did to her. He couldn't explain the hold she had over him but he knew it was cosmic.

But how could he tell her he was *the* Judas? The traitor. The one they said sold Jesus for thirty pieces of silver. The one that lies had been told about for centuries.

"Judas?" Eliza prodded.

His mind went back to that moment at the gala. She had stood before him and told him how she built an entire career around understanding the wrongfully convicted. Her entire self was dedicated to saving those who were innocent. Judas chewed the inside of his lip for a long moment and let his mind imagine what it might feel like to finally be understood.

He thought to himself, '*Don't make me regret this, Yesh.*'

"It's not my blood. I... want to tell you a story...one that is going to sound extraordinary and honestly... unbelievable. But I swear to you, Eliza... my *Ahavah*... every word is true. I swear on everything I hold dear," his voice trembled.

"Okay," she frowned. "Tell me."

Handing her a t-shirt from his closet, he whispered, "This will take a while. I'll make coffee."

Chapter Sixteen

The warm scent of fresh ground beans wafted its invitation into Eliza's nostrils, immediately alerting her senses. Her mouth watered for what she knew would be the most delicious cup of coffee she'd ever tasted. Watching from the marble bar separating the kitchen from the common living space, she admired Judas's agility as he expertly crafted the perfect brew.

Passing her the cup, his face was pensive, "You like it straight if I remember."

"That's right," she whispered gently, slowly sipping. There was delicious wizardry in the cup.

Eliza cradled the warmth in her hands and stared at him. Her mind swirled with questions about what kind of story he wanted to tell her. It concerned her that his demeanor had changed so quickly the second she mentioned the whip hanging on his bedroom wall. As he completed his mug of magical brew, the scattering of scars on his back didn't go unnoticed. He gave her a shirt and shorts but he dressed only in a pair of thick athletic pants; it was his home after all and Eliza had come to cherish his form.

Judas turned to face her. Eliza thought he looked sad and uncomfortable and it was so far out of his personality that it made her concerned for his mental health. She wondered if that protective childhood he spoke of was a euphemism for an abusive one. It wouldn't be the first time she heard a similar story.

Clearing his throat, Judas' voice broke their tense silence, "So...what I'm about to tell you—" He paused. "I know it's going to sound fantastic and believe me, you're going to think I'm a lunatic. But... I hope... by the end..." Another pause. "You can look past it and still...*care* for me because I really *care* about you," his dark caramel eyes misted with tears.

"Judas," reaching out, Eliza took his hand, "Nothing you can say will ever change the way I feel about you."

Judas closed his eyes, nodding.

"You asked about the pictures on the wall? It's not my family in those pictures, Eliza. I don't have any family... at least, I don't think I do." He mused for a moment in serious contemplation. Did he have relatives out in the world? He wouldn't know them, but surely his DNA was out there. Judas refocused, "Those men that resemble me? The reason they look like me is because... they *are* me," his voice soft and fearful.

Eliza was confused, "So, you had old pictures made to look like family photos? Can I ask—"

"No," shaking his head emphatically, "No... those pictures are old. But, they're of me. I'm in those pictures... all of them."

Walking to the wall, he pointed to the target of Eliza's interest, "This was taken October 3, 1862, the morning after Mr. Lincoln arrived at the Union camp in Antietam. I was working for the photographer, Alexander Gardner at the time. I set up the picture while Alex tested the lighting when he took this. It was so sunny that day and we had to move the officers several times because the President was so tall, he cast a shadow on some of the faces. After it was developed, Alex gave it to me as a gift."

Eliza narrowed her eyes on him in thought. There was absolutely no way what he was telling her was true. Did he just say he had his picture taken with the sixteenth president of the United States... over one hundred and sixty years ago?

"Judas," she chortled, "You can understand why that sounds absurd. I mean, that would make you, what? Over one hundred ninety years old? That's impossible."

"*Khara*," Judas growled under his breath.

"That! What is that word? I hear you use it a lot. It sounds... Hebrew," she exclaimed.

"Because it *is* Hebrew. I told you I speak many languages. It just means shit... right now it means shit, what do I do now to convince you I'm telling the truth."

"I forgot you know Hebrew." Eliza was impressed again, recalling how he had called her harzr shli, his treasure.

He rolled his eyes, sighing, "French, Arabic, Spanish, Hebrew, Gr eek...and.." He took a breath. "Aramaic."

Her shock was immediate, "Impressive...but, I mean...you come from Israel, so it stands to reason..." She stopped, narrowing her eyes on him once more, "Wait. Did you say Aramaic? As in the language of Jesus? That's certainly different."

Judas, relieved he was possibly making headway, latched onto the opportunity to move forward. Taking her by the hand, he led her to the sofa.

"You asked me about the whip hanging in my bedroom... it's real as is the blood it's stained with... but the blood isn't mine. It belongs to a friend of mine... someone I followed and learned from. Someone I loved who asked me to do a terrible thing that changed history as *you* know it. Something that I, in hindsight, would not do again."

"Who does the blood belong to?" Eliza shifted uncomfortably in her seat. Her heart racing as fast as her mind. It was crazy to think about what he was going to tell her, but the clues seemed to put themselves together like a completed puzzle. She was the child of a lifelong evangelical.

Israel. Aramaic. A teacher and a terrible act.

"I called him Yesh... but you know him by his common name, Jesus."

Eliza thought she might vomit. Shaking her head violently, she wanted to scream that he was insane, but what came out of her open mouth was near maniacal laughter. He had to be delirious if he thought she would believe that he was Judas Iscariot.

"There's no way. Judas... c'mon. Stop being ridiculous! You're trying to tell me that you're *the* Judas? The traitor?" Her laughter bounced off the walls of the apartment. When she finally got control of her lawless amusement, she found Judas not joining in the obvious joke, but sitting stoically, the tears streaming from his bitter eyes. The guilt of her childish delight poured over her like a cold shower. She half expected him to throw her out of the apartment but when he opened his mouth, the most beautiful song fell from his lips.

Abun D'bashmayo, Neth Q'adash Smokh
Tithe Mal kuthokh, Nehwe Sebyonkh
Aykano D'bashmayo, Oph Bar'o
Hab-lan lahmon D'sunqonan Yowmano
Wa-sbuq lan, Hawbayn, wa-htohayn
Aykano dof hnan, Sbaqan l-hayobayn
Lo ta 'alan l-neyuno, Ela faso lan Men biso
Metul d'dilokh hi Malkutho
W'haylo, W'thes 'buhto
L'olam 'olmin

Tears fell in streams from Eliza's flushed cheeks as she sucked in a shuttered breath. She felt the beauty, the longing, and the pain in Judas' hauntingly crystal voice. It was as if her soul was splitting from her body as his lilt sliced a chilly knife through her. Her bones rattled. She wanted to believe him and she was sure he needed her to, but her brain still overrode her heart and logic screamed of the impossibility.

"That was beautiful," choking, she clumsily swiped at the falling rivers, "What was it?"

Judas opened his eyes, "The Lord's Prayer...in the language of my people."

He paused.

"I am no traitor." He touched her face tenderly, "*Ahava...* I didn't mean for you to cry."

"I want to believe you... but, how? And...what are you?" Eliza asked with caution. Ridiculous ideas of vampires and Hollywood monsters flooded her mind. She still wasn't sure if he was serious or just mad.

His voice, chipped with derision, chortled, "This is a gift... given to me by my best friend, Yeshuda." Looking skyward he yelled, "Something I have asked for him to take back!"

Judas looked down into Eliza's questioning eyes, "*Judas,* he said, '*Judas...I need a favor. If you do this for me, I will grant you something that all of the others would be jealous of... because you, Judas, are truly receiving of the message of my Father. You and Mary, my only family.*' I told him he didn't need to repay me for a favor... I would give it willingly. Anything he needed, I would provide!" Judas became angrier with every word. "I'm sure you can guess what favor he asked of me. To turn him in! Give him to the priests... allow him to be humiliated and murdered. He said '*It's the only way, Judas!*' You have no idea what it's like to watch someone you love be tortured in front of you."

His words ripped Eliza's heart. She empathized with the feeling because she was watching it firsthand. She saw agony fill him as he spoke and her heart swelled with painful sorrow, "You were...there?"

He nodded, the ravenous tears threatening to burst from his eyes, "I was."

"But...I thought," her voiced trailed into silence.

"I killed myself?" his eyes rose to meet hers as the rivers ran into his beard. "I found that man hanging...I don't know why he was there or if he did that to himself and it didn't matter. The rumor of my betrayal was already circling but I couldn't allow Yesh to be alone. I needed to stand by his side. I took the man's clothes and replaced them with my own. By the time he was found by others, no one recognized him anyway."

Reaching out, Eliza took Judas' hand.

"I watched them tear my brother apart," a sob caught in his throat. "That Scourge on the wall? It was his. I stole it so no one else would be given the same fate." He huffed a small chuckle through his falling tears, "Symbolically, of course. The Romans had multitudes at their disposal. I wanted to save him, Eliza. But he said it was the only way. So, I stood in the crowd...cloaked and hidden. I watched as they nailed his wrists to that wood...my soul tore from me as they lifted him into the sky and I wailed like a child when he whispered his last words! My friend died and I helped him do it."

She moved to sit next to him. She still wasn't sure if she wholly believed him, but recognized that his grief was real. Judas had been through something traumatic. Reaching out, she gently touched the small scars on his back. When his eyes met hers, her question was asked without words.

"No," he wiped his face. "I got those while serving on a British navel ship. They were starving a prisoner... I thought it was cruel, so I gave him some of my bread."

Eliza didn't react but her insides were spinning. He spoke of this other life so calmly, so convincingly that a part of her was starting to believe the outlandish. His skin was warm under her hand and she had felt his breath on hers just hours before. He was real, that was unequivocal, but she had to know.

"What was his gift for you?" she whispered. "Yesh, that is."

Lifting his chin, he looked down at her with unfocused anger, "Eternal life. Immortality. I never age. I can never die."

Chapter Seventeen

T he pink in the early morning sky faded as the sun crested over the horizon. It promised to be another hot summer day as Eliza stared at Judas. The revelation that he was, in fact, *the* Judas Iscariot from legend and lore, overwhelmed the exhausted woman. As if he could sense her fading skepticism, Judas offered one last gift of confirmation.

"I can prove what I'm telling you is true," excitedly he motioned for her to follow him to the kitchen. Taking the thin knife used for deboning out of the mahogany base, Judas held his forearm out exposing his wrist. Eliza saw the two small scars just below the palm of his hand only seconds before Judas shoved the knife into his wrist and pulled it toward his elbow. Exposed flesh flayed open and blood poured from the four-inch-long slice. The knife made a loud clang in the sink as Judas dropped it, yelling in pain.

Eliza screamed, "Oh my God! Judas! What have you done?!"

Panic set in as she frantically raced around him grabbing at what towels she could find to stop the bleeding.

"Eliza!" he roared. "Wait! Please calm down, I'm okay! Watch."

Judas held his arm over the sink as blood flowed in waves down the drain. But slowly, as he held his arm steady, Eliza saw the laceration was pulling itself together, and the flow of sanguine fluid became a trickle before her eyes.

"What in the hell..." She blinked and all that remained was a thin, dry scab.

Now she really might faint.

"You...you..." she stuttered in shock. "You're telling the truth."

Regret consumed him. By the expression on her face, it was looking like the truth may not have been such a good idea. Judas wanted to take it all back until he watched her face light into a smile.

"I have so many questions. I don't know where to begin. So...all of this," she pointed to the pictures and displayed art, "is all... *real*?"

Judas was astonished. Cool relief washed over him. Finally, for the first time in his long life, Judas felt comfortable and at ease seeing her acceptance. He didn't have to hide who he was or lie about his history. The sensation was completely exotic and wholly exhilarating.

His laugh was lighthearted, "Yeah. Stuff I've collected as I've moved around. This," he pointed to a mask painted green with antlers like a stag, "is a druid ritual mask from Britannia. And this.." Pointing at a healthy potted tree near the access to his balcony, "Is an olive tree I've cultivated. It's a direct ancestor from one I picked fruit from in Galilee."

Eliza's head was spinning. It was too much information, too little sleep, and too little food for her body. She wanted to know everything but the mountain of questions was insurmountable. How would she wrap her mind around all of this? It seemed like a fever dream. Grabbing the lukewarm cup of coffee from the bar, she gulped the entire mug in one large mouthful.

As though he could feel her vibration change, Judas took her hand, "Are you okay?"

"I need to sit down... and some water, I think," walking back to the sofa, she flopped on its soft cushions. Reality was nothing and everything. What did it mean to be immortal? He clearly bled, but did he get sick? Was he immune to diseases? Could he eat anything he wanted? The thought of him being able to have chocolate cake for every meal made her a little jealous.

Handing her a large glass of water, Judas sat on the floor in front of her, "I know you have questions... a lot of them. I want to tell you everything."

Eliza thought of the most basic thing to ask, "The story we've been told, the one the entirety of the Christian world believes... is any of it true?"

"About me?" Judas shook his head, "No, it's not. Yesh asked me to turn him in. He said it was part of his Father's plan. If I didn't, the world would fall into despair, and his message would never be heard. You have to understand, I didn't want him to do it! I begged him to reconsider. Mary and I both did, but he wouldn't hear us. After he died, the rumors spread... Simon, Peter, and James pointed their manipulative fingers at me."

"What about the thirty pieces of silver?" she was on the edge of her seat in anticipation. The entire worldview of millions, including her father, being a complete fabrication was spellbinding.

Judas huffed, "It was a setup to feed into their narrative. They told the priesthood I should be rewarded for my actions. I never took that blood money, but they sure as hell told everyone I did."

It took Eliza a few moments to think of something else to ask. She had so many questions and still didn't know where to start.

"Are there others... like you?"

"Immortal? I only know of one... Adam's first wife, Lilith. She and I met in Greece around the third century after Yesh died—"

Eliza raised her hand to stop him, "Wait a minute. Adam's first wife? That story is true?"

"Yeah, it is," Judas laughed. "But, she's no demon and she doesn't steal or eat children. Can she be dangerous? Absolutely. I definitely wouldn't piss her off."

"This is just so..." her eyes widened in awe. "Why would you tell me this? Why me?"

Inhaling deeply, Judas held his breath for a long moment. His chestnut eyes looked at her with a longing that melted her insides and she thought her heart would jump out of her chest when he finally spoke.

"Because...I'm pretty sure I'm in love with you."

Chapter Eighteen

"I can't explain how I feel except that you connect with my entire being, Eliza. I have been on this earth for two millennia and have never felt my soul resonate like it does with you," Judas rose on his knees to meet her face. "The very sensation of your skin on mine is holy."

Eliza's tears flowed like waves down her chin. She had no way of knowing if he really meant the words he said, but they felt real in her heart. She couldn't deny that from the minute she shook his hand in her father's office weeks ago, she felt the fire between them when they were close and the pain of distance when they weren't. But she never thought she could say what she needed.

"My *ahavah*... please talk to me. I can't stand to see you cry," kissing her cheek, Judas wiped her tears with his gentle hands.

"I love you, too."

Her voice came as a soft breeze in his ears, but her words were strong as stone. Joy burst from every pore of Judas' body as his mouth collided with hers and they devoured each other. Eliza drove her hands under his loose-fitting pants, pulling them to the floor. Following her lead, Judas stripped her of the borrowed clothing until she was once again naked in his hands.

Eliza gently tugged her lover toward her but he shook his head.

"No. I want you above me. I want to watch you own me like you deserve," rolling under her, Judas slid his throbbing erection into her flooded entrance. No hesitating. No delay. She groaned in delight as his length filled her, sliding into place like a missing piece of her finally where it belonged.

Rocking back and forth, she planted her palms firmly on his chest. His hard body writhed in sync with each motion of her hips. Her full breasts heaved with every thrust and Judas reached out to hold them.

Eliza felt like a goddess atop her mountainous conquest and with every stroke her core made on his shaft, her lover begged for more. His protective hands explored her body until one settled in a grip on her ass and the other found her swollen clitoris.

He rubbed her between his fingers and locked his eyes with hers. The harder she rocked against him, the faster he stroked her pleasure center. She felt the imminent wave of orgasm building and her nails dug into his chest.

"Yes, my ahavah..." he cried, "Me too..."

Eliza ground herself harder and deeper onto his shaft and he gripped her tighter, relishing in their friction. She screamed delightfully as she watched his golden eyes roll in blessed euphoria. For the second time in less than twelve hours, the sounds of their climax and saturated skin mixed with the satisfied cries of pleasure reverberating off the walls. Together they came in earth shaking orgasm until she collapsed onto his chest, gasping for breath.

Once she had regained her ability to process thought, Eliza began to lift her body off of him in an attempt to unsheathe his still hard erection from inside her. He took hold of her arms and gently pulled her flat against his chest again.

"I'm not ready to be without you," he whispered against her hair.

For the next hour, Eliza lay on her lover's broad chest listening to his heartbeat as he caressed her soft skin. She realized for the first time in her life, she had a real feeling of fulfillment. She never thought of her life being remiss of anything. She had a nice home, a successful career that made her happy, and friends who were as close as family.

But, her time with Judas was different. They had a connection that was synchronous and symbiotic; two sides of the same coin.

Judas ran a finger tenderly around the curve of her ear and Eliza giggled.

"Sorry about that," he mused happily, still stroking her neck.

She breathed his scent deep, "No, not that. I was just thinking..."

"About?"

"Where do I start?" she smiled. "What have you been doing...all this time?"

Judas raised his chin in thought, "I moved around...a lot. I've lived almost everywhere. Before telephones and televisions, it was a lot easier to spend decades...even centuries in the same place." He winked, "No evidence showing up on the internet."

Eliza stared in child-like amazement. She was taken in by the thought of seeing the world in a cyclical lifespan of development and death over a multitude of lifetimes. But she realized as quickly that, as entrancing as eternal life sounded, it would be bittersweet; knowing you would continue on while any family and friends you might have would be gone in the blink of an eye.

She glanced at the picture of Lincoln, "So, you *met* Abraham Lincoln?"

"Yeah," his gregarious laugh filled the room.

"That's...amazing," she replied breathlessly. "Anyone else? How many famous people do you know...or...did you know?"

He pushed wisps of hair from her face, "I mean...a few, I guess. More so when I moved here...Yesh, notwithstanding, of course." He chuckled, "It's not like I sought people like that out...we just crossed paths. For instance, I met Ella in New York City in nineteen forty while she was performing in a club one night. She came to the bar, ordered a gin fizz, and struck up a conversation."

Judas shrugged in a nonchalant manner that blew Eliza's mind.

"Ella?" her widened eyes as she stuttered, "You're...you're talking about Ella Fitzgerald? *The* Ella Fitzgerald?"

He shrugged again, "It's not that big of a deal."

"Not that big of a deal? It's Ella Fitzgerald!" she exclaimed, jaw dropped wide.

"Eliza, understand, it's not been a thousand years of notables and parties. I left my home and wandered for years trying to make sense of everything that happened. I staged my own death for the sake of keeping those I loved safe. I've watched the rise and fall of entire empires. I've fought in wars that were never meant for me. I joined the Crusades just to see my homeland one more time...I fought in France, twice. I've seen more death than Samael, but," his finger traced the outline of her face. "I've also been witness to the most beautiful sunrises over vast oceans and felt hope in the darkest of places and love where I didn't think it existed."

The idea was too much to process and Eliza had so many more questions now. Before she could stop herself, she whispered, "What was he like? Yesh?"

Judas' eyes fell at the mention of his name, "He was brilliant. Loving. A visionary that only wanted the best for all of humanity. He opened our eyes to everything there is and will ever be. Unfortunately, his message has been garbled and bastardized to fit so many hateful and evil agendas... it's never ending. He wouldn't want anything of this vitriol...so few of the churches built in his name get his message right...that is the saddest realization so far."

Eliza mused over his words and had to agree with him. Even with her background as a child raised in the evangelical space, she knew the message didn't make sense. How do you both love and hate someone at the same time? How could you pull messages of damnation from a man's words that only spoke of acceptance? But, where she grew up, it happened every Sunday.

They stared into each other's eyes for what seemed like an eternity. "So...do you get sick? Like... have you ever had the flu?" she propped her chin on his chest, staring adoringly at him.

Judas howled with laughter, "I confess to you that I can never die...that I've lived countless lifetimes and you ask if I get the sniffles?"

"Well," Eliza choked a giggle, "yeah. I mean... it's a valid question."

He tightened his hold, "You're right. It's valid. Yes, I've had the flu... measles, chicken pox, smallpox, bubonic plague, scarlet fever, and strep throat. But, none of them last long. I guess one of the few upsides of everlasting life."

"Wow. Okay...some of those are painful. Can you feel pain?" she asked, curiosity sparkling in her sapphire eyes.

"Yes! Of course. I felt every inch of my little display over the kitchen sink earlier. I'm certainly not immune to pain," he chortled.

She had more questions but they were flying so fast in her mind it was difficult to grab one to ask. A sly grin pulled at the corner of her mouth, "Why would you choose *Christian* as your surname? Kind of on the nose a bit, right?"

Judas smirked. It was an expression that she found both satisfying and sexy at the same time.

"I've had lots of names."

"Okay, but why that one?" she narrowed her eyes on him.

"Well, I can't very well use my real name, can I?" he mused.

Eliza, the former prosecutor, pressed him, "But, why Christian?"

"You aren't going to let this go are you?" Judas' chest tightened in laughter.

"Uh huh," she shook her head, laughing, "we will definitely be circling back to that one until I get a real answer."

The tip of her chin still buried in the cup of her fist on his chest, she was quiet for a long moment watching him watch her. She felt a sense of safety in his gaze. It was as if a forcefield surrounded her and if the world crumbled beneath her feet, it would prevent her from disappearing in the ashes.

"That word you use... *ahavah*?" she tried to imitate the inflection of his tone when he spoke. "What does that mean?"

An enormous smile spread over Judas' face and she heard his heart beat faster. He was nervous or excited; maybe both, she thought.

"It means," he swallowed hard. "My love."

Chapter Nineteen

The mid-morning sun pulsed in rays as the pair held each other on the sofa. They could have forgotten about responsibility and the world outside for an eternity but the high-pitched ring of a cell phone forced them back into reality. Eliza jolted out of Judas' arms, clamoring toward her blazer, still draped over the leather side chair.

Scrambling to pull it out of the pocket, her face visibly fell when she saw her father's name on the screen.

"Shit," she muttered before answering with a flat, "Hi Dad."

Judas could hear Paul's muffled voice from the edge of the couch. Rising, he met Eliza as she paced a small path between the bar and living room before kissing her on the top of her head. "Tell your dad I said 'hi'," he whispered with a breathy voice in her ear and winked.

The comment elicited a stifled giggle and a wide-eyed look of fake admonishment. She was glad he couldn't read her mind because she might be embarrassed to admit to him that the tenor of his voice also brought a delightful shiver down her spine that made her damp moisture bloom between her thighs. Eliza forced herself to refocus her attention on what her dad was saying.

"Betsy. Are you listening to me? Where are you and what time will you be in the office? We need to talk about last night."

She sighed, watching Judas' tight ass as he pulled together ingredients for more coffee, "Yeah, Dad... I'm listening. But... I don't think we have much to talk about. I meant what I said last night...either pay

Georgia what she deserves or you can find yourself another coordinator."

"Elizabeth Catherine! Don't you dare threaten me—"

A mix of shock and anger poured over Judas's face at Paul's bellowing. He stepped forward with his hand out; to do what, he wasn't sure. The reaction felt naturally reflexive but Eliza shook her head gently, pursing her lips in a look that told him *'I've got this.'*

"I'm serious, Dad. Put in the paperwork this minute or I'm finished. I'll end my leave of absence and go back to my *salaried* career. It's a good deal, Dad. Because you won't find anyone that will take over my responsibilities for the amount I'm compensated." She disconnected the call.

Judas stood in shock. He watched this woman cater to, placate, babysit, and manage her father for weeks but never to the level he just witnessed. It was impressive.

"He's already typing the pay adjustment. I'll check with payroll after I get there to make sure they back-pay," tossing the phone on the bar, Eliza turned on her heel and walked to the bedroom.

Judas followed, "What was that with your father?"

He leaned on the doorframe, watching her dress.

Sighing, Eliza plopped on the end of the king-sized bed to button her shirt, "I was looking over the campaign accounts from last month. I noticed something weird with the payroll, so I did a little digging. Turns out, Georgia, the intern that... *caught* us..."

She looked up just as Judas's cheeks flushed.

"She's being paid three dollars less an hour than the other intern... who, of course, is a guy. I confronted him about it, which just devolved into an argument about how my worldview is skewed because of my liberal college education," jumping from her seat, she pulled on her jeans. "Among other things." Her voice trailed off.

"What do you mean, other things?" Judas retrieved a towel from his walk-in closet, wrapping it around his hips.

She tucked her blouse into her pants, and rolled her eyes, "Just shit he always says. I don't understand how the world really works. She should be grateful that she even has a job. If she were more of a *'good Christian girl'*", she could find a good man to marry her and she wouldn't need to work."

Judas was taken aback. Paul's words seemed to be not just insults about Georgia but about his own daughter as well. Judas himself came from what could literally be called old school thinking and he never— in his exceptionally long life— thought the same way as Paul did. Her father's attitude was at best, wholly disrespectful of all human beings and at worst, dangerous in the worst ways. Why would anyone want a person like him in charge?

Why? Because a lot of people were just like him. They hated women because they feared them.

Looking at Eliza's fierce expression and knowing her unwavering dedication to serving those around her, Judas thought to himself, if he were Paul he would fear this woman for certain. This woman was dangerous in all the right ways.

Chapter Twenty

"Good afternoon, Miss Lydia," dropping the carry-out cup next to her computer mouse, Judas' bright smile was glowing. "Thought you could use a pick me up."

The older woman's cheeks were brightening with color, "Well, now Judas...isn't that just thoughtful of you." She took a sip, "Oo! My favorite...Earl Grey."

"Even remembered the lemon," he winked, and Lydia's face was beaming pink. Heading around the curve of the desk, Judas stepped toward the hallway when he heard the receptionist's voice trailing after him.

"You be careful back there, sugar. Mr. Arthur is on one with Eliza right now."

"Perfect," Judas muttered under his breath. He had to wonder if whatever argument they were having now had anything to do with the phone call this morning. He rounded the corner of the hall, hearing the voices rising as he got closer to the door.

"I don't appreciate my daughter berating me like a child! You need to remember who is in charge here young lady," Paul's fervor hung in the air.

Pausing for a moment, Judas quickly took notice Beau wasn't outside the room. He rapped two hard knocks on the door before slipping inside, and it was just in time to hear Eliza's daring retort.

"Oh, I'm always clear on who's in charge... *Dad*. God forbid that you would take any advice from me... someone who studied political theory... or is it because I'm a woman? I'm just supposed to be at your demand when you need me or just when you need a mess cleaned up?"

The vitriol was almost tangible.

Paul's face boiled and he flew around the mahogany desk, his finger wagging, "I'll take no more of your sass, do you hear me, Betsy?"

The pair were statues as they stared the other down. Judas watched Paul's chest rise and fall in fury. For a split second, he thought the man was going to strike his daughter.

A thought roared in Judas' head, '*It would be the last thing he ever did.*'

Paul's eyes widened suddenly, as if Judas appeared out of thin air, "Judas. Good, you're here. Betsy was just telling me that the plans for the next week's fundraiser have changed." Turning on his heel, he returned to the large executive chair. "The Associated Republicans have secured a larger venue for us, which means you're going to need to put a few more on your staff."

"I can do that," Judas cut his eyes in Eliza's direction but she was more interested in the office ceiling for the moment. "Can I get early access? I'd like to have a blueprint of the room so I know who to place where."

Paul waved his hand dismissively, "Of course, of course. If Chet would get back from wherever he's disappeared to... his girl can pull plan sets from the city."

"His *girl*," Eliza mumbled softly, rolling her eyes, but Paul ignored her. "I don't think Uncle Chet will be back today, Dad. The text said it was a family emergency."

Still pretending he didn't hear his daughter, Paul scrolled his phone, "Ah... yeah, looks like we may not hear from him until tomorrow. I'll get *Amelia* to give you the access."

"I'll take you to her," Eliza offered. "I think I need some fresh air."

A feeling of awkwardness fell on the room, spreading thick on every surface. Luckily, Judas knew Paul would be leaving to play golf soon and would go straight home after. It was a break that would do both father and daughter some good. Shutting the door behind him, Judas struggled to catch up with Eliza.

"Hey! Hey, hey, hey..." Reaching out, he took her arm and spun her to face him. His eyes darted in all directions making sure they were alone, "What was that all about?"

Her heart fluttered like a schoolgirl at his touch, but Eliza's lips were pursed tight, "Nothing. It's over...I really don't want to talk about it. Actually, I just want to introduce you to Amelia and get out of here."

"Okay," he nodded. "Lead the way."

Chapter Twenty-One

The brown bags overflowed with their contents and Judas struggled to pull his keys from his pocket. All the ingredients for a romantic Italian dinner balanced heavily on his hip as he finally slipped the key into the lock, turning the tumbler. Judas kicked the door shut when he felt the soft vibration of his phone in his back pocket.

"Khara," groaning, he quickly dropped the sacks on the bar but was able to answer the call before it went to his voicemail, "Hello?"

There was a short silence.

"Hey... Judas," the man's steady voice replied carefully, "Chet Branson."

Judas checked the caller ID for confirmation, "Mr. Branson, how are you, sir? Everything alright? I heard there was a family emergency. I hope everyone is well."

"Oh, yeah... everything is... fine," Chet confirmed. "Just... my daughter, Nevaeh is a little... under the weather. It'll all be fine."

Judas thought for a moment that the man sounded a little distant. Maybe the illness was more serious than he wanted to discuss or maybe everything was indeed fine. He didn't know Chet well enough to tell. From their brief interactions, he seemed to be most of what Paul was not; friendly, personable, and well-liked by others. "What can I help you with, sir?"

"I haven't been able to get in contact with Paul. I need to talk to him about a project he worked on. You wouldn't happen to know where he is?" Chet asked.

Judas grinned, "Oh, yeah. He's playing golf with some members of the state police board." He glanced at the antique clock hanging over the sofa, "Actually, he should be on his way home now."

His voice lightened, "Great! Okay. I appreciate that. What about Eliza? Would you happen to know where she is?"

Judas' voice caught in his throat. The mention of her name sent waves of eager anticipation through his body. He dreamed every moment of her being near him. But even when they were in the same room, she was never close enough.

'Hopefully, already on her way here,' was his thought, but, "I think she's in a meeting right now," came from his mouth.

Chet's voice was rushed, "So still at the office. Sounds good. Well, I can catch up with her tomorrow. I appreciate your help."

The line disconnected.

Dropping his phone on the countertop, Judas pulled pots out of cabinets and filled them with water and sauce. The apartment quickly warmed with the aroma of basil and garlic saturating the air as tomatoes bubbled gently on the flame. The text he received from Eliza five minutes prior said she just packed an overnight bag and would be on her way.

The way the phrase *overnight bag* sounded thrilled him. He would have her again, all night, to himself. He never thought she would accept when he made his offer of sanctuary so they could be alone last week. While sneaking around behind Paul's back made their relationship a little more exciting in the beginning, the feelings Judas was sure they had for each other couldn't be kept a secret forever.

He filled the boiling water with the pasta and cut the vegetables for a salad. Judas pulled ivory plates from the cabinet along with silverware and wine glasses, placing them on the small wooden table in the breakfast nook. Back to the boiling pasta to strain.

Judas poured himself a glass of wine and stared at his phone as he sat on a bar stool. He reviewed the schedule for the following week and answered emails from his security team. He realized he missed a text from Beau nearly an hour and a half prior saying that Paul sent him home from the country club. Judas could only roll his eyes and reply that he would be paid for his time anyway.

He mumbled under his breath, "Why have a bodyguard if you don't allow him to do his job?"

He finished his glass and started to pour another only to realize it had been nearly forty-five minutes since Eliza told him she was on her way. It was almost seven o'clock on a Thursday night and traffic was heavier than normal, but she certainly should have been here and parked by now. She wouldn't have to park on the street. Judas made sure of that and gave her the code to the parking garage under his building.

Judas picked up the phone to call her when it vibrated in his hand. Her beautiful name flashed on the screen like a beacon in the dark.

"Ahavah," he cooed, "Where are you—"

"Judas!" she screamed.

Her bellow was like an electric shock to his body. He was immediately ready for a fight, "Eliza! What's wrong?"

He heard her wails and they nearly brought him to his knees. He couldn't help but grab his keys and run to the door before he remembered the food on the stove. He raced back to the stove to shut off the burners as her crying intensified and he recognized the sounds of sirens in the background. He ran out of the apartment, skipping the elevators, and raced down the six flights of stairs; his feet barely hitting any ground.

With his phone still in his ear, his core crumbled as he continued to listen to her sobs.

"Baby... talk to me. What's going on? Where are you? Baby, you need to tell me where you are!" His feet echoed in the expanse of the parking garage as he charged for his car. He slid on the leather seats of his Audi and the engine roared to life. But where is he going? Before he put the car in drive, he tried again, "Eliza! Please...ahavah. Talk to me—"

She finally caught her breath and her voice was short like a drum staccato, "It's. Dad. He's. Been. Shot. Judas. Oh. God. Judas!"

The tires of the car squealed as Judas raced past the gate guard arm, "I'm on my way."

Chapter Twenty-Two

The automatic doors of Baylor University Medical Center swished open as Judas ran into the emergency room waiting area. The time it took him to drive here was too much. His racing mind was uncontrollable as he played Eliza's screams of despair over in his head. He didn't know what he would be walking into either. Was Paul dead? Had Eliza been with him? Was she hurt? Judas would never forgive himself if the latter turned out to be true.

"I'm looking for Paul Arthur or his daughter," he told the thin nurse in the pink scrubs at the desk.

"Judas?" a faint whimper squeaked behind him. Judas spun to find Eliza, wrapped in a gray blanket, her face ruddy and swollen from crying.

Waves of relief crashed over him and he pulled her into his strong hold, "Oh my God. You're safe. It's okay, you're safe." He wasn't sure if he was reassuring Eliza or himself.

She wept in his tight hold and he stroked her golden hair. With every deepening sob, Eliza took in Judas' scent, which began to bring a sense of calm to her. Her cries ebbed more than flowed as her body relaxed.

A portly paramedic with bushy brown hair and a mustache handed Judas a cup of water, "I think she should drink this. She's been in a state of shock since she came in with her father."

Judas, not accepting the water because it would mean taking an arm away from her, spoke in a firm tone, "What happened? She said her father was shot?"

The round medic nodded, "GSW to the left anterior shoulder and posterior right lung. They just took him into the OR. I wanted to let her know."

Judas nodded sharply and the man walked away. Paul was shot twice; once in the front and once in the back. He wondered from what range the assailant fired and how large a caliber. In his life, Judas witnessed hundreds of wars and saw the life drain from men whose convictions convinced them they were on the side of justice. He never chose conflict even though at times, it seemed to hunt him with an ancient and ruthless disregard.

Eliza's mind raced as she allowed Judas's protective embrace to warm her. The chill of fear and despair are forced out of her body by the shield of electrifying security that radiated from him. She is under his guardianship now and she can finally make sense of the chaos playing out around her. She looked into the dark honey eyes of her savior and saw her own relief.

"Ahavah," he whispers, "What happened?"

He guided her to a chair but fdidn't let her out of his hold. She sat next to him, pulling the blanket tighter, and leans into him; his firm form supported her from completely crumbling under the weight of her thoughts. Her voice was stuck somewhere between her chest and teeth and distant when she tried to speak.

"I..." she pulled at the blanket, "I was in the car on my way when I got a call from a neighbor... they... said an ambulance was at Dad's... and police. I got there as quickly as I could... they were just about to leave with him."

Eliza stared at the phone in her shaking hand, "I called Uncle Chet... he told me to keep him posted. I think he's still dealing with his own stuff."

Judas reaches up to wipe a tear from her eye, "It's okay. Your dad's here now. They'll take care of him. He will be fine."

He knew his words would only soothe her pain temporarily. He didn't actually know if Paul would make it out of the operating room alive or not, but he had to keep hope alive inside Eliza. Judas didn't have it in him to allow reality to force its way inside her just yet. The stout paramedic was back but this time a slender man in a beige suit with a navy tie accompanied him to the pair.

"Ms. Arthur?" the man in the suit flips open a notebook.

Eliza's tear bleary eyes blink up in the direction of the voice, "Yes?"

"I'm Detective Grable with the Dallas police department. I know this is a difficult time right now, but do you think you could answer some questions?" Detective Grable pulled a pen out of his white Oxford shirt.

Judas noticed the officer's calloused hands and it reminded him of a carpenter he once knew. He felt Eliza trembling under his hands and he tightened his hold gently.

"I think so," Eliza wiped her face and stiffened her back. The public-facing, professional Elizabeth Arthur is starting to emerge. She's the strong one, the confident one, the one that can conquer the universe.

"Ms. Arthur," Detective Grable turned a page in his notebook. "Your father, Paul Arthur, is a lawyer, is that correct?"

She nodded, "Yes, a real estate attorney."

The detective scribbled on his pad before looking more intently at Eliza, "Wait. Didn't you work in the prosecutor's office a few years ago?"

Judas watched a smile cross her lips. He understood her micro-expressions and knew the act is one of necessary politeness. It's similar to the way she would greet her father's constituents.

"Yes," her voice is professional, "I mostly worked on special victims cases."

"I thought I recognized the name! Oh, Ms. Arthur, I am sorry about your father," Grable is the perfect amount of empathy without any pity. "Did he have any enemies that you can think of?"

Eliza glanced at Judas for assurance and he shook his head.

"No... not that we're aware of," the tears are starting to well in her eyes once more, but she fights them back relentlessly.

"I'm sorry, I didn't get your name," the detective's question is directed at Judas.

He stands to shake Grable's hand, "Jude Christian, I'm Mr. Arthur's head of security."

Grable's eyes widened, "Oh. Not a lot of attorneys with a personal security detail. Did he have a security issue, Mr. Christian?"

"No," Eliza's eyes look up at the men, "Mr. Christian was hired several months ago as a preemptive measure for my father's campaign for the state senate."

Judas gave the detective an assuring nod. It actually quite surprised him that Paul didn't have any threats against him. On a good day, he is a demanding, sexist, know-it-all, bigot; but Paul didn't always have good days.

"No threatening letters, texts... emails? No one is getting out of hand at a fundraiser or event?" Grable writes more in his little book.

'No one except the man who was shot', Judas thought to himself.

Judas shook his head, silencing the thought, "We had an incident at a rally last week. But it was contained quickly. So far, everything has been pretty normal."

Grable continued scratching in his pad. Judas can't imagine anyone who would hate Paul enough to want him dead. He was a profiteering loudmouth with an abrasive personality, but in Judas' experience, there were millions just like him; especially since the advent of the internet. But, there isn't anything special about Paul or his life; except Eliza.

"Just a couple more questions, Ms. Arthur," the detective paused. "Is your father seeing anyone?"

Eliza snickers with a sound so sardonic the men felt it, "I wish he were... but no. My father's only relationship is with his campaign."

More notes before, "Does he own a gun?"

"Yes," she chuckled, "After all, he is Texas born and bred."

"Does he own anything special or old?"

Judas could sense that the detective was leading her somewhere but before he could respond, Eliza was quick with her sharp retort, "Why are you asking? Do you think my father was shot with his own gun?"

The officer looked from Eliza to Judas, "Ma'am...we won't know for sure until the ballistics are back, but, from the x-rays, it appears he was shot with a black powder weapon."

Shock washed over her face. Eliza's head spun as she tried to concentrate on the implications. She was thankful for Judas' warm hand on the small of her back, tethering her to Earth.

"Yes, he owns old guns...but none of them are loaded. They're displayed around the house. I don't even think he has the supplies to shoot them," she shook her head.

A feeling of aggravation and uneasiness settled over her. It terrified her to think that her father's hobby may have in some way contributed to his attack but she couldn't let it affect her right now. As they watched the police detective walk back through the double doors of the ER, Eliza cleared her mind to prepare for the battle that awaited.

Chapter
Twenty-Three

J udas watched Eliza pace the cold floor of the OR waiting room. He could offer no comfort to her right now because she wasn't willing to accept any from anyone. She was quiet, reserved, and stoic. He knew she was just holding her breath until her phone vibrated and it was her turn to get information from the desk. It took five hours, but finally, the wait was over.

Eliza pulled Judas by the hand as they wove around scattered chairs and people.

"I received a text," her throat was like a desert.

"Name?" the bespectacled nurse asked.

Eliza drew a deep breath, "Paul Arthur...I'm his daughter."

The woman jabbed at keys on her computer, gazing at the monitor over her glasses, "Yes, he's been moved to recovery. If you'll please wait in consolation room one, someone will be in to speak with you."

Judas turned in the direction of her finger and nodded his thanks.

They sat in pregnant silence for a long moment in the small room. The tension between them was thick, weighing on them like the world on the back of Atlas. Judas left his position of protection by the door to take a place next to Eliza. It was as if the bottom fell out of a bucket.

"What happens if he dies?" she whispered, leaning into his shoulder, her eyes too tired to cry.

His grip enveloped her, "No, ahavah... not those thoughts. He's going to be just fine... your focus is being by his side."

"Who... would do this, Judas? Dad is... an asshole in the best of times, but," she paused. "I need to find out who did this."

"Eliza—"

The door swung open to a man in his mid-fifties in green scrubs; his face mask dangling from his neck, "Ms. Arthur?"

The pair stood, shaking hands with the doctor as quick introductions were made. He was abrupt and to the point. Paul had been shot twice; once in the shoulder, just missing his heart, and once in his back. The bullets were removed without incident but it seems as though he fell when he tried to outrun the assailant, hitting his head on something hard like a corner of a table or the floor. Paul was suffering from swelling in his brain.

"Oh my God!" all color drained from Eliza's face and Judas stood closer in case she might faint.

"Your father is in a medically induced coma. Right now, it's wait and see." He placed a reassuring hand on her elbow, "We'll know more in the next twenty-four to forty-eight hours. I am sorry I can't tell you more right now."

He looked at Judas, "He'll be moved from the recovery room to the critical care unit within the hour. You can see him then."

Judas bowed his head in thanks as the door closed. He felt the energy shift as Eliza melted into his arms, sobbing. He felt her anguish and pain as if it were his own and wished he could free her of it. He would find out who hurt Paul. It wouldn't be out of loyalty to his employer, but out of love for the man's daughter.

"Shhh..." he soothed. He felt her breath slowing as her cries abated.

She rose from his hold touching his damp shirt where her tears saturated the soft fabric, "Thank you, Judas. For everything. I'm not sure I would be half as coherent if you weren't here with me."

He had to laugh, "Eliza, I think you are capable of conquering the world if you set your mind to it."

Her dewy eyes rose to meet his, "I have to find out who did this."

"No, you don't," Judas shook his head vehemently. "The police are perfectly equipped to handle it. Please, Eliza. Let them do their job."

The thought of her playing detective while someone with an aspiration for murder was out there drove him to the brink of madness. If there was someone with a grudge against Paul, he wanted Eliza to be as far away as possible. He knew if he pushed her too hard, she would dig in and do it anyway. Which, if he were being honest, that's probably exactly what was happening.

"I'll tell you what... you and I," he put a hard emphasis on the *I*, "we'll do some digging... tomorrow, as a *team*. Between the two of us, I'm sure we can get closer to what really happened tonight. Deal?" He stared so hard into her glistening eyes, that he almost lost himself.

Eliza considered him for a long moment before an answer tumbled from her lips.

"Deal."

Chapter Twenty-Four

Judas was a sentinel from the doorway, watching Eliza hold her father's hand for an hour. It was the middle of the night and she refused to leave his side. After all the disagreements, coddling, and admonishment of poor judgment and even more terrible behavior, she was always the faithful and dutiful daughter. Judas knew this woman was otherworldly, but her strength and loyalty seemed infinite. He could only think of one other person he met in the vastness of his life that she came close to in veritable fortitude; and he loved them both, albeit, in differing ways.

Around three, Eliza took Judas by the hand and out of the presence of her father, "Hey... I'm not going anywhere, but you should go home. Get some sleep."

"I'm not leaving you," he argued.

"Judas," her smile graceful, "I feel the emptiness when you're gone too. But I'm perfectly safe here in this hospital. Please, do this for me."

He relented because he would do anything those gorgeous eyes wished for him.

Judas opened the door to his home and the scent of cold food met him. Taking a step inside, something crunched under his shoes and he quickly flipped on a light. He looked down to find a simple white envelope wedged into his tile entry.

He tossed his keys on the bar and then ran his thumb under the fold to find a check written out to him for five thousand dollars. The signature read Paul Arthur with *Thank You* scrolled in the memo line.

"Thank you?" he said aloud in the empty room. Was this a bonus? Even though his payroll records had Paul's signature, his salary was directly deposited into an account and he never received a paper check. It was odd for sure, but Judas was too tired to deal with it at the moment anyway. His focus was getting back to the hospital as soon as possible, fully rested and ready to work. He wouldn't allow Eliza to be alone for very long.

After tossing the food in the garbage and filling the dishwasher, Judas found himself in the confines of his shower. He couldn't help but think about how much he missed sharing it with Eliza. Closing his eyes, he imagined her lips making trails on his skin, her body awash with the hot deluge of water. His imagination ran wild and his body reacted to the images. He flipped the temperature handle over to cold before eventually exiting to an empty bedroom for an unsettled sleep.

Judas laid in the darkened room staring at the ceiling. Rolling over, he curled into the soft pillow, and breathed deep, forcing his eyes to close. The faint scent of soft honeysuckle and musk filled his nostrils and he buried his face further into the pillow that held her smell. Closing his eyes tighter, Judas did his best to relax his mind into sleep. Feeling his body loosen, he waited for the warmth of slumber to overtake him.

As if a strike of lightning shot through him, Judas sat bolt upright in the bed. Throwing the loose blanket from his body, he grabbed his phone from the bedside table and flipped through his calls. Something was off about Paul's assault, he could feel it. Judas scanned his call log for clues but to what, he didn't know yet.

Then there it was. His heart raced and nearly jumped in his throat remembering the conversation. Chet Branson's name and phone number with a timestamp of five minutes after five the afternoon prior shone on Judas' face in the dark like a beacon. The phone call itself was strange but remembering the conversation was more so, especially now, given the most recent events.

The pit in the bottom of his stomach was growing. Was Chet the one who tried to murder Paul? He certainly had enough time; there were almost two hours between his call and Eliza's call to Judas. But why would Paul's longtime partner and seemingly only friend try to kill him? Judas reasoned why people who just met him would want him dead, but a long time ally? He was missing something.

Judas thought of the mysterious check. There was no way Paul would cut him a check for that amount of money without a solid reason. Hurrying back to the kitchen, he looked the document over carefully for any signs of forgery. But to his dismay, it was printed on a computer with the signature as part of the check writing program; it hadn't been actually signed by anyone. He threw the piece of paper back on the bar in anger.

The recognizable feeling of dread boiled in his stomach. If Chet was the shooter, there had to be a reason. What had Paul done that his friend decided an execution was the only option? He thought of Eliza. If his suspicions were true, she would be devastated, after all, the Branson's had been her only family since her mother's death. Judas didn't want to be the one to upset her more, especially now, but what choice did he have?

Sleep was no longer on the table. If he was going to be the one to tell Eliza the man she considered as close as an uncle tried to murder her father, he would need more than his gut feeling. Judas redressed and now in the wee hours of the morning, he drove to the office to get his proof.

Chapter Twenty-Five

The building was still dark when Judas unlocked the heavy wooden doors of Arthur and Branson around four a.m. while sipping his second cup of coffee. Knowing that he would be alone for at least the next few hours, he contemplated where to start. If someone other than Paul had written the check that he found on his floor, it was possible that the cameras would have caught them entering the office. Turning down the dark hallway, Judas made his way into the security room.

With Paul's campaign in full swing, Judas was happy he forced the man to add the recording capabilities to the office's surveillance program. He was shocked to learn their system was mostly outdated and only held on to video for twenty-four hours. Judas thought for sure that Paul was the kind of man that would want to spy on his employees if only to make sure they were earning the money he paid.

For the next three hours, Judas played and replayed the digital recording from the previous day. Every employee, every hour, ran like a movie before his eyes; but he was really only interested in one person. To Judas' irritation, Chet Branson never showed. He never entered the building. Could the pit of suspicion in his stomach be wrong? Was the phone call a coincidence?

Even though he was alone in the room, Judas shook his head. He had been witness to more than a millennia of history and experience.

He could feel it in his soul that Chet was involved. Lost in his thoughts, he nearly didn't hear the soft knock on the door.

"Jude?" The soft voice was gentle.

Judas shuttered slightly, swinging around in his chair, "Oh! Lydia...I'm sorry. I didn't hear you."

The older woman looked much smaller than normal as her head hung low and she wrung her plump, wrinkled hands. Judas could see her eyes were damp from tears that she most likely had cried all night. She was an original; the first employee of Arthur and Branson and probably the most respected. She was mother or grandmother to everyone and handled Paul's tantrums like an expert. Now that he thought about it, it's probably where Eliza learned a lot of her skills.

"I was wondering if you had any news about Paul? I figured you had been with our Eliza all night," her eyes begged him for a good word.

He nodded, "He came out of surgery fine. He has a head injury, so they're keeping him still for now."

"How is Eliza? She must be just beside herself," Lydia dabbed her eyes with a tissue from her pocket.

It broke Judas' heart to see the old woman hurting. As much as Paul could be a complete asshole, he could tell that she loved him almost as much as Eliza did. Judas stepped toward her, wrapping his arms tenderly around her.

"It's okay, Miss Lydia. He's going to be fine," he soothed.

Lydia coughed a short sob, "Oh, I know. He's a tough old mule." She leaned back from his hold to look Judas in the eye, "He can be hard to get along with, but he's a good man. And he loves that little girl more than life." Smiling through the remnants of tears, she teased, "It's something the two of you have in common."

Judas blushed, "Now, Miss Lydia. I wouldn't let that rumor get back to Mr. Arthur."

"Pfft," she chided him. "He's a lot of hot air. And I've got my own eyes, young man... no rumor to be told."

Smiling down at her, he gave her one last gentle hug, "How about I make you a cup of tea?"

***

After Lydia was calm enough to return to her desk, Judas set out of the office for the day. The elevator seemed slower today and it annoyed him. He was anxious to get back to the hospital and to be rid of the gnawing in his gut. Having hundreds of years of experience told him the feeling of restlessness wasn't something he could ignore. His intuition told him that Chet was the shooter and there wasn't any doubt in his mind. The problem was he couldn't find evidence that the partner had been inside the building in the last twenty-four hours. He was missing something. As the faint ding of the elevator rang, a lightbulb went off in his head.

Judas researched Paul Arthur thoroughly before his interview. The prospective state senator ranked thirty-third in his Odessa High School class of 1982. He graduated Texas Christian University with a bachelors of business administration before attending law school at Baylor.

While studying to be a lawyer, Paul married Catherine Douglas, a debutante from a wealthy family who had their fingers in most all aspects of Texas life including oil drilling. She was a full-time nursing student and part-time beauty queen. Paul was completely smitten. Their only child, a daughter, was born three weeks after Paul received his degree.

Two years later, Paul and his law school buddy, Chet Branson opened their firm, Arthur and Branson, specializing in real estate and tax law. The business rolled in and the pair easily found themselves at the top of the Dallas social hierarchy. Judas found their names in numerous newspaper articles and even on the cover of a few local and professional magazines. To anyone, whether in their inner circle or from an outsider's perspective, all is well both personally and profes-sionally.

The question hung in the air: Where did it go wrong?

Judas followed the turn by turn directions of the car's navigation system. Turning into a sloped circle drive surrounded by lush foliage, he eased the Audi to a stop in front of Paul Arthur's home. He sat for a moment staring at the crime scene tape and contemplating his next move.

He considered for a moment that Eliza might not like him snooping around her father's home but under the circumstances, he had to be sure that his gut was correct. Something between Chet and Paul occurred here, he was positive. Checking his surroundings, he jogged up the brick staircase to the front landing. After cutting the seal with a small pocket knife, Judas used its tip and his American Express card to open the door.

The foyer looked much like it had the night he and Eliza poured Paul into his bed to sleep off his overindulgence with the exception that every surface seemed to be covered with a light layer of powder in a variety of colors. Judas realized that the Dallas police department was exceptionally thorough with fingerprinting every exposed area of the house; at least when it came to a well-known political candidate. Moving carefully, he walked into Paul's study just off the foyer.

The room was a complete wreck with overturned tables and papers strewn over the floor. As Judas walked deeper into the chaos, he noticed a large pool of dried blood staining the usually ornate ornamental rug just under the picture window. It was too much blood to be from any of his injuries individually and he knew it must have been where Paul was found. Turning back to the ornate desk, Judas reenacted the scene in his mind.

Paul was sitting in an armchair either working or reading when the assailant, Chet, entered the home. Startled, Paul asked his friend what he was doing there and it was then that Chet raised the gun, pointing it at his colleague. Did Paul stand? Or did he sit very still staring at the gun? Judas saw that the chair had the tiniest bit of splatter, so he must have stood. He probably confronted Chet, either demanding to know why or perhaps he pleaded for his life. Either way, he takes two steps forward before Chet fires the gun. The scattering of books and paperwork indicated that Paul turned his back to run, but was shot again, this time falling into the corner of a heavy-looking side table, head first.

The scene showed him everything except the reason why. Judas rifled through some of the papers scattered on the floor, but nothing jumped out at him. After intentionally wandering downstairs and not seeing anything else out of place, Judas decided his detour was also a dead end. Slipping out the front door, he looked around one last time just to be sure he left everything as it was when he arrived. It was then he saw it. The tiny slip of paper was wedged in the delicate branches of a neatly trimmed Boxwood.

It looked like trash, but Judas knew that Paul was a control freak. He would never allow any amount of refuse to collect or remain on his very expensive landscaping. Stretching his arm through the slats of the handrail of the landing, Judas plucked the paper from the evergreen.

Unfolding it, he saw it was a note, clearly in Paul's handwriting. *Dra, 469-555-4495.* It seemed meaningless, but he decided to keep it anyway. It could be a clue or it could be worthless, right now he didn't know which. Stuffing it in his pocket, Judas slid back into his car. The engine revved as he sped away from the quiet neighborhood to find Eliza.

Chapter Twenty-Six

"Dad, I need you to wake up," Eliza pleaded softly, stroking her father's hand. The small room was alive with the beeping, buzzing, and dings of medical equipment. The wood and vinyl chair butted as close to Paul's bed as she could make it, Eliza positioned herself so she would be the first thing he saw when he woke.

If he woke.

She couldn't allow the thought to cross her tired mind. She focused her attention on the rise and fall of his chest and any movement of his eyes. If she could have willed it, she would have made them open. Yawning wide, Eliza's body fought the urge to sleep.

"Dad, please," she whispered.

"You should probably go home for a while," a deep voice spoke behind her. It was familiar and comforting like hot tea on a rainy day.

Turning quickly, a smile couldn't help but spread over her lips, "Judas."

"Can we talk? Somewhere... not here?" his brow furrowed. His eyes darted from where Paul lay back to her.

Nodding, she placed her hand in his, allowing him to guide her out of the room. They walked in abated silence through halls until arriving at an empty surgery waiting area. Judas looked around and seeing no one, he opened a door to a small room labeled *Quiet Room*.

Eliza's eyes gazed into his, looking worried, "You don't look like you got much sleep... if any."

Shaking his head, he motioned to her to sit, "I didn't. I have some information and I need to tell you before I say anything to the authorities."

"What?" her heart raced. She couldn't imagine what he might know; he had only been gone for... what, six hours? It felt like weeks. But she had to admit that her mind wasn't firing on all cylinders, as it were. She'd only had an hour of sleep in the last day. She remained standing because she didn't think her ass could handle any more of the uncomfortableness the hospital seats provided.

Judas cleared his throat, "When I returned home, I found a check someone put under the door of my apartment. It was for five-thousand dollars with a note of thanks in the memo line.

Eliza's head twitched as though she was shooing a fly, "I don't understand. Who from?"

"That's the thing...it's signed by your dad. But, it's printed... like off the computer," he stared into her tired eyes. "Eliza, you know your dad doesn't pay me like that and certainly not for that amount. Then there's the phone call I received before all this happened."

She frowned, "From?"

"Mr. Branson."

She could tell Judas was struggling to speak, much like when he told her his truth. Was he trying to hide something else?

"Well," she urged, "What did he say?"

"Khara," his eyes looked skyward as he muttered under his breath. "He wanted to know where your dad was. And you. When I tried to ask if his family was alright, he hurried to get off the phone."

Eliza's eyes narrowed. The words he spoke to her made sense and yet, they didn't. What was he trying to imply? Exhaustion weighed on her face and she struggled to concentrate, "So, what? He and dad have a couple of cases they're working on together. He probably wanted to follow up since he was out of the office today." Then she quickly corrected her timeline, "Yesterday."

"Eliza, who else besides your dad, Mr. Branson, and their payroll department have access to the bank account?" Judas pressed her.

"Well, I guess I could get into it if I had the need," Eliza shrugged.

He nodded, "Why call me to find out where your dad was? Why wouldn't he just call Paul directly?" Judas wanted Eliza to come to the same conclusion he did because he didn't have the heart to say it out loud. Although, he was becoming acutely aware of the realization he might need to do just that.

She stared at him intently for a moment before laughing, "You think Uncle Chet shot my dad? Oh my god, Judas! That's ridiculous!"

He didn't think it was ridiculous. As a matter of fact, he thought it might be exactly what happened, the only question was why? What could Paul have said or done that would have pushed Chet Branson far enough that he wanted his partner dead?

"I don't think so," his brow furrowed, "Have your dad and Mr. Branson had any arguments? Disagree over anything? Even something small?"

"No! Absolutely not," her chortles were strained with exhaustion. "Judas, I know my dad is a lot to deal with, but you have to understand that Uncle Chet is the only family we have. I grew up with his three boys...I was there when Nevaeh was born!"

Judas took her by the hand, leading her to a chair. He recognized the weariness, "I know, but families fight... sometimes brutally. Are you *sure* there's nothing?"

Eliza's face flushed with color, "Yes! How many times do I have to say it?! There's no way! I'm done with this!"

Holding onto her arm, he continued to air his suspicions, "I'm sorry, Eliza, but I'm not buying it. I went to his house. The scene tells me that whoever did this *knew* your father. That he was comfortable with whomever came inside. Paul wasn't expecting the person to hurt him." Judas watched her wearied eyes carefully before he took the crumpled paper from his pocket, "I found this in the bushes outside…does it mean anything to you?"

She looked at the note, shaking her head. She had a headache starting, "No. Nothing."

Flying out of her seat, she pushed through him toward the door. But as she laid her hand on the handle, a cloud of thought fell over her and she turned back.

"Wait a minute," pausing, her stare turned hard as steel, "If you think that Uncle Chet wrote that check… why would he do it to thank you?"

"What?" Judas asked, confused.

She drew a sharp breath, glaring, "Why would Uncle Chet thank *you*? You don't work for him… or do you?" Her eyes narrowed, "Is there something you're not telling me?"

Eliza crossed her arms tightly to her chest. Judas knew her body language and right now it told him that she was pissed. It was a look he'd witnessed a hundred times in the last weeks; except in those instances it was always directed at Paul.

"Eliza–" stepping toward her, he watched the lightbulb come on in her mind.

"I don't believe that Uncle Chet did anything. He's not that kind of person. He could never do something like that, but someone did. And then you got a check saying thank you. You helped them them. Whoever it was, you helped them, didn't you? That's why you're acting so… guilty. You told them where to find my dad!" she charged and her voice bounced off the walls of the tiny room.

Judas' eyes went wide with panic, "I told Chet. He asked and I didn't think anything of it. I didn't know this would happen."

"Or did you? Because if what you're saying is true… which I don't believe it is… but *if*… then you shouldn't feel guilty," her words sizzled. Eliza's mind was firing thoughts and ideas and assumptions faster than she could articulate. A horrific thought of betrayal seeped in from the darkest recesses, clouding her already manic mind. Even though she wasn't consciously aware, the stories she grew up with resonated like a distant vibration, leaving a biased haze over her every thought. "I know he's not the greatest guy, but he's my dad, Judas! I know you probably hate him, but trying to eliminate him to make your life easier is psychotic behavior. Honestly."

Was her father set up? Did Judas help?

"Ahavah... please let's talk. Let me explain what happen–"

"No!" she yelled. "I don't want to hear it! Stay away..." Her voice broke as she pushed him away and fought back the growing lump in her throat, "Kind of feels like history repeating itself, doesn't it." Turning back to the door, she yanked hard and Judas heard a painful whisper fall from her mouth, "You really are a traitor."

And with her words, jagged and sharp like a weapon, his whole world crumbled.

Chapter Twenty-Seven

The silver Audi darted between cars, switching lanes with no regard for traffic lights or turn signals. Judas' knuckles were white and his fingers numb as his grip on the steering wheel tightened like a vice. He wanted to drive into the next brick wall he passed but knew it wouldn't give him the relief he wanted. The sweet release of non-existence was always on his mind, but now that the woman who held his very soul had pushed him away, the obsessive thoughts of death filled him.

Foregoing the elevator again, Judas charged up the stairwell, his booted steps echoing off the concrete walls. Sadness and fury congealed into a stone mountain of emotion that rested on his thick chest. He wasn't sure if he should curse the heavens or cry to them. As he entered his apartment and slammed the door, he did both.

"Damn you, Yesh!! You left me here! Why!? I did what you asked and for that history says I'm a monster!"

Judas paced the space between his living room and kitchen, the pounding behind his eyes beating fast as the pressure in his head rose. Every muscle in his body tightened and a primal scream escaped as he swept his hands across the bar sending various papers and a couple of wine glasses flying. "I wish you were here right now! I'd tell you to fuck off with your *gift!*" he picked a wine glass off the floor, smashing it against the wall. "Fuck you, Yesh!"

He panted desperately as hot tears fell from his eyes and the sobs echoed on pale walls, "I want to go home! I'm so... *tired.* I just want to go now! Take me home, you miserable asshole!"

Fire of anguish burned in every cell of his body. For centuries, Judas walked this world mostly alone. It didn't take him long to realize that he could never explain his affliction or situation to anyone he got close to, but with Eliza, things had seemed different. For a fleeting moment, he realized what was missing from his life for so long. It was her. But even now as her words played like a tortured echo in his mind, his soul still felt connected to hers and it made the pain unbearable.

Picking up the glass coffee table, Judas flipped it into a far wall; its thick corner slicing into the drywall with a crunch. The throbbing in his temples quickened as he grabbed the crystal decanter filled with scotch. As he pulled it back to launch it at the same wall, he immediately decided against it. Instead, he knocked off the heavy lid, tipping the opening to his mouth. With four heavy gulps, the expensive amber liquid was gone.

Dropping the carafe to the floor, he furiously rummaged through the glass enclosed cabinet containing bottles of all shapes, sizes, and a variety of colored liquids. Pulling out a skinny bottle containing vodka with a label written in Finnish, Judas pulled out the stopper, guzzling a long pull.

"You know, Yesh... *my best friend...* I know you're listening. You've always just sat and listened. But I'm tired of talking and asking! Just let me come home!" He took another swallow and collapsed against the wall. "It's the least you can do. Especially now. I let this woman... this amazing, glorious woman of the cosmos into my heart..."

He pounded his chest like an ape and the sound was thick, "My heart, Yesh. Not unlike I let you in you. My *brother.* Remember, Yesh? Brothers."

His head slammed against the wall as tears poured from his eyes in frustration.

"She's a lot like you. She's kind... warm... forgiving... patient. I think you'd like her. She's got these eyes... they're like diamonds on the Galilee on a sunny day." A sardonic laugh erupted and the scorching sorrow flowed from his eyes, "Why? Why, Yesh? Why would you do this to me? I did everything you asked..."

He took another drink from the bottle and a thought emerged in his mind. It grew quickly like billowing storm clouds until it was a tornado in his thoughts. He wondered if it would work. He felt a little pang of guilt just having the thought, but, what else could he do? It was the only thing his desperate mind could conjure. But, it was a dark thought. A dangerous thought. Something he always hid like a well kept secret that he feared if spoken aloud would come true.

He had the number. He'd actually been in possession of it for years. Why, he couldn't say. He often thought that maybe they could get a drink together, talk about life and home. It was a romanticized thought because Judas knew it would be a terrible, very, *very* bad idea to sit across from *him*.

Smiling to himself, he worked up the courage to vocalize it.

Taking a final gulp of the vodka, he threw the bottle aside, "I don't want this life anymore! Not without her!" He paused, taking a deep breath, "Alright... fine. You aren't going to let me die? I know someone who might... should we ask the Morningstar? Do you think he'll take my call?"

Judas looked to the room in silence. The thought of making that call played in his mind for centuries and he thought for sure it would evoke some response from his long deceased friend and teacher. Tears flooded his face and he leaned hard into the wall behind him. He remembered the sound of Yesh's voice as he spoke to a small group of them about his angelic half-brother.

"Helel is misunderstood, but my father was right to banish him. Now he seeks to destroy everything our father built..."

"Why, brother? If Helel is truly sorry for his disobedience, why won't your father take him back?" Judas asked and James nodded his agreement.

Yesh smiled a distant grin; one that spoke of longing and pain, "Helel was not given the same choices as we are."

"Oh Yesh... I wish you would have given me a choice. I did what you asked. I always did," his voice was hoarse. Reaching for another bottle, he pulled a random choice from the cabinet, but this time, he couldn't focus on the label. It didn't matter, he pulled the stopper anyway and filled his mouth with the contents. There was no burn this time, but the licorice vapor filled his sinuses.

"The green fairy," he mused, dropping the bottle to his side. "C'mon Yesh, let's say we call your brother. I know he's around... I need..." Judas' voice cracked with emotion. "I need something to take this pain away, brother. I won't be able to go on without... her," he swigged another mouthful and his eyelids drooped heavily. "I'm not... strong enough."

Judas' last conscious thought is the warmth of a calloused hand covering his eyes and a distantly familiar voice commanding him to sleep.

Chapter Twenty-Eight

S he stood just inside the door staring at him.

The stillness of the room compounded her frustration while she quietly seethed. Monitors were beeping. The hum of the central air system was a low counterpoint. The placidity of a room with no movement. Eliza wondered what to do next. Her exhaustion didn't allow her to be furious at Judas' ridiculous accusations for long because she wanted to know if any morsel of it were true. She opened her fist to find the tiny note still gripped tightly. She recognized the handwriting as her father's.

A tiny nurse breezed in silently as Eliza stared at her father. She watched the young woman check the intravenous lines, inspect all the air tubing for any kinks, and straighten his sheets. Eliza admired those who cared for others like this nurse. She couldn't imagine the things this woman had seen and didn't want to, but Eliza appreciated her for who she was. A realization washed over her in that stark, quiet moment: she and this stranger were very much the same.

Eliza herself, as a young teen, fluffed the sheets on many occasions while her father lay passed out on his bed after enjoying one too many drinks after golf. She often made sure his airway was clear and that he wouldn't choke himself in the night. It was a scenario that often played in her head, especially after her first CPR training class. She had just been hired for the summer as a lifeguard at the country club. The photos in the book were nothing compared to the nightmares she imagined in her own mind. She didn't want to find her father like that. Ever.

The next morning she cooked him breakfast and filled his favorite cup with hot coffee so he could fend off the hangover. Even after she moved away to college, Eliza called to check in on him no less than three times a week. She remembered praying every night that her father didn't miss her and wasn't as lonely as she imagined. And even now, she was holding his hand through every step of his campaign. Even though most days he didn't deserve it and, secretly, she hoped he didn't win. Mostly because he didn't deserve that either.

But as much as she was his caretaker, she was realizing she really didn't *know* her father. She never questioned his lack of sobriety even though his drinking laughed in the face of his good, man-of-God-son-of-Texas facade. Not one time did she ask on those calls home, who the female voice was in the background. And she would never, ever dare inquire about his business or clients. Her eyes turned hard as she stared more closely at Paul.

She heard Judas' voice in her ear *"Ahavah... listen to me. Something doesn't fit..."*

The lonesome hole in her heart grew bigger but she forced herself to turn off those feelings for the moment. He was accusing Chet, *Uncle Chet*, of something so horrible, something so distasteful and unbelievably vile as murder; or rather, attempted murder. Eliza, more than anyone, knew the dangers of accusing someone with the presumption of guilt. For the last five years of her career, she had been trying to bring justice to the wrongfully convicted. She witnessed firsthand the gates of socioeconomic and racial inequity closing on those most disadvantaged. Judas, of all people, should know what that's like.

The words she said to him. *Traitor.* There was nothing more hurtful that she could possibly say to him... but...

How dare he.

How dare... he.

He. He, who?

The confusion set in. Her extremities tingled with exhaustion and she knew she would need to get some rest at some point today or her body would give out. The tiny cat naps she was able to sneak in were wearing off fast.

He, who?

Dark thoughts were oozing their way through her mind as she contemplated the question. Inky, oily sediments drifted to the surface and spread like wet, dirty silk. She couldn't fight the images of her father and his repugnant behavior. Closing her eyes, she dropped her father's hand. In her mind, she watched Paul grope Georgia in a room full of people. She heard his words echo in her head and a mist of conspiracy lurked over all of it.

Had Uncle Chet grown tired of his behavior? If that were so, there must have been an argument. There was no way that he wouldn't have tried to talk sense to her father. Uncle Chet was the calmest, kindest person she knew. Nothing ruffled his feathers, not even in a courtroom. He was the polar opposite of her father. If he had done this, there was no doubt it was hard earned by her father.

"Ahavah... listen to me. Something doesn't fit..." Judas' words echoed in her ears again.

Eliza's lids slowly opened as she rose from her seat next to her father's bed. She knew what she had to do. Throwing her small purse over her shoulder, she marched out of the room and didn't look back.

Chapter Twenty-Nine

Eliza's stop at her apartment was a short one. It took her a mere thirty minutes to shower, refresh, and dress in some clean clothes. And for the first time in a long time, she really didn't care about what she was wearing or where she was wearing it. Her black slim-cut jeans, boots, and T-shirt would be just fine. After spinning her blonde locks into a bun on the top of her head, she was out of the door and back in her car.

For the full twenty-five-minute drive to her father's office, she contemplated what she would say to everyone once inside. Eliza didn't think she could do all the small talk, but she knew everyone would want the details on Paul's condition and how she was doing with all of it. She knew in her bones what she wanted to say or rather what she didn't. She didn't want to speak with anyone. Eliza was on a mission to find out why her father was shot and who did it. The repetitive, inane questions about anything else were useless to her. Familiar streets and buildings passed by in a swirl as she considered that she could not truly disregard anyone's concern. She would placate everyone with phrases like "He's doing well" and "Oh, I'm hanging in there" when in reality she was still deciding whether she would scream or cry at any moment. With any luck, she'd arrive after everyone had left for the day.

It was nearing five o'clock when she stepped off the elevator and into the familiar surroundings of Arthur and Branson. She made a quick note that Lydia wasn't at her desk, a blessing, but it meant the older woman was probably doing her nightly walk-through before she locked up for the night. Eliza slipped down the hall and into her uncle's office without a sound, slumping against the large oak door. She stood in agonizing silence for what seemed like ten minutes before she heard Lydia's sweet hum stride past the office where Eliza was concealed and back to the front. She opened the large door just a crack to peek out into the dimly lit hallway and heard the secretary's key turn the outside lock. Eliza waited another few minutes before deciding she was indeed all alone and crossing the hallway to her father's office.

Sorrow and dread hit her in the chest as the enormous door swung to reveal her dad's sanctuary. Cards and notes covered the tops of his tables and desk. Eliza peeked at a few of the names, noticing they were from employees or clients. The get-well wishes burned Eliza's heart. Judas was wrong about Uncle Chet and he's wrong about her father. Sure, Paul Lindsey Arthur was as difficult as a colic, sleep-deprived baby, but he didn't do anything to deserve this. No one deserved to be shot in their own home.

Eliza jostled the mouse next to Paul's laptop and the screen sprang to life. Her fingers hovered over the keyboard because she didn't know where to start as she stared at his desktop files. She rolled her eyes in consternation at the sheer volume and general chaos of Paul's filing system. After scanning the fifty or so small icons, she located his banking records and opened them. She spent the better part of two hours skimming each line item going back three years. It was only when she saw an electronic transfer of funds that she stopped searching.

"Transfer to nine-seven-two-nine," she muses. "What is nine-seven-en-two-nine?"

Eliza shook her head and closed the file not knowing if it was significant or not. She moved on with her task of picking apart her father's life, electronically, until her neck was stiff and her eyes burned. When she finally scrolled to the bottom of the extensive list, she opened a file labeled *Privileged*. She double-clicked the file and to her surprise, a password lock popped on the screen.

"Seriously, Dad? Anyone can open this computer up and get any information you have and this file is protected?" she scoffed to the empty room. "Whatever."

Eliza poked the keys, plugging in Paul's password.

Access denied.

She frowned, trying again; it's possible with everything that's happened in the last few days she'd forgotten her own birthdate.

Access denied; one try remaining.

"What the hell?" Eliza huffed out a breath and stared at the flashing box on the screen. Her dad had used the same basic password for as long as she could remember, why was this one different? She sat back in the large leather chair. All evening she'd clicked through, scrubbing every single file Paul had and it made her wonder what was so damn important that this one had to be locked. Her fingers hovered over the keys again when something in her brain clicked. She typed in four numbers. Nine-seven-two-nine.

Access granted.

What Eliza opened was difficult to make out even though she recognized it as a banking spreadsheet. At first glance, it looked like a private account that her father seemed to have made sporadic payments into every several months. Nothing too large, usually a couple of hundred dollars each time, with larger deposits of one thousand dollars a couple times a year. It also looked like an interest bearing account and Eliza is mildly impressed with the rate it had . She scrolled through each sheet but didn't find any abnormalities.

Still confused as to why the account was locked, it was when she clicked on page number ten, that she found a note that drew her attention.

"Withdraw for four-thousand, five-hundred dollars paid to Dra," the crease between her brow deepened. "Who is Dra?"

The deeper into the file Eliza searched the more confused she became. Various deposits spanning two decades and the only money being removed went to the same person. She was wracking her memory to pull that name from her head but kept coming up empty. Eliza looked at her watch; eleven-thirty. Deciding that the computer and the puzzle within it were currently a dead end, she shut the machine and headed for the door. She pulled out her keys to lock the office behind her when she heard the shuffling of feet that made her freeze.

The office hallway was mostly dark with dappled light coming from well placed lamps on the side tables. She listened closely for the sound again, but the blood rushing in her ears was louder. It drowned everything out and for a moment she convinced herself it was just her imagination. Eliza pulled in a slow breath that caught when she heard the rustling of papers and a drawer being shut across the hallway.

She was definitely not alone.

Chapter Thirty

I t didn't take Eliza but a few seconds to regret not telling anyone she was in the building. She stood frozen in place, her ears straining to hear the slightest sound in the office across the hallway from her. Drawing a deep breath, she gathered what composure she could muster, shoving the near complete exhaustion from her bones. Eliza scanned her father's office for anything to defend herself. If this was an intruder, or worse, the person who shot her father, she would put up a fight. Before she could talk herself out of whatever nonsense she was about to be a part of, she snatched a letter opener from a side table before cracking the door. The table lamps along the corridor cast small shadows along the walls and while most of the time she would have never noticed, they now felt creepy and intimidating.

Her footsteps, muffled by the dense carpeting, crept quietly to the oak door. Leaning her ear against the cool wood, Eliza's fingers gripped the small blade tightly. With a final push of courage, she flung the door wide.

Eliza stood shocked, "Uncle Chet! What are you doing here so late?"

"Oh, I... um... I was looking for a file I forgot to grab earlier," he stammered before noticing the letter opener clutched in her hand. "I'm sorry if I scared you. I didn't realize you were working tonight." He motioned to her hand.

She let out an exasperated chortle, "I'm not... I mean, I am. It's complicated."

Chet nodded before resuming his search through a desk drawer. Eliza watched as he plucked a single manila folder from the very back and flipped through the first few pages. Satisfied that he got what he came for, Chet stepped toward his niece.

"I'm sorry I can't stay and chat, sweetheart. I really have some things I need to take care of before morning," Chet slid past her.

Eliza's next words came from her before she thought them in her head, "Aren't you going to ask me about Dad?"

She watched the man freeze in place, but when he turned back to her his expression confused her. Fury raged behind his dark blue eyes and his grasp on the folder tightened. In the dimness of the light, Eliza watched all of his muscles tighten like a coiled snake ready to strike. For as long as she could remember, she couldn't think of a time when her uncle was ever outwardly angry.

"Eliza," Chet said, his voice taught, "I am sorry about Paul."

A deep crease formed in her brow, "I know, Uncle Chet. You just haven't been by to see him... or me."

"I can't, Eliza."

Chet had to be hurting as well, she thought. Maybe seeing her father in that room with all those tubes and monitors was just too much for him. She could understand that, but after her blow up with Judas, she really could use the support. She felt the hot tears creep back into her eyes and she fought them back with everything she had, but a few escaped anyway.

Brushing them away quickly, Eliza nodded, "I understand."

Chet hesitated a moment but finally came closer, wrapping a strong arm around her, "I am sorry, sweetheart. Really. You know I love you like my own. I really do."

He turned away from her as the elevator chimed. Chet entered and turned to face her once more. The light of the elevator was much brighter than the rest of the room and it was in this light that Eliza could read the tab of the file. Written in black ink and in her uncle's handwriting, she could see the last three digits of a four digit number. Her heart raced and before she could utter a word for him to stop, the door slid shut and her uncle was gone.

Eliza thought about going after him, but by the time the elevator emptied on the first floor and came back to her Chet would be long gone anyway. She felt a little defeated and even more curious. What was it in that file that was so important that it couldn't wait until morning? And why did he wait until he thought everyone had gone for the night before coming to get it? She knew he had not been into the office since her father was shot, Judas had said as much.

Judas.

She shook the thought of him from her mind. She didn't have time to think about their last talk. She was so angry with him for accusing one of the only people she considered family of shooting her father. He didn't know Chet. He didn't know what a kind, loving, wonderful, man he was. Chet would do anything for his family.

Judas didn't know anything about her uncle. But like a slow moving fog, the picture of Chet with the thick folder clutched in his arms drifted slowly back into her mind. Another pervasive thought formed... Judas didn't know Chet, but maybe neither did she.

Chapter Thirty-One

The bits of dawn peeked through the uncovered window of the apartment as Judas' eyes, crusted from dried tears, broke open. He shifted his gaze from one side to the other in an attempt to take account of his surroundings. Moving his arms, his hand stopped short of a skinny bottle at his side, still half full of green liquid.

"It's not going to work, brother," he said to the room, "Too little, too late, I say."

He grasped the bottle, putting it to his lips.

"Go back to hell, Yesh," he whispered before finishing off the bottle. "I'm done. Do you hear me? I'm calling him today... one way or another, I'm done."

The words came out painful and slurred. Judas didn't know what time it was nor did he care. His only plan was to either drink himself to death, if he could, or until he worked up enough courage to make the call; whichever came first. Tossing the thin bottle aside, Judas stumbled to the kitchen and pulled out two more. Bourbon, a classic.

He staggered with his prizes back to the living room, looking around at the chaos of overturned furniture, broken pictures, and empty bottles. He wanted desperately to care about the state of his surroundings, but he just couldn't. He was numb and he was glad for it. Twisting the lid off the first, he threw the stopper against the wall and filled his mouth.

Falling into the sofa, Judas took another long pull from the bottle, "I heard you last night, Yesh. I heard you whispering in my ear. I wake up and am I home? No!"

He shakes his head madly.

"No, I'm not! I'm here... in this place. Without Eliza. I gave you everything, brother. Everything! More than two thousand years you took from me... what was your plan? For me to watch humanity forever?" Another large swallow of the liquid was gone. "Then what? This feels more like a punishment than a gift." No doubt about it.

Judas had no fear of ending up in hell one day. This was darker and more tortuous than any fiery pit he could ever be thrown into. This was true hell.

Chapter Thirty-Two

Eliza sat up straight with a start. Pools of drool covered her arm which was, at this moment, very, very asleep. Straightening from her slumped position, she shielded her eyes from the bright glare of the search page on her home computer. Her back ached and her neck was stiff from lying on the desk for so long. Squinting at the clock, she realized she'd only been asleep for a few hours, at best.

She wiped her mouth with the back of her hand as she leaned back in her office chair to get her bearings. After leaving the office, she'd spent the better part of the night searching different combinations of the four digits and the entry in the bank log, Dra. After finding absolutely nothing, the researcher in her had dug through every article she could find about her father and his law firm. She didn't find anything she didn't already know, her snooping was fruitless and she was more exhausted than before.

But like an annoying little gnat, a few intrusive thoughts were still buzzing in the back of her brain. They poked and prodded and tickled until she couldn't ignore them anymore. The folder Uncle Chet was holding. Why did he have it and why was it labeled with the numbers nine-seven-two-nine? What about a bank account was so secret, that it was protected with a password on her dad's computer? Although, she had to admit, it was a terrible password. And why didn't *she* know about it? Eliza had to get answers, but first, she had to check on Paul.

The phone to the nurse's station rang twice before a woman with a thick southern drawl picked up. Eliza could tell immediately that the person on the other end wasn't a native of Texas but probably more Deep South like Mississippi or Alabama. After an introduction, the woman's accent became thicker, more than Eliza thought possible.

"Oh, good morning, darlin'," the voice, as sweet as southern tea, cooed. "I'm April, his nurse for the day."

"How's my dad?" Eliza asked.

"I'm pleased to report that he had a restful night. Doc's already done his rounds... your daddy's going to have another CT today. If all goes well, Doc's gonna pull him off the meds and get him to wake up," April smiled through the phone.

Waves of relief washed over her but there was something else behind the emotion. It was something she didn't expect and it even took her by surprise. She felt... afraid. But of what? There was a good chance that by the end of the day, her father would be awake and he could tell them who shot him. She should be ecstatic, but she wasn't. She felt like she was running out of time.

Shoving every concern to the back of her mind, she drew a deep breath, "Thank you, April. That's wonderful news...I'll be by later today."

Eliza hung up the phone and decided to waste no more time getting the answers she needed.

***

The thirty-minute drive to Southlake felt like it took hours and until she turned onto Continental Boulevard, Eliza thought she'd never get to her destination. In the last ten minutes, the morning sun faded behind billowing clouds and the Texas sky turned a dull shade of grey. A thunderstorm gathered in the distance and she couldn't help but see the parallels between her thoughts and the impending squall.

Eliza slowed at the tall iron bars of the gated neighborhood. Adam's Lane was a sprawling development of brick mansions, green lawns, and good schools. After punching in her own code, the one given to her the moment she could drive, she curved around the quiet streets until she found her destination. Eliza stared for a moment at the five bedroom home with its black shutters a stark contrast against the pale sand colored brick.

There was a time when, inside its walls, Eliza found pockets of solace. Barbeques on the back patio while she and the other kids swam in the cool water of the pool until late into the night. The smell of homemade tomato sauce bubbling on the stove in the kitchen while she played game after game of Mario Brothers in the downstairs den. The comfort of nights tucked into the four-poster bed at the end of the hall on the second floor. So many memories. So much time passed.

Hesitating before she rang the doorbell, Eliza braced herself. She didn't want to accuse anyone of anything, but she needed Chet to show her what was in that file. Time was short and something inside her told her she needed her answers before her dad woke.

She pushed the bell.

Within a few seconds, a thin woman with healthily tanned skin and brunette hair opened the door. Eliza noticed her beautiful face becoming taut at the sight of Eliza's presence.

"Aunt Reba, are you okay?" her brow furrowed with worry.

Reba swallowed hard, "Sure honey, I'm okay. What can I help you with, sweetheart?"

Eliza took immediate notice that her aunt never moved to invite her inside. As a matter of fact, she seemed to position herself in a way that would demand a steamroller to move her.

"I wanted to talk to Uncle Chet—"

"Chet isn't home," his wife cut her off tersely, pursing her lips tighter.

Eliza nodded, "Oh, okay... I think he has a file I need for work. Would you mind if I looked in the office for it?"

"Not right now, honey. I think maybe you should go back to the hospital and sit with your daddy," Reba looked as though she was choking back vomit.

"Aunt Reba, what's going on?" she furrowed her brow.

Tears welled in the tired woman's eyes but, before she could shut the door, Eliza heard another familiar voice in the distance, "Who's at the door, Mom?"

She was relieved for a moment when Dave Branson's tall frame came into view behind his mother and Eliza couldn't help but to smile. The sensation was short lived when her adoptive brother began yelling.

"What the hell are you doing here!?" he barked.

"Davy, no. Stop!" Reba turned, putting her hands on her eldest son's chest. "She doesn't have anything to do with this."

Eliza stared through the decorative screen door at the pair in shock and it didn't go unnoticed by Dave. His face softened a bit but his eyes glared. She heard Reba whisper something to her son before he took several steps backward.

"Aunt Reba, what's going on? Where's Uncle Chet?" she pleaded.

The woman grasped the door with a shaking hand, "You sit with your daddy."

"Aunt Reba," Eliza began, but before she could utter what she wanted to say, something else came out of her mouth, much like with her uncle the night before. "Nine-seven-two-nine."

The woman froze midway through her action and was the deer in the headlights.

"You know," Eliza whispered. "What is it, Aunt Reba? What's in that file?"

The last thing she saw before her aunt shut the door were the tears pouring from her eyes.

Eliza walked back to her car more confused than ever. She had no idea why Reba wouldn't let her in the house or why Davy was so quick to attack. What was she missing? And where was Chet?

She pulled away from the home, glancing in the rearview mirror at its beauty. She wondered for a moment if she would ever feel its warmth again. But, the idea was fleeting as a constant reel of questions overtook any other ideas she might have. She drove aimlessly out of Southlake and back into Dallas the whole time trying to piece together the puzzle in front of her.

When she finally regained her focus, Eliza noticed signs for Katy Trail. A pang of guilt and pain hit her heart as she drove closer to Judas' apartment. After everything she'd learned, or hadn't learned in the last couple of days, it all gave her pause about her uncle's involvement. She couldn't believe he actually pulled the trigger, but he at least knew something about her father's shooting. Of that, she was more convinced than ever.

And then, of something else.

Regret poured over her in sheets like heavy rain. What had she done? She was so tired and so heartbroken. She hadn't been thinking clearly. She had just reacted without a thought. She had let the words tumble out of her so casually. She had been so cold and cruel. The most hurtful thing she could have hurled at him and all he was trying to do was help. She had taken out all her hurt and all her fear on the only one that was there for her. She had crushed him with her words without a single thought of hesitation and she had done it on purpose.

Judas had simply tried to warn her. She'd called him a traitor.

He had trusted her with his deepest secret and she had used it against him.

My god.

What had she done?

She owed him an apology. She just hoped it would be enough.

Chapter Thirty-Three

Eliza stood outside the door to Judas' apartment. She stared at it, almost too afraid to knock. Would he slam the door in her face? Would he even open it for her at all? She was certain he must hate her.

The last words she'd spoken to him had been the most hurtful words she could've ever imagined saying. She'd stabbed him with them like a weapon meant to slice him as deeply as possible. Eliza had watched him slice his own flesh before her eyes only to see the wound heal itself within seconds. She had a heavy, dark feeling that the wounds left behind by her words would be less easily mended.

She'd made assumptions in her grief and she'd been so terribly wrong. Her heart ached to think of what she did to him in that moment, but she had to try to salvage what she could of their relationship, if that was even possible. At a minimum, he needed to know that she knew she was wrong. She had to tell him that she knew he was the innocent one in all of this mess. He was innocent all the way back then in his first life and he was now.

Right now, in this life that he should be sharing with her.

That was it. That's the thought that spurred her on. He should be in her life. Eliza loved Judas on a level she never knew was even possible and she wanted him in her life every single day. She had to fix this. He had to love her back. She prayed she wasn't too late, that she hadn't screwed this up too profoundly to take it all back. He had to know how deeply sorry she was.

With that thought, Eliza raised her fist and knocked on his door. For several minutes there is nothing but silence. She was about to knock again when she heard stirring inside. A few thuds and curses later, Eliza was greeted by a very haggard looking Judas. He was sporting an untrimmed beard and deep, dark circles under his eyes. Seeing him look so broken tore her heart into pieces.

"Oh, Judas," she murmured as she reached out with a gentle hand and caressed his cheek.

His eyes light up with recognition of who stood before him. He spoke in a hushed tone dripping in awe, "Ahavah."

Without hesitation, they reached for each other and embraced. Having her in his arms again was the single greatest moment thus far in his wretched, cursed life. He breathed her in and begged her not to disappear from his grasp. He was certain she was a dream.

Is this it? Did Yesh finally take him? Is this heaven?

He held her face in his hands and looked down on her angelic features with tears brimming his bloodshot eyes, "Are you real?"

Eliza laughed at his awestruck gaze, "Yes, I'm real. And I'm sorry, Judas. I'm so, very sorry. I never should have said those terrible things to you. I was hurting, but that's no excuse. You deserve so much better than that and I'll do anything I can for the rest of my life to make it up to you. Can you ever forgive me?"

No words would convey how deeply he craved her forgiveness for the tortured soul he was. How badly he needed her to see past all his faults and love him anyway. He pressed his mouth into hers and relished in the sweet taste of her lips on his. He had missed her taste, the soft glide of her lips against his own, and the feeling of her body against his.

Eliza, while equally drawn into their embrace, registered a less sweet flavor to her lover's kiss. She leaned away from his lips, gazing into his red eyes. She glanced around the room before her and saw it for the first time since arriving. It stood in absolute ruin with shattered glass and empty bottles of liquor all around them.

Meeting his eyes again, Eliza asked, "Are you drunk?"

Falling to his knees before her, Judas clung to her and howled in slurred speech, "Oh, Ahavah. Please forgive me. Please, love. I'm not worthy of you. I beg you, let me love you though I don't deserve you."

She stared down at this seemingly broken man before her, "You don't owe me apologies for anything. You've been nothing but wonderful to me since the moment we met."

Judas let out an anguished cry, "No, my Eliza, Ahavah. My love. No. I'm a terrible, horrid man who doesn't deserve the brightness of your love. Please, my Eliza, please say you can love me!"

Part of Eliza wanted to laugh at his hiccupping pleas because they were so completely absurd, but she knew he wasn't in the right mindset for that. Instead, she knelt down to his level, both of them still in the doorway, and took his face in her hands.

"You have spent more years than I can even fathom trying to prove yourself when you never did anything wrong to begin with. You aren't just a good person. You are the most kind, caring, genuine person I have ever encountered in my life. You are worthy of all the love in the world." She smiled at his droopy, bloodshot eyes somehow still full of his greatness shining through all the alcohol, "I can't offer you the love of the entire world, but I can offer you mine. It's yours, Judas. You can stop fighting now. I'll stand beside you always."

Judas stared back at her, hearing her words and knowing their gravity even with the entirety of his liquor cabinet coursing through his veins. He sniffled as a sob bubbled up his throat and in his drunken stupor responded, "You are everything I have waited all this time for."

These words would normally have sent Eliza swooning if, immediately after speaking them, Judas hadn't collapsed all of his weight into her arms. His head cradled in the crook of her neck, Judas sobbed drunken tears of relief and gratitude as she struggled to support his barely functioning body.

Patting him on the back, she attempted to help him stand, "It's okay, love. Let it all out. I know you've been strong for so long, but if we could just get you up and on the couch I think that would be great." Eliza groaned as she helped him heave his body up into a standing position. She let him brace himself on her shoulders as she helped guide his stumbling feet to the couch.

Finally, they made it to their destination and plopped down together. Eliza out of breath from the effort and Judas smiling at her with tear stained cheeks. He reached one finger out and poked Eliza right on the nose.

"You," he slurred, "are just so pretty."

She couldn't help but laugh, "Okay, Casanova... how about we get some coffee in you?"

"Just so pretty, pretty, pretty," he drunkenly sang as the top half of his body slumped toward her.

Kissing his forehead, Eliza leaned him back toward the pillows on the couch to rest while she walked into the kitchen to prepare some very strong coffee. She pulled down the French press. Placing it on the counter, she grabbed the electric coffee grinder and her favorite of his selection of coffee beans. While she set to work preparing his roast, she took further inventory of the state of his home.

Judas was so orderly and neat. Seeing his shattered belongings, sink full of empty bottles, and dirty laundry strewn across the already littered floor was jarring. He truly lost all sense of himself when he thought he had lost her. Her heart ached for him when she considered what she'd put him through over these last days.

But then...

It also filled her with warmth through her entire being.

She was loved. Truly and deeply.

Eliza spent her entire life being ruled by the one person in the world who should've loved her beyond measure, yet her father was too selfish to have ever spent a single second truly loving her. A part of her had always known this. However, this was why she worked so hard to continue supporting him when she knew he was wrong, even disturbed. She'd made excuses for him and justified his atrocious behavior. Even now, as he lay unconscious in a hospital bed, she'd held his hand even though she knew that he likely wouldn't do the same for her. All because, deep inside, she was still his little girl begging him to love her. Needing his love to prove her worth.

Judas showed her, however, she wasn't that little girl anymore. She was a woman who had value in her own self.

Paul spent her entire life trying to mold her into something that he might find suitable. He wanted to make her into something she never had any desire to be. He judged her every decision and made her feel unworthy. Always lacking and unsure.

With Judas, she was free of the constraints she had been tethered by her whole life. She could be unapologetically herself and that was enough. Even when she was wrong or careless or plain hurtful, he could see her for who she really was and he loved her. Warts and all.

Judas loved her mind and her thoughts. He loved her imperfections and her quirks. This man loved her more than he loved himself. She didn't need validation from anyone else, anymore, because Judas had shown her she was capable of being whole on her own and he loved her for it.

He loved her so much that losing her made him want to burn his own world to the ground.

He loved her so much that she was finally able to love herself, just as she was.

Drunk or not, she wanted to tell him how much he had brought to her life. She needed him to understand how truly revolutionary he had been in her world. Carrying his now ready coffee to him waiting on the couch, she practiced how she was going to express all of this to him. When she rounded the corner of the couch she stared down at the beautiful man that loved her and found him slumped over on his side, mouth hanging wide open with a little bit of drool pooling on the cushion beneath his head as a soft snore rumbled from his chest.

For a long moment, she just stood over him watching him sleep, then sighed, "Get some sleep you crazy fool." She draped the blanket from the back of the couch over his comatose body and leaned down to gently kiss his temple, "I love you more than words can say." She sipped the coffee that was meant for him and wandered back to the kitchen while her soulmate snored behind her.

Chapter Thirty-Four

J udas suddenly opened his eyes wide and sat up on the couch.

Eliza.

He was certain she had been here. Had he dreamed of her? Judas rolled to his side and smelled the pillow his head had been resting on, the sweet jasmine of her perfume still lingered on the fabric. Then he was hit with both the smell of coffee and bleach.

It was real. She was here. She'd come back.

The joy in his soul propelled him from the couch and he turned to face the kitchen. He appraised the space around him and saw that it sparkled and gleamed as if the last few days had never happened. All the remains of his mental breakdown had been erased and the smell of coffee lingered as he entered the kitchen space. He tried to mentally count the messes she must've cleaned up for him and his stomach plummeted. He was terribly mortified that she had to see him in that state. That she'd had to clean up his messes that were of his own making. His head fell into his hands as he let the humiliation wash over him. He did not deserve her. Never had and never would.

But she came back anyway. He knew it. The rest of his memories may be fuzzy around the edges but he knew he saw her face and she was the only person that would willingly put in all that work to put his home back together.

He rushed to the bedroom, peering inside. Sleeping beneath his sheets was the only woman who had ever made his continued existence a gift. His heart swelled with gratitude to see her in his space again.

He didn't want to wake her but he had to be near her. He was certain he would crumble to pieces if he wasn't. He slowly approached the bed and gently sat by her side.

As carefully as he could, Judas grazed his fingers across her cheek and whispered, "You, my Eliza, are the greatest gift I have ever been given. You alone have made all the years of solitude worth it. I promise you, I will never stop proving my worth to you."

She smiled as her eyelids fluttered open. Turning to face him, she took his hand from her face to hold it in her own.

Complete and total devotion shone from his eyes as he looked down at her, "I didn't mean to wake you, my love."

"I'm glad you did," she said, her voice husky from sleep. "Are you feeling better this morning?"

He broke their eye contact glancing toward the floor, "I am feeling grateful to have you here, but I'm also feeling very embarrassed. I'm sorry you had to see me like that. I'm sorry you had to clean up my mess."

Sitting up, she took his face in her hands, forcing him to look at her, "It's okay to not be perfect all the time. You might be some kind of biblical immortal that I'm sure has a grand purpose in this world, but you're also still a human. You're allowed to act like one."

"I've been in a dark place without you," he whispered.

It was something in his voice that made her pause. Maybe it was the in way he said the work dark or she could've been reading into it, but for a split second, her blood ran cold. "Judas, what do you mean?"

Shaking off her concern, he forced a smile, "Nothing...my choices were pretty bad the last few days, but they could have been worse."

"I'm sorry I wasn't here. And for everything...I haven't exactly been myself either. I know you were just looking out for me," she replied.

Her words warmed him from the inside out. He leaned forward and laid his lips against hers. Pressing his forehead against hers, he whispered, "Thank you for loving me."

"Right back at ya, baby," she replied with a sleepy smile as she leaned into a long, deep kiss. She gazed into his face, "Question... um... I saw all the bottles and I need to know... Were those all full?"

His cheeks flushed and he nodded in acknowledgment.

Her eyes grew into huge saucers, "Holy shit, Judas. That's massively impressive and completely terrifying all at once. Just exactly how much alcohol does it take to make an immortal drunk?"

Her words were light hearted and teasing. It made him chuckle and he knew that they were going to be okay.

"Copious amounts," he answered.

She giggled in response and felt her heart swell to know that she was still welcome in his life. Her time here in his apartment had allowed her to finally sleep for a solid chunk of time. She had been able to clear her head and rest her heart. His presence was sanctuary.

Judas reached his hands into her hair and pulled her as close against him as he possibly could. She felt the flames of her desire for his body blooming in her and groaned against his lips. The sound of her need nearly drove him mad. He began to move toward her body, but she pushed him until his back fell onto the bed.

Climbing over his body, Eliza straddled his lap. Grinding her hips into him, she felt his hard length rubbing against her and it made her feral. She grabbed the waistband of his sweatpants, working them down his hips. She wanted to leave no doubt in his mind that she loved him and wanted to do nothing but give him everything he wanted for the rest of her life.

Freeing his erection, she smiled greedily before kneeling between his knees at the edge of the bed. She watched his face as she lowered her mouth to him, wrapping her lips around his length. She thrills to see the absolute bliss spread across his features. Slowly, she worked her way down his shaft, teasing him with her tongue the entire way.

He hissed out his appreciation, "Oh fuck, Eliza."

Smiling around his girth, she continues to work her magic. She lets him slide all the way to the back of her throat again and again. She is thrilled to hear his moans of pleasure. Faster and faster she plunges him down her throat until she can feel his muscles tighten in anticipation of release.

Before she could finish him, he sat up from the bed, pulling himself from her mouth, grabbing her arms. Pulling her to meet his mouth, their lips locked. He kissed her like he was trying to devour her and with the way she made him feel, he very well may have been. Tearing her clothes from her body, he laid her across the bed and stared down at her. Every inch of her exposed skin was like seeing the holy grail before him. Everything he could ever want or need displayed in front of his eyes.

Slowly, he trailed his fingers down her flesh leaving behind scorching paths of need across her skin. She trembled beneath him purring her desire. Leaning toward her, he watched her beautiful face as his fingers found the slick, wet evidence of her arousal. He slid his fingers inside her and nearly came undone as she gasped his name.

"Judas..." she panted, "Please. Please."

Her desperation sent his head into a flurry of desire. His hands, magical in their ability to draw every ounce of pleasure from her body, moved faster to bring her to the edge of orgasm. One trailing along her nakedness, the other expertly stroking her most sensitive nerves. He needed to see her come undone. Needed to know that he was the same kind of ferocious need for her that she was for him. He needed to be the home of her pleasure just as she was the home of all his love and adoration.

"Come for me, Eliza," he whispered and watched her skin flush the most erotic shade of pink. "Feel how much I love your body. Let it all go and come for me."

As if his words were the secret to eternal satisfaction, Eliza's body obeyed without question. Her thoughts went fuzzy and her body churned with ecstasy as an orgasm swept over her in waves of warmth.

She screamed his name and it took him past the point of no return. As the tides of her pleasure receded, he pulled his hand away and positioned himself between her thighs, wet with her arousal. Bringing his fingers to her mouth, he groaned as she wrapped her lips around them and sucked. Taking in the taste of herself, she nearly exploded as he moaned, the sound driving her near another climax without even a touch from him.

Pulling his fingers from her mouth, he claimed the site with his own lips, kissing her as if it were the only thing that could save him. Mouths still connected in their frenzied kiss, he slid into her and they both cried out. Again and again, he drove into her. Their bodies moved together, writhing in a sweaty mess of limbs grasping for skin, desperate for more. Clinging to each other as if their lives depend on it.

There is sex. There is making love. This was neither.

It was a deep, needy hunger that could not be encompassed with any words. It was beyond normal human functions. This was carnal.

Their bodies moved together as if they were one. Each knowing exactly how to grind and rub against the other to maximize all the pleasure building between them. Every nerve in their bodies was alive and burning through them. The climax spread through every cell as they reached their peak together. She cried his name. He buried his head in her neck and breathed in her scent. Orgasm thundered down on them until they collapsed into a panting, sweating pile of flesh.

Their minds were buzzing with the divine bliss of satisfaction, but they could still recognize the familiar warmth of home. It was right there, bound together in the most intimate of ways. This was home.

No, this wasn't just sex.

This was salvation.

Chapter Thirty-Five

"I really should call the hospital," Eliza's voice drifted over the sunlit air between them. They were both spent and all Eliza wanted to do was live in Judas' embrace until the end of time. She'd found her home and she knew that nothing would ever change that.

Judas granted her a small kiss on her forehead, "We should go to the hospital. You need to see him."

"I don't think I can," her head shook. "Something's wrong, Judas... but I just can't put my finger on it."

"Tell me."

She paused for a moment, "I don't know what it is... a feeling, maybe. I don't think Dad getting shot was any kind of random act of violence. And..."

"What?" he pressed.

It was the crutch of their argument days ago. Eliza didn't know how she was going to admit to him, a *sober* him, that he may be right. Chet may very well be involved in the crime. But in the end, she had to swallow her pride.

"And I think maybe there's a chance Uncle Chet may have some involvement... albeit a small chance... but he definitely knows something," she admitted, waiting for the *I told you so*; but it never came.

Judas sighed, "I'm sorry, Eliza."

"It just... sucks," she huffed.

"Can I ask," he bit his lip in hesitation, "why do you suspect him?" Judas had to admit to himself that he was a little scared to ask the question. He didn't want her to leave angry, this time it really would kill him, but he needed to know what changed her mind.

"I found him in the office, after hours. He said he forgot something, but the file he took with him had the same number on it that I found in a password protected file on Dad's laptop. Then I went to the house to ask him about it, but he wasn't home and Aunt Reba wouldn't let me in...even Davy yelled at me," the statement poured out of her like a confession. "There's something no one is telling me... and I've got to know what it is."

"Did you check out all the files on Paul's computer? Even the deleted ones?" Judas asked.

"Yes."

"What about any recycle bin activity or download history?" he urged.

"All clear," she replied. "I spent hours combing over every keystroke on that machine. The only thing I found that doesn't make sense is a spreadsheet for a bank account, nine-seven-two-nine. I have no idea where this account is or what it's for. But, that same number was on the file Chet took from the office and Reba knows about it, I'm sure."

Judas' eyes narrowed in thought, "Good job, Nancy."

"Nancy?" Eliza asked, perplexed.

"Nancy Drew? Literary amateur detective?" he smiled.

Eliza couldn't help but laugh, "You've read Nancy Drew?"

"Read? Yes," Judas sat on the edge of the bed, "But I also own probably the largest private collection of the books that feature the character."

If he could have seen her face in the dim room, Judas would have doubled over at her look of shock. Was he being serious?

"No you don't," she laughed.

Finding her hand, Judas pulled her from the bed, "Oh, Eliza, there's so much for me to show you." He put his lips on hers for a moment before continuing, "We've got plenty of time for all of that... right now, I want to know about this bank account."

She eyed him skeptically, "Okay... but we'll be revisiting this whole Nancy Drew conversation."

After a quick shower, a clothing refresh, and a quick call to the charge nurse, the pair were back in his car with the hospital in their sights. Paul was still coming out of his medically induced coma but was responding to external stimuli. Eliza's heart raced faster the more she thought of seeing Paul. If he woke up when she was there, what would she say to him? Could he tell her who tried to kill him? She wasn't sure she was ready for the answer.

With his free hand, Judas laced his fingers in hers and he could feel her anxiety pulsing through them, "Tell me about what you found."

"It's odd. Dad has never been one to really secure anything on his computer even though I know we've both lectured him about internet security," glancing in Judas' direction, Eliza watched his head bob in the affirmative. "But, he still uses my birthday, probably easy for him to remember, I guess. Except for one file. Just one. But Dad being who he is, he used the account number as the password."

"What's in the account?" Judas ran his fingers over hers; they were soft like silk.

Eliza shook her head, "A lot of deposits... nothing that stood out. And withdraws. Big ones. All of them are going to someone or someplace called D-r-a."

"Dra?" he asked, puzzled.

"Yeah, not sure if that's a name or initials. Just Dra. But, it gets weirder," she continued. "That file? The one Chet was holding? It was thick, Judas. Really thick and I'm sure the tab had the same account numbers written on it. Nine-seven-two-nine."

She repeated the numbers like a mantra.

"Wait a minute," Judas declared sharply, pulling his hand away from hers. Reaching into his pocket, he pulled a small wallet-money clip combo from it and worked a green paper from his thin pouch. Tossing the wallet onto the dash, he unraveled the paper to reveal a check. "I knew it! Take a look at that."

He held the check between two fingers, offering it to Eliza. Wrinkles formed between her brow as she scanned the document.

"I don't understand," she said quietly.

"Look at the bottom. The account number," Judas pointed to the row of numbers just under the signature line. Eliza read the entire line and gasped when her eyes saw the last four digits.

"Nine-seven-two-nine," she choked.

"That's the check I found under my door when I got home that night. If your father is the only signatory on that account, then it clearly didn't come from Paul. Someone else wrote that check and forged your dad's name," he replied. Judas had a good idea about who wrote it and why, but that was a can of worms he wasn't ready to open again.

"Judas, I need to get into that account. I need to know who or what Dra is... and I want that file," Eliza demanded. "I know it's the only thing that will tell me why someone shot Dad."

Without warning, Judas veered the Audi onto an offramp then into the parking lot of a near empty Whataburger, before slamming on the brakes. The plan was fully formed in his mind before he had time to stop the car.

"Jesus, Judas! What's wrong?" Eliza gasped, still clinging to the dashboard.

"Your dad's a lawyer," Judas said, his eyes darted as all the pieces fell into place.

She looked at him incredulously, "Yeah, so am I. The point?"

"You're *both* lawyers," he offered.

Eliza's eyes rolled, "We've established that."

She wasn't getting his point and it made him smile. He turned to her, "Your father has a will, correct? I bet you do as well."

"Of course. Dad set up a trust years ago. I'm the sole beneficiary," her brow furrowed deeper.

"Eliza," Judas cleared his throat. "When was the last time you knew of a lawyer not having all of his affairs in order? I'm willing to bet Paul also has you listed as his Power of Attorney, in case something were to happen. Say... he's incapacitated?"

Her heart fell to her knees; this man was a certified genius. She looked back down at the check in her hand, "North Texas Bank and Trust."

Before she could utter another word, Judas already had the car turned and back on the freeway.

Chapter Thirty-Six

The tiny, unassuming white building of the North Texas Bank and Trust sat meekly between a cluster of similar retail spaces. Much taller office buildings with mirrored windows surround the bustling area like guardians. Once inside, Eliza and Judas waited for a young woman, with a long braid of chestnut hair to finish with another customer before they stepped forward.

"Welcome in! How can I help you today?" her Texas drawl dripped with sweetness.

Eliza read her name tag. "Hello, Ashley, I'm Eliza Arthur and my father has an account here. Unfortunately, he's been in an...accident," she paused. "I'm his Power of Attorney on record and need his bank statements for the past month so I can reconcile the account. Can you help me?"

"Oh, I'm so sorry about your daddy, Ms. Arthur," Ashley said before a soft smile smoothed her lips. "He's such a nice man...and I'm just so excited he's going to be our next state senator. I'll just have to check your identification and match it with the records real quick."

Removing her wallet, Eliza handed her driver's license to the woman as she punched in keys on her computer. Eliza assumed she was pulling the trust paperwork to confirm the claim and match names. Once satisfied, Ashley nodded to herself before turning back to Eliza and Judas.

"I'll get all of that printed for you in a jiff. You can just wait here, I'll run back to the printer," she instructed. They waited in pregnant silence for several minutes before the teller returned to her post with a small handful of neatly stacked and paperclipped papers. "Here you go! And you tell your daddy, we're all praying for him here."

Eliza painted on her most charming smile, and Judas almost laughed. Almost. Just as suddenly as the amusement fell over him, it just as quickly dissipated. He felt sad for her in a way. How many years had she been putting on that fake smile of hers? Certainly long enough to fool her father and everyone else, but not him. He could see right through the mask and into the pain she held underneath. If he could, Judas would die a thousand deaths if he never saw that mask again.

"Thank you," she replied before turning sharply toward the door, Judas on her heel. They were barely outside the tinted glass doors and Eliza's eyes were scanning every word. Judas read quickly over her shoulder and found something interesting.

"There," he pointed to the bottom of the page. "A check for four thousand five hundred dollars written to Dr. Abigail Dupree. I wonder who that is."

"I don't know," the crease between Eliza's eyes furrowed deeper. But like a light in the darkness, a switch flipped, "Dra!"

Judas exclaimed understanding, "D-R-A. Dr. Abigail. But why is he paying her these large amounts of money? You said they went back years on the computer, right?"

"They do," Eliza nodded, looking up at him as they walked to the car. "But, who is she?"

Judas held the door for her, "Paul's not sick, is he?"

She waited for him to slide behind the wheel before answering, "No way...and if he was ill for this long, I'd know it. Judas, these payments are going back at least a decade, maybe longer. And there's no pattern to them, as far as I can tell. Two checks one year, five the next. It's so weird."

She paused to think for a moment.

"That number...didn't you find a phone number at my dad's?" she asked excitedly as a plan was rumbling in her mind. She didn't know who this person was or what connection she had to her father, but Eliza was damn sure going to find out.

Judas took his wallet off the dash of the car, "Yeah, it's right here."

Eliza nearly snatched it out of his fingers and was dialing before he could get a word in. When the phone began to ring, she put it on speaker so he could hear as well.

One ring, two rings...

"Good afternoon, Arlington Medical Group, how may I direct your call?"

"Hello," Eliza's voice was smooth and professional. "I am wondering if there is any way I can get an appointment with Dr. Dupree. I know it's last minute, but I was hoping she could see me on short notice."

Judas' eyes went round like oversized marbles.

"Are you currently a patient?" the voice on the other end asked.

Eliza's plastic smile returned, "I'm not...at least not yet. But, Dr. Dupree comes highly recommended and if there's anything you can do, I'd really appreciate it."

"Let me check."

"What the hell are you doing?!" he whispered hoarsely as the receptionist clacked on her keyboard at the other end of the phone.

Eliza covered the receiver, "Getting information."

"By scheduling an appointment with a woman you don't know? We don't even know what kind of doctor she is!" Judas protested.

She shot him a look of bewilderment. While her plan wasn't fully formed when she dialed the number, Eliza was fairly confident that she wasn't dealing with anyone who handled medical issues exclusive to men.

"Are you still there?" the gentle voice asked.

"Yes, of course," Eliza shot a warning look at Judas.

"Well, I don't have anything today, but I can get you in at eleven am tomorrow, if that would work for you?"

A grin spread across her face and she winked in his direction, "Eleven is great."

The gesture caught Judas off guard. It was simple, provocative, and conspiratorial. It sent a shot of electricity through him and made his heart flutter with excitement. She was sexy as hell even in the most inane moments.

"Name for the appointment?" the receptionist asked.

Without hesitation, Eliza replied, "Beth. Beth Christian."

The words hit Judas so hard in the chest that he couldn't breathe for a moment. He worked hard to contain his momentary shock as she finished up the call, but he knew she could see it written all over his face.

Disconnecting the call, she bit her lip, "I had to give them a name. I couldn't give my own just in case."

Judas felt the slow creep of a smile cross his face, "That... um... it just caught me off guard."

Her face flooded with pink as embarrassment filled her mind, "I'm sorry if that was too much."

Judas chuckled out his disbelief that she still didn't understand how much she meant to him. He didn't say a single word. Leaning across the front seat, he wrapped his fingers around the nape of her neck, winding his fingers in her hair and pulling her face to him. His lips connected with hers as his tongue gently urged her lips to part. He held her there against him as she cradled his face in her hands.

Finally, he leaned away just enough to rest his forehead against hers. She was breathless from the love she felt in his kiss.

"Eliza," he breathed, his voice barely a whisper, "I want nothing in this world more than to give you my name. Hearing it now, I just...

I thought my heart might actually beat out of my chest. I have never heard sweeter words in all my life."

She smiled, kissing him again. Gently, just a little peck against the soft skin of his lips.

"Well, that's pretty impressive," she said, "because you're like... really old."

A deep laugh left his chest as he leaned back staring across the front seat watching her. He could still see the stress of the last few days etched into her skin, but he could also still see the radiant glow that emanated from her at all times.

Staring into his eyes, Eliza continued, "Right now, my world is upside down and I don't know what is going to happen. I do know, though, that I am yours and if you ever wanted to share your name with me, your *real* name...I would wear it with pride."

Judas was sure she could see his glow of love for her shining from the depths of his soul in that moment.

Chapter Thirty-Seven

"I 'll wait out here, okay?" Judas stroked Eliza's arm just outside the heavy door. On the other side, his employer fully woke from his coma an hour ago. From the report from the nursing staff he asked for two things. First, a morning paper so he could catch up on any stories that were written about his *accident* and second, his daughter.

She nodded hesitantly and stared at the barrier between her and her dad. Eliza knew there was more to the story of what happened, but getting Paul to talk about it, she knew would be entirely different. She drew in a long breath, holding it for a few seconds before slowly releasing it and going inside.

Color had returned to the man's face, but Eliza thought he looked so much older than when she left him two days ago. His usually well-groomed gray hair was messy and he needed a shave. The breath she let go of just moments before, Eliza wished she had back because she now felt like she was choking. He was difficult, and obnoxious, and hard to handle and her gut told her that a hundred people probably wanted him dead for good reason. But, he was her father. He taught her how to ride her brand new pink bike with the silver glitter banana seat when she was five. He took her for ice cream when she lost her first tooth. She remembered how gently he spoke to her and how he smelled when she nuzzled her face into his neck while she cried after he told her that her mother was gone.

He could be a real bastard, but she hoped he could still have good in him somewhere. She needed her father to be redeemable.

A tear slid down Eliza's cheek.

This was her dad.

She brushed the tear away just as Paul's eyes blinked open and his head lolled in her direction. His smile grew as Eliza stepped closer to the bed and took his hand.

"Betsy. Oh, my beautiful angel," he cooed.

Her expression was tight, "Hi, Dad. How are you feeling?"

"Oh," waving a dismissive hand, he chuckled. "Little bit of a headache, but not enough to take this old dog out."

Eliza laughed softly, "That's great, Dad. Have you eaten? Are they getting you up yet?"

She knew she would have to ease into the real questions she wanted to ask.

"Why yes...as a matter of fact, doc says one or two more days here in Club Med and I'll be good as new. Which is fine by me because I'm already behind on the campaign trail. But, thank the good Lord I'm still polling ahead of Marquez." Paul sat straight, "As a matter of fact this little accident is going to play in my favor."

Eliza's face contorted in horror, "Accident? In your favor? What are you talking about?"

"Well, the papers are running with their own theories...everything from the Democrats trying to take me out to some maniac-criminal illegal. Any way you play it though, my poll numbers keep rising!" his excitement was growing. "We need to use this, Betsy...keep the fires going. Let's send out a press release that lets my followers know that I'm going to be back on the road next week and that whoever this bastard is, the Dallas police department has my full backing and we will take our streets back and make them safe again."

She stared blankly at her father. He had to be joking...was he *happy* about the attempt on his life?

"Dad, you can't be serious—"

"Betsy, Marquez doesn't stand a chance. Damn snowflake is too soft on crime...people want clean neighborhoods. Safe neighborhoods. God back in schools. The way it used to be...with the damn troublemakers in their own countries, where they belong. I'm going to give them that," his words grew like a Southern preacher on a pulpit. "Speaking of safety...where is Jude?"

"He's outside," she muttered as her eyes blinked in disbelief.

"He's a good one," Paul nodded. "Probably hasn't left since I came in here. You don't find loyalty like that from an outsider. Hard to come by...tell him to come in here so I can reward the boy."

She thought someone else had control of her limbs as she turned back to the door, inviting Judas inside. The idea her father would use such an abhorrent act of violence as a whistle for the constituency was sickening. But, so was the whole political game and she hated that she put herself in the middle of it. She could've said no, she should've said no when her father asked her to manage his campaign. As if he actually asked. He didn't; he told her she would be great and that was the end of the conversation.

Her father's voice yanked her back into the moment, "Jude, I wanna thank you for standing by my side through this. You're one of the good ones."

Paul held out his hand to Judas. Glancing in Eliza's direction, he watched her eyes roll in disgust, but Judas clasped Paul's hand tightly and shook it.

"Of course, sir," he replied, still a little confused by the context.

"Well, now, down to business," Paul dropped his hand. "Betsy, we need to gather a big press conference for my release. We need to show these people what kind of man Paul Arthur is."

Eliza sighed, "Dad, what we need is to know who shot you."

"Well, I have no idea," he said quickly.

Eliza's brow furrowed. From what Judas described and the reports from the police, her father would have surely had to know his attacker. There were no signs of forced entry and his office was an apparent mess. She felt an odd sensation rise from her toes, filling every pore of her skin, and sinking in her mind. Some might call it instinct, but it was the same feeling she had as a prosecutor when a defendant was lying to her.

"What do you mean, you don't know. What happened that afternoon, Dad?" her question came out more icy than was her intent.

Paul paused, "First off, young lady, I don't like your tone. Second, I don't remember what happened."

"I'm sorry." Her lips drew into a thin line, "Is there anything you do remember?"

She forced her voice to soften.

"Well, I," Paul shrugged. "I was in my office, reading. Then all of a sudden there was someone there with a gun...that's all."

"Can you give the police a description?" she urged, unsure how far she could push him before he shut her down. "Don't you want this person to get what they deserve?"

Waving his hand again, Paul sat a little more straight against the hospital bed, "Now honey, this is just a mess that we need to let the police handle. And yes, I'm sure when or *if* they are caught, they'll get what's coming to them."

"Dad," Eliza's voice was full of warning.

"He was wearing a mask," her father replied flatly and Eliza took the hint. He would give her no more answers on the topic. "Now, Betsy, please make sure the press is ready to go the second I'm released. We're going to need a statement to hand them, but I'll also be taking questions. Also, can you pick up my good navy suit from the dry cleaners? I heard once that wearing blue portrays strength. And, get Lydia to call someone about the house...I need that cleaned up before

I get home. We can talk about next Thursday's speaking event tomorrow...although, I think I want to pull together one of those town halls in North Dallas the week after."

Eliza huffed, "Fine."

"Sweetheart, come here," Paul cooed. As his daughter drew closer, he took her hand, "I'm alright, honey. I know you're worried about me, but I'm fit as a bull in a pasture of heifers."

He smiled, "Jude, you go ahead and take a day or two. You've spent enough time here...you send Bobby or Beau over to stand watch until I get out of here."

"Yes, sir," he nodded, still a little confused.

"And, can you make sure Betsy gets home okay? She's looking a little pale," Paul squeezed his daughter's hand.

As the pair turned to leave, Eliza heard her father pushing keys on his cell phone. But instead of cycling back into a losing argument, she walked into the white and gray hallway, and allowed the heavy door to shut behind her. Every few feet, Judas glanced in her direction, but didn't dare interrupt what was stirring in her mind. He felt the anger boiling inside her. They walked side by side in silence until reaching the door of his car.

"Goddamn it!" she snarled.

"What the hell happened in there?" Judas demanded finally.

Eliza whirled on him, but the second her eyes met his, the tension released from her face, "My father...being a complete ass. He cares more about this damn election than anything else, including his own safety. But, what's worse? Now, I think he's hiding something."

Her voice trailed into nothing and he stared intently into her face. Judas was concerned that Paul was taking the threat against his life so flippantly, but he was more worried about Eliza. He already knew her determination to get to the bottom of this ordeal, but now his uncertainty grew with her solidifying tenacity to uncover the truth.

Judas leaned close, "Let me get you home. We can tackle Paul's diversions tomorrow...after your doctor's appointment, *Mrs. Christian.*

The sly grin from Judas was the final hammer. Eliza's rigid facade broke as her lips cracked into a small smile.

Chapter Thirty-Eight

Eliza watched rain spatter the dingy windows of the Fort Worth Women's Health Center as she sat mindlessly flipping the pages of an outdated issue of *Southern Living*. The medical office, located on the fifth floor of a sprawling complex, was located near the campus of the Texas Health Methodist Hospital. Sparsely decorated, the large waiting room featured beige floral print walls, standard issue commercial tile floor, and padded seating that were purchased sometime in the mid-nineties.

After checking in, Eliza was given a clipboard with five forms to gather family history, insurance information, and health information releases. But after making up false information for ten minutes, she gave up and returned the paperwork and pen to the receptionist, and instead picked up a magazine. She was unsure of what she would say when she was called back but figured she could wing it. It was at this moment that she wished she had allowed Judas to come upstairs with her. He always brought her a sense of calm, but she reminded herself that he might raise suspicion.

"Beth Christian?"

Eliza's head snapped to the petite redheaded nurse holding her chart just outside the entrance to the exam rooms.

"Yes," she stood and moved toward the woman.

The pair crossed the threshold, zigzagging down a couple of hallways until they reached their destination. Eliza's insides trembled with anxiety as the nurse took her pulse, blood pressure, and oxygen level.

The woman's voice broke the bubble of silence, "Alright, if you want to get into that gown, Dr. Dupree will be in shortly."

With a quick movement, the nurse left and Eliza was alone. Too nervous to sit still for even a moment, she paced the small room reading and rereading several posters for cancer detection and menopause symptoms. Thirty minutes later, a sharp knock rattled the door and a tall woman, around Eliza's height with silvering blonde hair strode inside. Her white coat was neatly pressed and monogrammed. Eliza took in her entire presence, taking mental notes.

"Good afternoon, I'm Dr. Dupree," the woman announced, taking a seat on a rolling stool. She looked over to where she expected Eliza to be seated on the table, but she wasn't. "Oh, goodness. Hon, I'm going to need you up here," she patted the exam table.

"I thought we could discuss treatment for a moment," Eliza replied.

Dr. Dupree nodded, "Of course. Tell me, what brings you to see me today."

Eliza's heart thundered in her chest, "I was given your name by Paul Arthur."

She watched as the doctor's face became stone. She slowly closed Eliza's fake chart and took out a notepad. She scribbled quickly across its front page as she spoke.

"I don't do that here," she pulled the paper loose from the pad. "You'll have to come to this address. I have an opening tonight at ten."

Dr. Dupree handed the note to Eliza and stood to leave. Eliza read the address but still had more questions.

"Excuse me?" she said in her most innocent voice. "I don't understand. He told me to see you here."

The doctor turned back, "Yes...to make first contact. But, I can't do the procedure you're needing in this office. He knows that and he should have explained it to you." Dr. Dupree paused, "If I could offer you some friendly advice? Stay away from men like him. They aren't going to marry you and you're not going to have a lifetime of security and cotillions."

Eliza looked at the note in her hand again. What was she saying? Why would she think that she was promised anything? Immediate understanding fell over her like a bucket of ice water but it wasn't cold enough to contain the rage that was beginning to simmer in her core. It was all starting to make sense. Eliza jumped from her seat, pushing her way to the door of the small exam room to block the doctor's exit.

"Miss, meet me there at ten o'clock—"

"I have one more question," Eliza cut her off.

Dr. Dupree's eyes flared, "I will answer your questions later tonight."

"No. You'll answer them now...or I leave this office and tell the front desk and the medical board what you're doing," Eliza snapped boldly.

"Who the hell do you think you are?" the doctor's jaw set.

"Eliza Arthur. Paul Arthur's *daughter*," narrowing her glare on the doctor, Eliza watched her take a stumbling step backward. Dr. Dupree raised her hands defensively as if Eliza was getting ready to strike.

"I'm sorry...I didn't know he'd...he'd," the woman gagged. "Oh my God...that's disgusting."

Eliza's face wrinkled in disbelief, "What are you—no! No, I'm not pregnant."

She watched the relief sweep the doctor's face.

"I want to know about this arraignment you have with my dad, though," she ordered.

The doctor shook her head, "I can't. I can't do that...this...this is healthcare. No matter what they say."

"Yes, you will. Or I will make good on my promise, whether I agree with what you're doing or not," growling through clenched teeth, Eliza pointed to the doctor's shoes. "Or are you more worried about losing your meal ticket?" She whistled through her clenched teeth, "Those Louboutin's must have cost a fortune."

Tears welled in Dr. Abigail Dupree's eyes. Both she and Eliza knew this was the end of the road and it didn't matter if they could have been on the same side at one time. Right now, Eliza held all the cards and that hand was a Royal Flush.

"I met Paul years ago. We ran in the same circles and he knew I worked in women's health. He had a girlfriend at the time and he said they made a mistake and needed my help...if I could get her in, he'd pay for the privilege. That's when abortions were legal here," tears streaked down the doctor's aged face, making trails in her foundation. "When this backward ass state followed the Supreme Court, they threw us back to the dark ages."

Dr. Dupree pointed at the note in Eliza's hand, "I had to start doing them in my home. I have a clean room...all the equipment. I make sure all the girls are safe. Believe me, your father isn't my only client. "

Eliza's heart sank. Abigail Dupree was a woman old enough to have seen the birth of women's healthcare rights and their subsequent death. She really believed what she was doing was right, and Eliza couldn't disagree. It was a tragedy that while men could make any decision under the sun in regard to their own bodies, the other half of society wasn't given the same rights. It made her furious.

"Don't you see?" Dr. Dupree pleaded. "It's not about the money...if I stop, where will these girls go when they're in trouble? What makes me angry is that the more money someone has, the bigger the promises they're told."

Eliza patted the doctor on the shoulder, "I'm not here to out you. Your secret is safe with me. But, do me a favor?"

"Sure. If I can," Dr. Dupree dabbed her eyes with a tissue.

"If another woman comes in here saying my Dad sent her...call me," handing the doctor one of her business cards, she nodded. "I'm also tired of wealthy men getting away with what they please."

"I can do that."

Eliza made her way out to the parking garage to find Judas leaning against the door of his Audi. Her mind was reeling with Dr. Dupree's confession but when she saw him, a blanket of peace and comfort fell over her. Judas was her solace and she knew that whatever came of all of this chaos, he would be waiting for her on the other side.

As she drew closer, he stood to meet her, "So? How did it go?"

"I don't think I've been more angry at my father in my entire life," she replied as her phone buzzed in her hand. "Hang on a second. Hi Lydia..."

Judas watched Eliza's eyes grow wide then shrink again into a glare.

"What do you mean he's turned himself in?" she asked in a measured tone then waited, listening. "Tell him not to say a word to anyone. I'm on my way!"

Judas' eyes locked with hers, asking the unspoken question.

"Uncle Chet just confessed to shooting my Dad."

Chapter Thirty-Nine

While still in the parking lot, Eliza thought it was a good idea to talk to Chet alone. She asked Judas to wait for her in the car even though he protested heavily. Still, she insisted. Now, sitting in the room alone, she felt like maybe she should have let him win that little argument.

As an attorney, this was far from the first time she had sat in that chair. She had spent the better part of her adult life in and out of rooms just like that one. She made deals, she passed judgment, and she comforted the wrongly accused. The room felt like nothing more than familiar territory, but was also so different.

Everything was colder than she remembered it being. The stark grey of the concrete walls. The sleek metal of the table in front of her. The damp air blasting from the overhead vents. Her own heart. All of it frigid and her body trembled as the cold permeated into her bones.

She wrapped her arms tighter around herself, watching the door as she awaited the arrival of one of her most beloved family members. The idea that she would ever be here with Chet Branson sitting on the other side of the table seemed impossible to her just yesterday. But, there she was; knowing that the man she grew up with, the man that helped raise her and played a more fatherly role in her life than Paul ever had, just confessed to attempted murder.

Allowing the feeling to wash over her in waves of remorse and pain, she was startled as the heavy clang of the door announced Chet's entrance. Coming into the room with a defiant posture, the second he saw Eliza sitting before him his shoulders dropped and his stoic expression turned to one of immense shame. His head hung to his chest and Chet avoided all eye contact as he shuffled to the table, taking his seat across from Eliza.

His voice was soft and sounded on the verge of tears as he spoke, "They told me my attorney was here."

"Just little old me," she replied.

"Eliza," his eyes still locked on the cold, hard floor, "I don't know what you want me to say."

She took a deep breath, releasing it slowly, "I want you to tell me everything."

Chet huffed out a sardonic laugh, "No, you don't. Trust me when I say this. You don't want to hear this from me. I love you, Eliza, and that is exactly why I won't do that to you."

Leaning her elbows on the table, Eliza moved closer, "I know about Dr. Dupree."

Chet's head jerked up and his nostrils flared as he sucked in a sharp breath. He didn't speak, but Eliza saw the thoughts and questions swirling in his mind.

"I did some digging and I went to her. I know what he's done, but I need your confirmation." She swallowed back the last bits of fear in her gut before laying it all on the table, "I am willing to represent you and make sure you don't lose any more time with Reba and the kids, but I need your full honesty first. I need to know every detail of what happened."

He stared across the table at her for what felt like an eternity. He considered every possibility and contemplated all his options. Then dropping his head into his hands, Chet wept. She watched as his shoulders shook from the sobs wracking his body and waited patiently until he was ready.

After several long minutes, he leaned back in his chair, staring at the ceiling, "God help me. Eliza, I didn't even think. I just reacted. I saw red and I knew I had to kill him. I fully intended to let him die on the floor. I wanted him to die and rot in hell for what he did."

Eliza nodded her understanding as she watched the tears pouring uncontrollably from his face.

"He ruined her life, Eliza," he choked out as sobs overtook him again. "He took away her innocence. He fucking put his hands on her and stole a piece of who she could have been for the rest of her life."

Eliza squirmed in her chair. She fully expected Chet to tell her that he found the banking materials, that he put the pieces together just as she did. She expected to hear that he was disgusted with the man he thought was a friend and just acted without thinking. She raised a hand to cover her mouth as the true gravity of this situation began to sink in.

Chet shook his head in disgust, "And then... then that goddamn doctor of his almost killed her. When she told us, Eliza... I lost it. What else was I supposed to do?" His voice rose as he looks Eliza in the eye, "He fucking raped her and then paid for some back alley abortion and she almost fucking died!"

The volume and weight of his words slapped Eliza across the face and her voice quaked, "Uncle Chet... who... who did he do that to?"

Chet closed his eyes as he realized how little Eliza knew. The words stuck in the back of his throat and he shook his head. When he was finally able to speak again, his words were dripping with heavy layers of anguish and ruin, "It was Neveah. My fucking seventeen-year-old daughter! I trusted that son of a bitch for decades and he fucking raped my daughter, Eliza!"

Eliza opened her mouth to speak but nothing came out. She heard the heavy thud of her pulse pounding in her head. The edges of her vision blurred as tears filled her eyes. Suddenly, she wasn't cold anymore because a white hot rage boiled inside of her. Her heart was shattered but her mind was set. She reached across the table and placed one hand on Chet's arm. He glanced up at her and she saw the toll this had taken on him. He was a broken man and there was no one to blame for that but Paul Arthur. Eliza cleared her throat, summoning every ounce of self-control in her body to keep herself from falling apart. There would be time for that, but she couldn't let it happen yet. She had too much work to do before she let the gravity of this truth tear her apart.

Squeezing Chet's arm, she made her uncle a promise, "I will make sure you are put in front of a judge immediately and bail is set. I will make sure that bail is paid in full from Paul's account. I will represent you every step of the way and I will make sure you don't serve a single day. What you did is nothing more than a public service and I wish you had succeeded."

***

Judas couldn't stand the thought of waiting for her in the car. He waited until she was safely inside then walked himself inside as well. Planting himself directly across from the access door he knew she would return out of and he watched, not allowing his eyes to stray from the doorway for even a second. When Eliza returned he would be ready for whatever reality came with her.

After what felt like a millennia, she emerged and his heart sank. Whatever she learned had ravaged her. Her normal flushed cheeks were pale and devoid of life. She looked like the shell of a person.

Judas rose to his feet, rushing to her side. Eliza's face didn't react as it usually did when she saw him. She simply stared ahead and took his hand as she marched toward the exit.

Once outside, Judas pulled her arm gently, forcing her to look at him, "Hey, what happened? You're not okay right now."

Eliza pursed her lips as she contemplated what she could bear to share at that moment. She knew if she even tried to tell him what she just learned she would crumble into a useless pile of heartbreak and she couldn't afford to do that yet.

She shook her head, "I can't talk about this yet."

Concern creased his forehead, "Ahava, whatever this is, we can navigate it together."

She felt the threat of tears but shook them away, "No. No, Judas. I can't yet. If I do, I'll fall apart and I can't do that yet. I have some things I need to do. When that is finished, we will talk."

The frustration of knowing she was holding in so much just to keep herself afloat was nearly unbearable, but he understood time is something she needed from him, "I'm not happy about that, but whatever you need. Until then, what can I do?"

She breathed in and out several times before walking to the car, "I have to run a couple of errands and I need to do them alone. Can you—"

"Eliza, I'm not letting you shoulder this alone," he interjected.

She stopped, turning to face him, "Look, what I just learned in there is so much worse than I even thought it could be. I need to do some things and I need to do them alone. I'm not asking. I'm telling you that this is what I'm doing. If you want to help, you can go to the hospital and you can stand guard outside Paul's room. You don't have to go in and he doesn't even need to know you're there. Just be there. In case."

Did she just call her father by his name?

He frowned. "Is he in danger? I thought it was just Chet involved. Who should I be watching for?"

Eliza huffed a bitter laugh, "Me, Judas. I need you to guard the door from me and I'm not even joking. I am going to try my very best to go do what I need to do without going there to see him, but I need you there to stop me if I fail. If I show up at that hospital, you have to stop me or I am going to end up right back in that jail, but I'll be on the other side of the table because I *will* kill him. I will march right into that room and I will finish the goddamn job."

The pain in her voice was palpable and he believed every word she spoke. Judas pulled her into a crushing embrace. Kissing her hair, he whispered, "Okay, Ahava. I will be there."

Chapter Forty

The wide Texas sky was clear and the sunshine beat down punishingly on Eliza's skin. She had been standing in her father's driveway staring up at the home she was raised in for ten minutes but she just couldn't make herself go inside.

Those walls were full of her childhood. Everything about who she was had roots in this home. She grew into herself from all the seeds of experience planted right here. She'd always thought she'd had a decent childhood, mostly tended to by nannies and Aunt Reba, with the occasional appearance by her father. The younger versions of Eliza remembered Paul as fun and outgoing. He was always laughing and entertaining a crowd. He seemed to understand how to delight her childhood sense of wonder in the world. It wasn't until she was older that those memories morphed into ones of tending to a drunken hypocrite. The man who espoused conservatism by day and drank away his nights. A man who made Eliza's friends uncomfortable when they caught him staring a little too long. A man that she wept for at night because she was afraid this might be the drunken stupor that finally did him in, making her an orphan. It was in those later years that she began to come to terms with the fact that her father wasn't a good person. He was selfish and cruel and hate filled. So why was it such a surprise to learn he was a rapist too?

How had she not known? There had to have been clues that he was more than just a drunken idiot. Did she just ignore them as he reminded her that family came before all else except God? She knew they disagreed on everything and most days, as an adult, she was sure she didn't even like him, but she never imagined he was capable of the terrible things she'd been told. Being totally honest with herself, she'd known he was a bad person for a long time but she didn't know he was a monster.

Looking up at the columned entry and tan brick facade, she wondered if anyone else ever knew the kind of deplorable being that lived inside. Were the other homes in their gated community the same? Did they all use these monstrous displays of their wealth to hide all the dirty secrets inside? Was this how all the families in the world worked? Everyone was just living lies to hide their demons?

But then...

She thought of Judas. He was good and pure and kind. He spent thousands of years hearing the world call him terrible things. His name was synonymous in society with being the enemy. A traitor. Yet, he remained good. He didn't let that taint or tarnish his soul. She knew he was proof of goodness and that was what she clung to as she walked to the front door and slid her key into the lock.

Her shoes tapped against the cold marble floor as she made her way across the grand entry to Paul's office.

'Focus on what you need to do here, Eliza,' she thought to herself. Taking a steadying breath, she flipped on the light.

She already made a phone call to connections in the prosecutor's office and Chet would be put in front of a judge to receive a bail determination before the end of the night. She'd also reached out to the bank and ensured the funds would be available to pay the bail the first second she could. Each phone call she made came with vague clues of understanding so that when she was ready to bring this case to court, the system was already tipping in her favor. The legal system really shouldn't be so easy to skew, but in this case, she was glad it was. Now, to further her position, Eliza was in Paul Arthur's home looking for any and all additional help to show his deserving guilt in bringing this whole thing on himself. Did she believe in the death penalty? Usually, no. Especially not at the hands of someone outside of the proper legal channels, but then again she'd never felt such a strong betrayal so close to home. When she was finished, the world was going to know Paul got exactly what he deserved and even that really wasn't enough.

She had no clue what she was looking for, but she searched through every drawer, cabinet, and closet until she was satisfied there was nothing here to help her. When she cleared the office, she moved on to the next room. And the next. And the next, until she had just one room left.

She wasn't sure how long she'd been s inside the home, but she hadn't received the phone call about bail. Arriving at the last room gave her pause. She stood outside of the doorway and stared at the closed door, willing her phone to ring and save her from this one. When it didn't obey, she sighed, turning the knob before walking into her mother's office.

Catherine Arthur had died in a car accident when Eliza was five years old and every memory of her was foggy. She wasn't even sure the memories were all truly hers or just her mind's retelling of stories she had been told over the years. She used to cling to any possible way to know her mother and spent many afternoons in her mother's space. Paul had kept it exactly as Catherine left it and it was the only room in the house that'd never felt like him. It was warm and full of rich fabrics. The sun shone brightly through the large bay windows. The entire space was light and airy. As Eliza grew older the space became just a reminder that she would never know the woman that created it and being inside only made her heart ache. Shaking her head, Eliza realized that it might make the perfect room for Paul to hide any indiscretions.

Eliza made her way through the desk first, carefully running her fingers over the pens and pencils tucked inside. Being here and seeing these things for the first time in so many years felt otherworldly. It was like going back in time only to realize you still can't change what once was. The pain of heartbreak was somehow both a new stab and an old friend all at once. Tears stung her eyes, but with a deep breath, she continued anyway.

Eliza tore through the room with care, being sure to leave it just as she found it while still leaving no stone unturned. Eventually, she reaches the closet. Taking a seat on the floor, legs crisscross like the young schoolgirl she was the last time she'd held her mother's hand, Eliza began unpacking boxes tucked away inside. Most of the paperwork littering the boxes was nothing more than day to day monotony. Long ago paid bills from now closed accounts, shopping lists carefully checked off through a trip to the store, appointment reminders scrawled across faded receipts. But then, resting beneath all the years of paper clutter, something else.

Eliza reached into the box to pull out a stack of leatherbound notebooks with worn pages and wear and tear of use. Laying the stack in front of her, she gently opened the cover to find line after line of delicate, handwritten journal entries. Glancing through each one, she could see the dates going back all the way to the year her parents married and carrying through to the year she lost her mother. She never even knew her mother had kept journals.

Her heart soared as she realized that her mother's entire life story was written out on these pages in her own words. Then, thumbing through the most recent journal, she came across the last entry. It was written the day of her mother's death. A chill slid down her spine and her lungs seized shut, leaving Eliza unable to breathe as the words on the page came into sharp focus before her.

Catherine Arthur may very well have been the first to discover Paul Arthur's dirty little secrets.

Chapter Forty-One

April 17th, 1995

I learned today that my entire life is a lie.

My husband is among the lowest forms of human life.

I have never been so naive to believe that my marriage or my husband are perfect. I have known for too many years that he has had other women. I was heartbroken at first, as I watched all my childhood dreams of what marriage should be swept away by his need to be the center of attention even in some other women's beds.

Eventually, though, I became numb to it. He provided for my life, wore me on his arm at societal functions, and gave me my darling Eliza. It was truly a perfectly suitable arrangement for these last several years. He stayed busy at work and out doing who knows what with who knows who while I got to be home with our girl. I got to be her mother without any interference from his archaic ways. I got to raise her on my own however I saw fit and he was gone too much to realize I was raising her to be the kind of woman that would never fall for a man like him. I got to raise her to be the kind of woman I so wish I was.

This morning that entire arrangement got blown to shit.

I woke this morning at my own leisure, no alarm to pierce my dreams, and drank my morning tea from the window seat in my office. That's my favorite place to be, after all, and Eliza wasn't home. She's staying the weekend with a friend and I can't tell you how grateful I am for that now.

Around 9 am, as I wandered my bookshelves looking for a new read to fill my afternoon, I heard the distinct whine of sirens through the neighborhood. Living where we do, that's not a common occurrence so of course it drew my attention immediately. I raced to the front door and flung it open wide to see what all the commotion was about. When the door opened, a lonely white envelope fell at my feet. There was no stamp or address written across it. It simply said, Mrs. Arthur.

Forgetting all about whatever neighborhood disturbance had caused the sirens, I picked up the letter and carried it inside. It was my own little mystery to unravel and the thought delighted me to my core.

Inside the envelope was a handwritten letter. I don't know why, but I felt instant melancholy as I sat in the kitchen to read it. Once the words took hold of me, the distant sadness became the greatest devastation of my life.

In a small neighborhood like ours, you come to know your neighbors well. Just around the corner, in a house just like mine, lives a family with a seemingly perfect life. A mother, a father, a teenage son, and a teenage daughter. I have spent afternoons at the club with the mother. I have sat across the table from the father at fundraising galas. I have watched the son play in their yard and the daughter travel the neighborhood selling Girl Scout cookies. I have watched them both grow up, but they are still children.

The letter in my hands was written by the daughter. Her name is Margaret and she goes by Maggie. She is poised and athletic. She is a member of her school's honor society. She has plans for her life that go far beyond this community.

Or, rather, she had plans.

Today, she left this letter at my door to let me know that my husband had been grooming her for a sexual relationship for the last year, since she was fifteen. He had manipulated her and taken advantage of her youth in order to have her under him. He had taken no care to preserve her innocence. He had gotten her pregnant and she was full of shame.

She wrote me this letter to tell me that she had thought he loved her, that they had something that would stand the test of time. He had convinced her of this until the consequences became real. It was at that point that he made it clear she was just one of many and that he would never be a part of her life. He had given her no option but abortion or a shattered life as a single mother. She chose her own option. The sirens I heard while retrieving her letter had been for her.

As I sat in my kitchen reading her words, the paramedics were carrying her body out of her home as her mother wailed on her knees in the front yard. She had taken her own life as a result of the shame and guilt buried in her and tended to by the monster I married.

He, a man of influence and with a position of power in our community, took advantage of and raped a child.

There is no return from this moment. He cost that girl her life and her future. I cannot spend another second in any kind of arrangement with someone who could do that.

I'll admit, I have drank away my day. Tears have poured down my face and into my vodka, as I have wandered aimlessly through my home for hours contemplating my next move. I think now, as the effects of the liquor have begun to fade, I will go for a drive and maybe visit Reba. She is good in a crisis and I think she can help me plan my escape with Eliza.

That is my only priority now. I want Eliza safely away from that man. I will take her into hiding if I have to, I just never want her to be exposed to someone as vile as her father ever again. By the time I pick her up on Sunday, I hope to have at least a place to go that isn't here. If we have to live in a tiny apartment somewhere we've never been, it will be worth it to never have to be here again. I have lived my whole life with privilege and, it turns out, when faced with a situation as dire as this one, I don't care about it in the slightest.

I don't want things anymore.

I just want freedom and to save my daughter's life from heartbreak at the hands of her own father.

Chapter Forty-Two

Eliza stood at the familiar door's threshold with a held breath. She didn't want to cry anymore today, but she also understood that was a promise to herself she wasn't likely to keep. It took just a moment for Reba to peer through the side window and open the door.

"Aunt Reba, may I come in?" her voice was heavy as she choked back more tears.

Nodding, Reba moved to the side and opened the door wider. Once inside, the two women stared at each other for a long moment. Eliza noticed her aunt looked a lot more aged than she had even a day ago. Her skin, always tanned and rosy from being in the pool or playing tennis, looked grey. And the small wrinkles around her eyes that come from years of laughter were deeper and pronounced.

"Eliza, sweetheart," Reba choked. "Thank you for helping Chet. You don't know what it means to the both of us."

A pang of guilt hit her heart, but Eliza managed, "Of course. It's the least I can do."

Reba nodded again, "Well, what brings you by?"

"Nevaeh. I'd like to talk to her, if that's alright."

Her aunt considered her for a moment, but agreed, "I think she would like that."

The pair walked through the foyer into the living room and past the kitchen. It was a path Eliza could draw in her sleep. She had so much she wanted to say and yet, the silence between them strangled her.

"I found my mom's journals," Eliza blurted.

Reba pulled in a deep sigh, before a wistful smile appeared, "Your mom was always writing in her books. She never wanted to forget anything...the good, the bad. It was important to her. I always thought she would have made a damn fine lawyer too."

"She wrote about him...the day she died."

Her aunt stopped in her tracks. The memory of Catherine's passing fell over her like a shadow and Eliza watched it darken the woman's eyes, "I'm so sorry, sweetheart."

Movement through the dining room door drew the pair's attention, as Dave came into frame in the doorway.

"Hey," he called out. Eliza's heart beat fiercely because their last meeting had been an all out attack, but in the same instant, she knew it was for good reason. He was only protecting his baby sister.

"I'm sorry for snapping at you," he apologized, holding out his hand. When she took it, he pulled Eliza into a tight hug. "And thank you for helping my Dad."

Eliza melted into that embrace. Dave and the rest of the Branson offspring were the siblings she never had and it was killing her that her father caused them any pain.

Pulling back, her eyes met his, "I will make this right. Uncle Chet isn't going to spend any time in jail if I have anything to do with it."

"We appreciate that."

Reba gave her son a tight smile, "She wants to talk to your sister."

His head nodded in agreement and the women set off up the stairs. They reached a dark oak door; a sign in glitter spelling out Neveah's name hung on a tiny hook at eye level. Eliza's stomach lurched as her eyes focused on the handmade keepsake.

"Veah?" Reba knocked lightly on the door. "You have a visitor."

"Come in."

Her aunt placed a hand on Eliza's arm and did her best to look at peace, but she knew it was a lie. How could anyone possibly be able to comfort another in a time like this?

Eliza opened the door to find Neveah sitting criss-cross on her bed with a book. Her room was still tidy, like always, and it smelled faintly sweet like caramelized sugar. She recognized it immediately as her de facto sister's perfume.

"Hey, Nevaeh...is it alright if I come in to talk?" Eliza's tone was soft as if she might scare the young woman and that was the last thing she wanted.

She nodded, "Yeah...I'd like that."

Eliza took a look around the room for a place to sit. Grabbing the plush pink office chair from the desk, she placed it close enough to Neveah that she could hold her hand, if she needed.

"Look, Veah—" she tried to ease into a conversation but was cut short.

"You want to know what Uncle Paul did, don't you?" Neveah's sharp green eyes narrowed.

Eliza drew a staggered breath, "Yeah, I do. But, if you don't feel like talking about it, that's okay."

The girl turned her face away, staring into the far wall as a heavy silence fell on them both. Eliza knew if sitting in the quiet was what her little sister needed right now, then that was what they would do, for as long as it took. She had more than enough time to just be still with her. Reaching out, she took Neveah's small hand and the two laced their fingers. They sat together, in the calm, for long minutes that stretched into a quarter hour then a half hour.

"I didn't realize what was happening until later," Nevaeh's soft voice broke their meditation. "I'd went by the office a few times, after hours, you know? Just to study or to pick up something for Dad." Turning her face to Eliza, she shrugged, "The internet is so much better at the office than the library at school."

Eliza nodded.

"He told me how pretty I had gotten...how fast I grew up. How much I reminded him of Catherine," her chin dipped to her chest. "Toby and I just broke up...so, it was nice to hear things like that from someone...even if it was just Uncle Paul."

Eliza squeezed her hand. But, while Nevaeh may have taken it as a sign of support for her, Eliza's stomach was churning at the mention of her mother's name and she was only beginning to realize how sick her father really was.

"I went in one night, right before school was out. I needed to get a term paper done for AP Bio, he was there. He told me I could sit in his office so I wouldn't be alone," Nevaeh's eyes filled with tears. "I remember he was drinking something brown...whiskey or something. He asked if I wanted one...I said no, but he said it wasn't a big deal. After a while, I said I needed to go home...I tried to stand up, but—" She looked at Eliza, "I've never drank before...I felt weird and I remember stumbling around. Next thing I remember is being on the floor with my pants down...he was on top of me." The silent tears streamed down her slim face, "I couldn't make him stop...I couldn't tell him no."

Eliza didn't speak and she didn't know if she could. She had watched her father get to the edge of being inappropriate at times, like at the campaign ball, with Georgia, and he'd clearly had relationships with women, but she didn't know that he would go that far. Or, maybe she didn't want to admit it. If it would have been any other man, she would have seen the signs, but he was in her blind spot.

The young girl's sigh broke their silence, "I missed my period earlier this month...I just knew. I called Uncle Paul and told him...he told me not to worry about it. Gave me Dr. Abigail's number...she was nice. But, I guess there was a complication and I got an infection. That's how I ended up in the hospital."

"I'm really, really sorry, Nevaeh," Eliza couldn't dam the tears any longer. "I truly am so sorry! Sweetheart, I promise you, he will never do this to another girl again." Her anger fused and she lifted Nevaeh's chin to meet her eyes, "Do you hear me? Never again."

Chapter Forty-Three

Judas stood outside of Paul's hospital room for hours. He promised Eliza he would be there and he never regretted a second of his duty to her. When he received a text from her that he was safe to leave and meet at her apartment, he hesitated but only for a moment. He felt the momentary grip of fear that she was only trying to get him to leave so that she could slip into the room unnoticed, but then he realized he trusted her more than she trusted herself.

He knew she would never risk her own life and well-being for the scum that was Paul Arthur. He knew that she might want to kill him and he might even deserve it, but she was too good of a person to carry through with it. The entire charade of guarding the room, to begin with, was only for her peace of mind.

Knocking on Eliza's door, he planned to tell her just that. He wanted her to know that she was never in danger of her own self. She was strong, courageous, and pure. But when she opened the door, all the words left his mind.

She was completely shattered.

Eliza worked for the last several hours to hold herself together, but with Judas in front of her, she felt the freedom to let it all go and finally fall to pieces. The tears began to pour from her face and she fell willingly into his open arms.

He held her tight against his chest and walked her backward into the apartment. Shutting the door behind them, he ran a gentle hand down her back, soothing her like a child. Her sobs vibrate through him and send splintering cracks through his heart. Kissing her hair, he scooped her into his arms, walked to the couch, and sat with Eliza cradled in his arms.

"Ahava, my Eliza," he cooed against her hair.

She buried her head in his chest, trying to speak, "He's a rapist, Judas. Paul... he's... a... oh, god, Judas..."

Her words sliced through him and he held her closer to him, still rubbing her back to comfort her. Though, at this point, he wasn't sure comfort was possible.

Leaning away from the sanctuary of his chest, Eliza looks into his eyes, "Judas, my father raped Nevaeh. That's why Chet did what he did. And I don't think she's the first one. It goes all the way back to my mother. She learned what he was and she was leaving. She was leaving and she died. Judas, I..." her voice catches on a sob, "It's so unfair. And I have stood behind him even though I knew it was wrong. Even before I knew how wrong, I knew it was wrong, but I still stood there making excuses for him. Jesus, it's all so fucking disgusting. He is a horrible, disgusting man and I helped him get to where he is."

The rage boiling through his veins made it hard for Judas to stay seated here holding his love. He wanted nothing more than to walk into Paul Arthur's room and tear him to shreds. Not only did he desecrate the bodies of young girls, but he splintered Eliza's heart into a million tiny pieces. The look of devastation shining from her deep irises was the only thing holding him in place.

Swallowing back his rage, Judas took her face in his hands, "You did nothing wrong, Ahava. You didn't know. You couldn't have known."

Eliza shook her head in frustration, "No, that's not good enough." Anger billowed as she pushed herself away from his embrace to stand, "Men get away with shit like this because people in their lives don't hold them accountable for the shitty things they do. I hate those people!" Furious tears pour from her eyes, "I was one of those people

I hate, Judas. I made excuses and told myself he could be redeemed if I just kept trying. I knew he was a terrible person. I knew!"

Eliza stood before Judas, shaking from her indignation. The sight of her looking so ravaged by heartbreak was almost more than he could take.

"Eliza," he whispered carefully, "You are *not* responsible for the sins of your father. As for the work you have done for him, you can't take it back. All you can do is move forward."

His words sank into her and her shoulders shook with another round of tears, "I just keep thinking of what he has done to these poor girls. And all the other women he's lied to to get what he wants. What he has put them through. What he has taken from them and... Judas, it just hurts so much because I can't take away the hurt he has caused them. I just want," her voice cracks with emotion, "I just want to make him pay!"

Standing from the sofa, he walked to her as she dissolved into inconsolable cries. Judas wrapped his arms around her, carrying her to her bed. He laid her down before crawling in beside her to hold her while she cried.

***

Judas had no idea how much time had passed, but eventually Eliza's tears dried and her body was still. Thinking she has fallen asleep, he gently places a kiss on her forehead. To his surprise, he was greeted with a murmur of acknowledgment and then a quick peck on the lips before Eliza sat up, breaking their embrace. She rolled to the edge of the bed and sat with her face in her hands.

"Come back, Ahava," he pleaded, knowing she needed this intimacy as much as he did.

She shook her head, standing, "No, I can't."

He watched as she walked around the room like a woman on a mission. She changed her clothes, ran a brush through her long hair, and swiped beneath her eyes in an attempt to wipe away the streaks of mascara trailing down her face. When she was finished, Eliza turned to face him.

She motioned for him to follow, "Get up, love. I need your help."

He moved to the edge of the bed to sit, motioning for her to come to him. Eliza obeys and positions herself to stand between his thighs.

Wrapping his arms around her legs, Judas hugs her to him, resting his face against her stomach, "I will help you do anything you need, but you don't have to do anything at all if you're not ready."

Eliza ran her fingers through his long, silky hair, gripped the strands, and pulled his head back to look up at her, "I am ready."

She had never been more radiant than she was in that moment, of this Judas was absolutely certain. Where just earlier she was wrapped in sadness and regret, now she glowed with resolve and determination.

"Are you sure?" he asked.

Sucking in a sharp breath, she releases it in a long sigh, "Every single person he has victimized deserves tears shed for their pain, but they also deserve vindication. That's exactly what we're going to give them. I gave them all the tears I have to give today, now I'm going to take their abuser and I'm going to ruin his life."

With that, Eliza released his hair and walked from the room.

Judas smiled as he watched her go. Two things were crystal clear in his mind. First, he loved that woman more than he ever thought possible and, second, that was a plan he could absolutely support.

Chapter Forty-Four

High heels and Italian loafers clack against the stark white tile of the hallway as Eliza and Judas round the final corner and approach Paul's hospital room. Judas' eyes cut slightly in her direction only to find fierce determination on his lover's face. Their strides slow and Judas raises a chin to the bodyguard stationed outside the door.

"Good morning, sir," Travis nodded back.

"Last night?" Judas asked.

The guard's shoulders raise then fall, "All quiet. No visitors all night...and Mr. Arthur seemed to sleep well."

"Is he awake?" Eliza's sharp tone cut across them.

"Yes ma'am. For a while now, I believe he is getting dressed and preparing for the press conference," he reported confidently. "Bobby should be back from his break soon, as well."

Judas patted the man on the shoulder in gratitude, "Travis, good job. Why don't you go to the cafeteria and get yourself a cup of coffee." His eyes cut quickly to Eliza, "I've got it from here."

As the former defensive lineman strode away, Eliza pushed the door to Paul's room open without preamble. The time for niceties was coming to an end and she wasn't going to play the game much longer. But, she had to be patient and that was something she was lacking.

The door of the private room swung wide and Paul startled as Eliza and Judas appeared. Her father continued to shrug on his suit jacket, "Well, good morning Darlin'. How are we doing out there? Big crowd?"

"It's starting to build," Eliza mused.

Paul turned to Judas, "And security...we're all good? The whole team is here, right? I'm pulling ahead fast in the polls, and we're going to ride this wave all the way to the capital."

His glee made Eliza's stomach churn.

"Yes, sir," Judas glanced quickly in her direction. No matter what was going on in her mind, he noticed she was doing an excellent job keeping her emotions in check. "Everyone is here and accounted for."

The enormous smile encompassed Paul's entire face. Clapping his hands together, gregarious laughter erupted from his chest, "Wonderful! Jude, my boy, tell Bobby to grab my bag. I think the people of Texas are ready for my return."

Stifling a chuckle, Judas waved the bodyguard into the room. Eliza's eyes darted nervously and fell on him as he handed Bobby the leather duffle bag and Travis reentered the room. She needed to give her dad one more chance. The small voice in her head reminded her he was her father and he would tell her the truth.

"Dad," she blurted. "Before we go out, we really need to talk about what happened that night. The police say Uncle Chet shot you. Why would he do that?"

Paul spun on his heel, his face ruddy and she thought her father's head might explode at such an invasive question. But, as quick as he was to anger, his demeanor shifted back just as fast. "Honey, I don't have any idea why they would say that. They're wrong...I mean," he stuttered, "I...I have no idea what kind of wild story is being told."

She stared at him for a long time, hoping her long pause would bring about the truth. *Just say it, Dad! This is your last chance!'* Her inner voice screamed inside her mind. But she was met with more silence and Paul's shadowy blue eyes.

He took her gently by the shoulder's and Eliza struggled not to recoil, "Sweetheart. Everything is fine, we're gonna win this election...and your daddy is going to bring you with him to the top!"

"Mr. Arthur?" a middle-aged man with a head full of salt-and-pepper hair and a white lab coat said as he strode confidently into the room.

"Doc Fayden, good to see you, sir!" Paul shook the man's hand. "I hope those are my walking papers...I've got a hoard of press outside waiting for my return."

Doctor Fayden smiled, "I know, Paul...and a state senate to wrangle." He turned to Eliza, "Make sure he takes it easy out there...even though he may not believe it, he needs lots of rest. Those stitches still need a little healing... just as much as that knock to the head."

"I'll do my best," she nodded curtly.

"Enough of all of that," Paul waved his hand at the pair, before shaking the doctor's hand again. "Don't forget to vote for decency, come November." He turned to Judas, "Let's go Jude."

Judas nodded and Bobby held the door until everyone exited the room. They walked in a single file line through the unit's hallways with Judas taking point and the large linebacker bringing up the rear. In the elevator, the large pair of men blocked the inside of the car like a barricade until they arrived on the ground floor. Just outside the large doors, reporters and a small crowd of onlookers are gathered in an adjoining courtyard.

"This is it! Look alive people," a charismatic smile spread on Paul's face as the doors swished open and a cacophony of shouted questions and flashing bulbs assaulted the group. Judas held his arm out to keep the reporters closing in at a minute's distance until he guided Paul to a small podium.

Once Paul was in front of the spectators Judas stepped away, pulling Eliza with him. He pointed at Bobby to follow and the man's eyebrow raised in concern, "Shouldn't someone—"

Judas cut him short, "Mr. Arthur needs space."

Eliza watched her father wave at the cameras, point to people in the crowd he pretended to know, and blow kisses to babies. She knew it was all a show and the curtain was getting ready to fall. Part of her didn't want to watch him do this again. She hated the falsity of this election at every step and didn't think she could handle one more second of it. But, the other part of her knew she needed closure. She needed to know that one more bad guy was gone and wouldn't hurt anyone ever again.

"Good morning my fine friends!" Paul's amplified voice hushed the crowd. "I appreciate you all coming out today. You know, there have been a lot of times in my life when I've questioned my path...my duty in this life. When I lost my sweet wife, Catherine, God rest her soul, I didn't know what I was going to do with myself. Here I was, a single father, to the most beautiful child God has granted." He smiled at Eliza. "I tell you, if it wasn't for that wonderful girl, I know I would have lost hope. That's what I want to talk to you all about today. Hope. We have an opportunity to bring back our good old days! Remember when you played stickball in the streets? Back when your neighborhoods were clean and safe? No drugs. No riff-raff. When police were respected?"

The crowd erupted in applause.

His voice grew stronger, "I tell you we have hope! We can make our family safe again! We can bring back decency and good old Texas values. Ryan Marquez and his leftist gang can't do that!"

The cheers from the audience grew and Paul's name was chanted over and over. He was almost giddy when he saw Lydia and a group of paralegals from his office standing near Eliza. His star had risen, and he knew it. The more his supporters encouraged him, the brighter he smiled. Not even when he looked out into the small sea of people and his eyes landed on Chet, Reba, and Dave, did his smile fade. Eliza watched her father swallow hard, the only indication of his worry before he cut his eyes in her direction, but her plain expression never changed.

"I can tell you're all good people here...including my longest friend, right there!" Paul motioned to Chet who stood stoically next to his wife. "Chet Branson everyone...we've known each other for a lot of years. Been through a lot together. It's the kind of friendship that you just know they've got your back. And I want to do the same for you all! I'm going to have your back in Austin!"

The whoops and yells of approval were deafening. Two men in dark suits stepped behind Paul and three of his guards made a defensive move to intercept.

Judas spoke into his microphone running through his sleeve, "Stand down and observe. There's no threat."

The three men's heads whipped in Judas' direction and he nodded at them. Taking a step back they maintained their positions. With all of the commotion the gathered crowd made, Paul failed to notice either of the two men, the directive of his guards or that he now was surrounded with four uniformed Dallas police officers. One of the suited men, a tall Latin gentleman in his mid-thirties, lay a hand on Paul's shoulder.

"Mr. Arthur?" he said as Paul spun on him in surprise.

He covered the microphone, "Son, can this wait? These people aren't a threat."

"Mr. Arthur, I'm Detective Reyes with the Dallas Special Victims Unit," Reyes announced.

Paul nodded aggressively, "That's all fine and good, but as you can see we're in the middle of something right now." He turned to find Eliza. She stood just a few feet from him with Judas' arm wrapped tightly around her waist. "Betsy! Come here, handle this."

A hush began to build throughout the crowd as people craned their necks around the press to see what was happening. Eliza and Judas stepped forward as Reyes cleared his throat.

"Mr. Arthur, I have a warrant for your arrest. Please put your hands behind your back," he ordered.

"What are you talking about?! I demand to speak with Chief Buccio! Better yet, Betsy! Get Mr. Castile on the phone! That's right, boy...I have the City Manager on speed dial," Paul's fury was palpable as he bellowed at the detective. "Betsy! Do as I said!"

Eliza shook her head.

Keeping his calm demeanor, Reyes' eyes narrowed on the older man, "Sir, the chief and Mr. Castile have already been made aware of this warrant. Now, I need you to put your hands behind your back."

The crowd was absolutely silent.

"What are the charges?!" Paul demanded.

"Sexual assault of a person under the age of eighteen," Reyes stated as a matter of fact before spinning Paul on his heel. He locked the handcuffs on Paul's wrists with seemingly little effort and the clutch of onlookers burst into yells of bewilderment and anger.

Paul screamed wildly, "I did no such thing!! Betsy! Betsy! You meet me wherever these so-called police are taking me! We won't stand for this!"

"No. I won't, *Dad*," angry tears welled in her eyes. "I know what you've done. All these years—"

"Betsy! Listen to me!" Paul struggled against the restraints and two of the uniformed police.

She shook her head, "No! You'll listen to me! You raped Nevaeh and you forced her to have an abortion! And you've been doing this for years! I'm done with you. You can rot in hell!" She turned away, but changed her mind, "And don't call me when you're looking for a lawyer...I'll be too busy representing Uncle Chet."

Eliza stepped away from her father and made her way to the Branson's. Chet wrapped his arm around her shoulders, holding her there.

Desperate, Paul screamed like an animal, "Jude! Jude! Are you going to let them do this to me?? Don't they know who I am?? Bring Betsy back here!"

"Sir," a wicked grin spreading across his lips, he leaned in close to Paul's ear. "I want you to know a few things before they take you away. One...Eliza, who is the love of my life, by the way, is the one that made all of this happen...she is quite amazing, you know? Using her contacts to take a dangerous man off the streets. Two, it's too bad Mr. Branson wasn't a better shot. Had you assaulted my child..." He leaned back to see the look of utter astonishment and horror fall over his former boss' face, pausing for a moment to savor every satisfying drop of the reaction. "And three...My name is Judas, but you'll always be the traitor Eliza remembers."

He turned away, returning to Eliza's side as Paul's howls of protest faded into the distance and a mob of reporters surrounded them. She slid her hand into his as Judas and his men pushed her and the Branson's through the throngs of people demanding information. Eliza understood this wasn't the end of the fight, but just the beginning. She would do everything in her power to save Chet and work just as hard to see her father serve time.

After escaping, Judas sent his team to follow Chet and his family home. Eliza had worked out a plan to keep the security staff on the payroll for another couple of weeks until the initial shock wore off and the press moved on to something else. She wouldn't have her aunt and uncle worry about someone sneaking into their neighborhood just to get a soundbite.

The coast was clear in the far corner of the hospital parking garage where Judas' car sat and the chirp of the unlocking vehicle echoed loudly in the concrete cave. Sliding in front of Eliza, Judas opened the passenger door. He hesitated for a moment to look her over in the dim, artificial light.

"What?" she asked.

He shook his head, "I think this is the first time I've ever seen you...at peace."

"I am," she nodded. "It's not over. Not for a long shot and my father may not even spend a day in jail... I know that. He's been exposed... and for today, that has to be good enough. But I promised Nevaeh he would pay and I'll keep that promise."

Leaning into her, Judas' body caged her against the car and he smirked, "You're a dangerous creature, Eliza. The world doesn't know who it's messing with."

His kiss was light on her lips.

Warmth traveled through her and she wrapped her arms around his neck. She stared into his honeyed eyes only to lose herself in their comfort.

"Let's go home, Judas."

Chapter Forty-Five

Six Months Later

Since discovering her mother's journals, Eliza had started keeping her own.

It all began with pouring over every single word Catherine Arthur had ever written on those pages. Eliza was hungry with a need to know everything. Some of it had been hard to read. Any mention of her father came with the sting of regret and deep hatred. Even the positive things written about him stunk of lies and betrayal. Eliza supposed that was a feeling that would be sticking with her for the rest of her life. At least she hoped it did because the idea of ever forgiving him was absolutely repulsive to her.

The journals weren't all bad though and there were actually very few mentions of Paul beyond the first year or so of their marriage. After that, it seemed Catherine had begun to get to know herself more intimately and, in turn, given Eliza the same opportunity. She now knew that her mother had loved playing tennis, had hated any kind of social gathering, drank hot tea with cream, and absolutely loathed pickles. Eliza knew that reading Danielle Steele was Catherine's guilty pleasure and that she dreamed of traveling the world. She loved to cook, but she hated to bake. Her grandmother, Norma, was her hero and Reba Branson was the very best friend she'd ever had in her life.

Most of all, though, she had loved Eliza and being her mother more than anything this world could've ever offered. Knowing that filled Eliza with both pride and an aching, relentless sadness. It would ebb and flow through her days but was ever present. Eliza was sure it was just an uncontrollable companion to losing a parent and found ways to coexist with it.

That is where her own journaling had come to be.

Eliza wanted to put her own life down on paper so that maybe someday, someone that loved her as much as she loved her mother could have the same kind of treasure.

She knew at the heart of that plan was another aching heart that would eventually have to live without her. She was in love with and loved by an immortal. Part of that burden is carrying on without the ones you have come to cherish in every season of eternity. When she was eventually gone from this world, she wanted to leave behind a record of their entire life together for him to have always.

Sitting there now, scribbling away on the edge of their bed, she knew that just a few more seconds would tell her if she might be leaving behind another treasure for him to have a little longer than he might have her.

Right on cue, Eliza's cell phone buzzes to life as her timer expires. Smiling to herself, she closes her eyes as she turns to the nightstand. When she opens her eyes and glances down, she sees the exact answer she was hoping for. Tears lined the rims of her eyes and she scooped the magical little device off the nightstand.

Bounding into their living room, Eliza stared across the space at the only man she could ever love. His head was bowed reverently as he carefully sliced mushrooms to add to the risotto he was preparing for dinner. For a long pause, she just admired him standing there. He was beautiful beyond words. Inside and out. Her heart gave an enthusiastic flutter as she gazed at him. Then another body part gave a flutter too because the things that man could do to her body...

Shaking off the rising hormones, Eliza walked across the space and sat on a bar stool across the counter from him. He looked up at her and smiled.

"My Eliza, are you ready for dinner?"

She smiled back and said nothing. She simply slid a positive pregnancy test across the counter.

He looked at the test and a million thoughts raced through his mind. Joy. Fear. Elation. Anxiety. In the onslaught of questions and emotions, his hand slipped and the knife sliced through his flesh.

He cried out at the pain, "Khara!"

Eliza gasped and came to stand next to him as he ran the bleeding finger under cold water. She'd hoped he'd be as excited as she was. They'd talked about the possibility of having children someday, but always in the capacity of adoption. Judas wasn't even sure it was possible for a thousands year old immortal being to have children, but it was in their plan somehow. Now, seeing the blank look on his face and the uncharacteristic slip of his knife, Eliza wasn't so sure.

As she came to his side and her whole body pressed against him, Judas quickly forgot all his questions. Suddenly, he could think of nothing, not even his bleeding wound, but the fact that her body had a tiny piece of them both growing inside her. He was filled with a warmth he had never experienced before.

Looking down at her worried eyes, Judas placed his not-bleeding hand against her stomach. She flushed at his touch and their eyes met.

"Is there really a baby in there?" he asked.

Eliza nodded.

A jubilant smile overtook his face and he leaned down to place his mouth against hers. Desire and love swirled inside him and the way he wanted her on a normal daily basis exploded into something even more ferocious. He needed to have her right here, right now. He wanted to worship this new body that was creating a new life within it.

Breaking the kiss, Judas reached to shut off the water, sure his cut had healed itself completely by this point. As he moved to touch her, Eliza cried out.

"Judas! You're still bleeding!" She grabbed paper towels and began to wrap them around his wound, soaking up the blood.

Desire moved to the back of his mind, as Judas turned his main focus to the cut on his hand. She was right. The cut was still wide open and pouring blood. It looked like it might even need stitches. Leaning toward it, Judas stared in awe.

He swallowed hard as he turned to Eliza, "I... I'm not healing."

Her eyebrows furrowed and concern took over her entire face as a million what ifs passed through her mind, "Judas, I don't understand."

He wasn't sure, but for the briefest of moments, he thought he felt the familiar clasp of a long lost friend's hand on his shoulder. The phantom touch didn't answer his questions, but it allowed a glowing feeling of possibility to take root in his mind.

Judas swallowed hard, staring at the beautiful woman before him. The woman he feared losing since the moment he met her. The woman that he wasn't sure he would be able to live without someday when she was old and gray and too elderly to carry on in life. This woman that he craved growing old with. And, now, this child. This growing life that he would undoubtedly love more than any life he could ever have. This child that he would also outlive.

Judas swallowed back his tears of gratitude, "I think it might be the answer to my prayers."

Without another word and with his wounded flesh ignored and forgotten, Judas swept Eliza into his arms and placed her on the counter before him. He spent the rest of the evening making her body shake with pleasure until they were both spent.

Until their dinner was burnt embers on the stovetop.

Until the certainty of forever became the possibility of a life well spent.

Epilogue

Mary, or Mistress Maggie, as her employees and the world's elite called her, spent the last several centuries wandering from country to country offering her services to the very wealthy. She learned a long time ago that rich men had very singular desires and were willing to pay obscene amounts of money to fulfill them. She lived well and got to degrade powerful men in the process. She considered it a win-win.

Helmut Von Albrecht was born into wealth but pretended to have built his business empire from the ground up. Having his hands in multiple industries, he fancied himself an innovator, but really he just had more money than any one person ever should and bought other people's ideas out from under them. On paper, he looked like a thriving success. In reality, he was a fragile man-child with mommy issues who paid Mary to tell him what a piece of shit he was.

Standing over him, Mary looked down her long leather pantsuit, twisting the toe of her black leather stiletto harder on the sensitive skin of his scrotum as he squirmed under her gaze.

"And what does a nasty little bootlicker like you say? Hmm?" she demanded in her sing-song cadence of an adult talking to a small child.

Helmut grimaced up at his mistress, "Thank you, madam."

"And will my dirty, nasty little pig disobey me again?" she arched an eyebrow.

Helmut gazed up at her with complete and total adoration, "No, madam. Never again."

She yanked at the leash connected to the collar around his neck, jerking him to attention, "What else do you need to say, slug? You forgot something."

Helmut yelped at the sudden tug and scrambled to find the words she was looking for, "I... Uh... Um..."

Mary spit in his face, "Apologize, you filthy fucking piece of shit."

Recognition lit in his eyes, "I'm sorry, madame! I'm so sorry and I will never do it again. I'm your slave, madame."

Mary smiled and patted her pet on the head, "Good boy. Now, kiss my feet please."

Helmut smiled with enthusiasm as Mary lifted the toe of her shoe from his delicate sack and allowed him to kneel before her. He bowed to place his lips against her sleek black stilettos and she watched as he relished the opportunity to worship at her feet.

Moments like this always felt strange to her, even after so many countless years of doing it. That these men, men who wear suits worth more than nice cars while commanding boardroom conference tables before the world's most powerful individuals, would pay her money to bow down to her. It was a mind-fuck of monumental proportions.

Mary started life doing everything right and above board. Following rules of piety and loving all. She had been in love with and married the king of kings and the kindest soul to walk the earth, or at least she had thought that of him a very long time ago.

But then he left her.

He'd not only left her behind, but he left her to live forever without any question of whether or not she would even want to. And, then, the rumors and the stories told about her as the centuries went by. Who she was became so distorted and false. They called her a whore and demeaned her at every chance. Eventually, she got tired of being called something she wasn't, so she just embraced the madness and became what they claimed her to be. That's when her life changed.

She'd learned that men, especially the powerful ones, only respected you when you had something to offer them; so, she offered. As it turned out, life as a whore was far more palatable than the life of a martyr. It wasn't always pretty and sometimes it was incredibly dangerous, but at least it was her choice.

Glancing up from the slave at her feet for a moment, Mary's eyes glided past to a television hung from the wall in Helmut's office. It had no sound, just the moving pictures from a twenty-four hour news channel. Normally nothing on TV would be a distraction for her, but her eyes connected with the image of a man on the screen and she couldn't look away. The image was fleeting and gone before she had time to fully process what she had just seen.

She yanked the leash, tossing Helmut to the side as she scrambled toward the tv. Grabbing the remote from the table below, she rewound the live footage back. Hitting pause, Mary stared at the face.

Standing in the middle of a full scale investigation into an American politician was a man she once knew as a brother. A man she thought had died with his sins during her first life. She had cried for his sacrifice back then. She still cried for him from time to time. He was one of those faces that would never leave her mind no matter how much time passed. He was the closest thing she had to family and she was staring at him, still alive after all this time.

Helmut's voice broke into her racing thoughts with a hesitating question, "Are we... done? I thought I was paying for the night."

Mary turned a withering look at the man on the floor behind her in his tighty-whities, "Did I fucking say you could talk?"

Helmut returned to his submissive kneel and stared at the floor while Mary turned back to the TV for one last look just to be sure.

Yes, there was no question.

"I thought I was the only one," she whispered to herself. She reached shaking hands toward the screen and touched the paused figure as if that might give her all the answers to her questions but it only brought a million more to the surface.

Without a second thought to her customer on the ground behind her, Mary walked straight out of his office and into the bustling hallway of his financial firm. She heard him yelling after her, no doubt demanding his money back for denied services, but she didn't care. She kept walking, mind spinning a million miles an hour, until she reached the elevator, then the lobby, then the cool mountain air outside.

When the cold hit her face, Mary could feel the tears welling in her eyes. She tried desperately to keep them inside and finally made it to her car. As she slid behind the wheel, she let go and the tears poured from her eyes, as furiously as the aching wails from her lungs.

All this time. All these centuries.

She thought she was alone.

If she had to search every corner of this world, she had to find him.

She was going to find him.

She gripped the steering wheel as resolve flooded her consciousness, "If it takes me the next thousand years to find you, I'm coming for you, Judas."

Acknowledgements

We would like to thank our editor, Kymmee for all the hard work that took place during the development of this first joint novel. We appreciate every scream, cry, headache, eyeroll, hair pulling, heartburn, and curse word that we know for a fact happened during the editing process. The next cuppa is on us and we promise to keep the conversation in one consistent tense the whole time.

Love,

Amanda and January

Additional resources:

"Lord's Prayer in Aramaic-Pray Before I Sleep." *YouTube*, EasyMind; WombatNoisesAudio, 1 Dec. 2021, www.youtube.com/watch?v=vAU2uOBM2pY.

About the Authors

Amanda and January are both former employees of a Paul Arthur type megalomaniac which is where the two met in 2017. Having discovered a mutual love for all things books, they have become close friends and business partners. Aside from writing their own individual books and co-authoring the Sinful Salvation series, they are co-owners of Wandering Reads, a mobile bookshop in the Ozarks. These ladies can often be found in local coffee shops plotting the downfall of the patriarchy and discussing the age old argument: coffee versus tea. January promises to teach Amanda how to use Ingram Spark while Amanda swears she will always screen record the really good TikToks so January never has to make an account. Together, they hope to continue filling the world with books by indie authors for many years to come.

Follow on Facebook
https://www.facebook.com/authorAmandaEast
and on TikTok
https://www.tiktok.com/@thewriteamanda

www.januarykelly.com

Follow on Facebook:

https://www.facebook.com/profile.php?id=100067850730415

Instagram:

https://www.instagram.com/januarykelly.author/?next=%2F